To my readers-

April 2020

So you're probably wondering why I decided to publish a second edition of my book; a book that hasn't sold well past my friends and family. In order to sell books, you have to market them well, and most of the time it can cost much more than a Self-Published Author can afford until the money starts coming in. The only downfall I have found in my decision to go on my own, is a smaller budget to market my book; the bright side though, is that there are "no rules" to my creativity in traveling my own path – hence the name of my website, *Author Without Rules.*

Once I really discovered what I could do with this gift God has given me, all kinds of thoughts came to mind of what I really wanted to do if given the chance to help others less fortunate than myself. My thought process was that God has given me this gift, and so much more with my amazing family and friends; I'm truly blessed! I told God, "If you provide the means, and I will make sure to "pay it forward." Straight up, that's our deal".

When this Coronavirus began its reign of terror on all of our lives, just like everyone else, I was scared and angry, that our lives as we knew it, was going to come to a complete stop for most of us. For the first time ever, my job in the Security field was labeled as "essential", so I'm fortunate enough to be able to keep working when others are not. But for all of those who know us, Jeff's disease automatically put him in one of the highest risk categories, so he would be grounded to the house; with the exception of traveling to and from his dialysis appointments. The real kick in the head came when his doctor added the restrictions that, anyone who is not a resident of our home is not allowed in for any reason until this horrible "social distancing" is lifted; and no one knows just how long it will be in place.

This virus has really made so many of us feel helpless; myself included, and so this is my way of doing something, but I really need all of you – my family, friends, and followers of my social media sites and my website; to please share this info. If you buy *Forbidden Desires* at $27.99, I will donate 100% of my royalties to help those affected by the Coronavirus. The more I sell, the more areas we can help. This promotion will last through August 31, 2020.

I'm publishing a second edition to correct the format as well as add this note. Publishing your own book does have other downfalls if you choose not to pay for an "expert" to do it for you. I wrote it all, I created my own cover, and I simply went to Barnes and Noble and followed their directions. Of course I made a few mistakes, so I will go back and correct them with this edition. The more you learn, the more you want to try to get it right; and because I'm proud of my work, I want to produce a better looking book.

My story means so much to me, and as any writer will tell you, our characters are very real to us; this particular story is quite dark, however, I do believe that there are many more fans than we will ever really know, who are drawn to stories with some very real human desires, intrigue, and fantasies; all characteristics many of us were told are "taboo", or are "subjects we don't talk about." The way I see it, as a human being and an Author, it's my story; I don't know where it came from, other than from my imagination and my passion for the 1950's Era. But, I suppressed it for so many years, and I wrote edits after edits – and after countless times of being so close to getting published by a traditional publisher, I decided that this story had to come out, and it was time to go out on my own – full speed ahead, and there is no turning back. My whole point is that reading a story like this is OK to enjoy, and it doesn't mean that we will go out and commit the acts in the story. I've decided that I'm that "edgy" and controversial writer, and I won't apologize for it.

When reading *Forbidden Desires*, remember, it's a *fictional* story. Readers enjoy fiction because we can escape from reality for a few hours; just as we do with movies and TV.

Thank you for your support; it means so very much to me, and please visit my website, where you can find the direct link to buy *Forbidden Desires*. I'm also working on a "Book Review" section where you can leave your thoughts on my story. Please see all my contact information on my site if you would like my free book marker.

https://snappyweaver.wixsite.com/author-without-rules

Acknowledgements:

To my Lord and Savior: I can't thank you enough for this gift of writing that has become my passion. I know that if it weren't for you, I could never create an alternate world to escape to when I need it most; this gift you have given me allows me to do just that. Writing is definitely cheaper than therapy, and probably more effective.

To my husband Jeff: Thank you for dealing with my quirkiness; I know it hasn't been easy, as it isn't always easy for me to deal with either; I'm still having to remind myself to embrace the real me. I have often read that creative people can be some of the most difficult people to live with, but here we are, over twenty years later and you're still with me; so I suppose it hasn't been too bad.

I love you for so much more than I could ever have time to express, but in this instance, I love you for your encouragement and your patience while I take this journey of the unknown; which is usually very scary, but I feel that it will be a very exciting journey that I want you to join me on each step of the way. Nothing would be the same without you.

To my Mom: Thank you for all of your love and support through this journey; the encouragement you have given me means more than I could ever express to you. I know that I have had "dreams" in the past as any kid or young adult who was just trying to find their place in this world, but I believe you understand what I desire to do for the rest of my life, and your support means everything to me.

To Father Richard: Thank you for the encouragement and help you gave me to embrace the gift that God has given me. As you know, there were several times where I was concerned about the content that flowed from my mind to the computer screen. Thank you for your humor and your non-judgmental, open mind. In addition, thank you for that idea that helped me take my story to where it needed to be.

To Dr. Brian Boggs, PhD: My dear cousin, as I have told you before, you're that little brother I never had. Thank you for your ongoing encouragement, that of which helped me keep the faith throughout this long process. Countless times you told me, "You will get published." I knew you were right, but it always helps to hear the positive. In addition, I can't thank you enough for writing my forward; it means so very much to me.

To all of my family and friends: I have been truly blessed to have each one of you in my life! Thank you for all the love, support and prayers. I hope that you all enjoy the book! God Bless all of you.

Forward by Dr. Brian Boggs:

T.S. Eliot once said there are two great tragedies in life: the first of which is not getting what you want and the second of which is getting what you want. And, of the two, the latter is far worse. Or, put another way, we always seem to want what we cannot have, until we get it and then we no longer want it … most of the time. So, goes the story of Robert and Vivian. He a powerful, rich, and handsome man; and her, a stunning waitress caught in an endless cycle of poverty and abuse. As Amy tells us, Robert can have any woman that he wants and often does. But, wait … there is catch. The one woman he wants is the only woman that does not want him – Vivian. She continually turns down his gentle advances. This only fuels the fire of his desire and her fear.

So, what can Robert do? Well, did I mention that he is rich? Well, of course – however, I failed to mention just how he got his money. He is the son of a late mob boss and as he comes to learn Vivian's ne'er-do-well of a father who has an outstanding debt to Robert's father. Oh, what to do with this kind of information? Will he try to collect on the debt? Maybe strike some sort of bargain? Or are his feelings genuine and he only wants to use this information – not for malice per se, but as the only way to get into Vivian's life. As Vivian makes her deal with the devil to be Robert's "live in assistant," the drama of confused love unfolds, but how will it work out?

The answers to these questions and so much more are thoughtfully portrayed throughout this well-written novel of tortured love and desire. Only Amy could have conceived of such a riveting plot that has depth and a connection to life.

Enjoy the book,

Brian Boggs, PhD.

Prologue

June 1950

Robert stared off into the distance after firing the last round from his Smith and Wesson pistol, trying to get the image of Vivian's tears out of his mind, just before she walked out on him with her suitcase in tow. That was the first time he had ever saw terror in her eyes when looking at him. Someone had convinced her that he led the same life as his father, that of which included money laundering, prostitution, rape, and murder. But Vivian was wrong about him, and she would see that if he just had the chance to prove it to her – and rid their world of the ones who are trying to stop them from happiness.

In thinking about the people who could have an issue with Vivian becoming Mrs. Robert Sterling, his face turned into a deep red color and his eyes narrowed as he reloaded his pistol and began firing it off. But then, the echo of his gun shots took him back to the first time he discovered that his father's business was much more than just owning a clothing store and a gentleman's club…

***

In early June 1936, with the summer sun beating down on his face, ten year old Robert Sterling wandered off alone to the wooded area of the Sterling Estates, as he often did. But this day would be different, as a woman's loud cries caught his attention and led him to the commotion through the trees. He came upon a Barren spot at the bottom of a steep hill with his heart pounding through his chest from running as fast as he could, and where he caught a glimpse of his father and five men he recognized as his father's associates, gathered around a short, stocky woman with brown hair just touching her shoulders and dressed in a plain light blue dress.

And then his innocent brown eyes fell upon a man dressed in a white shirt, soaked in blood that was dripping from his head and face and wearing black pants, standing not so far away from her. His wrists and ankles were in shackles and he was begging for them to let her go. He promised that he would get the money someway. But they weren't listening to him and two men began to rip the woman's clothes off as she continued with ear piercing screams, prompting the boy to cover his ears with his tiny hands, which barely muffled her volume.

Robert stood frozen in his sweat, dirty from head to toe, and so afraid to make a sound, that his breathing became shallow. What money was this man talking about? He wondered to himself. And why was dad just standing there while his friends kicked and beat that woman's naked body? His heart began to race to the point where he could feel the throbbing in his throat, he was afraid to watch anything further, but he was also too curious to walk away.

The largest of his father's friends was the biggest man he had ever seen in his life. Robert once compared the man's bicep to his waist, and was astounded that the man's arm was nearly the size of his twenty-six inch waist – the man was the Chief of Police, and the young boy decided he would grow to be big and strong like him! But as big as this guy is, why won't he stop them? He wondered.

Then Robert saw his father force the beaten man over to his limousine where they had the woman lying on the hood of the car, flat on her stomach with her legs wide open and two men holding her down, one on each side of her. Robert gathered his nerves about him and walked in closer – just in time to hear his dad shout at the man. "Just remember – you're the one who did this to your wife!" The two men continued to hold the woman down while two other men held the man in place, and forced him to watch as Phillip Sterling unzipped his pants and shoved his manhood inside the woman's ass, causing more ear piercing screams from her bloodied mouth. The man fell to his knees, sobbing and begging them to stop. The young boy began tasting the acid rising from his stomach as he became chilled, but instead of running, he stood in place, taking deep breaths to keep from getting sick.

Phillip finished with the woman and zipped his pants. He stood over the man with a cold stare, and said to him, "She's part of my property now- and time for you to say goodbye", he told him with emphasis. The shaken little boy continued to watch as Phillip pulled the man up by his hair and then shouted just inches from his face, "You weren't man enough to take care of business and pay me what you owe, so I will take it from the wife – you lousy piece of shit!"

His thunderous voice echoed off in the distance. It was then that Robert noticed a shovel leaning against the car and his father then nodded at one of the men. "Get him to finish on the digging." The Chief unlocked the shackles to his wrists and ankles, while ordering the man to finish digging the deep hole that was started. Why is he digging a hole? Robert wondered to himself. Suddenly, Phillip turned around and spotted his young and curious son. Still, Robert couldn't move – even as Phillip inched toward him.

As his father walked toward the frightened boy, he lit a cigarette and calmly approached him. He looked back over his shoulder at the man digging the hole and then his eyes cut back to his wide eyed, curious son. Robert looked up at his father's white shirt, covered in blood and dirt, and then he quickly looked back at the ground – trembling and afraid to speak.

Phillip gently laid his hand on his son's shoulder. "This is nothing but business, son." Robert slowly lifted his little brown eyes to his towering father and asked, "Why is that man digging a hole?" Phillip looked back over his shoulder at the man and then his eyes cut back to his son, he came to one knee, and with emphasis, he answered, "I said it's just business, boy." He then gripped Robert's shoulder and gritted his teeth when adding, "You never saw a damn thing here", he growled. Robert's lips quivered as his tears began to fall. "Do you understand Robert Phillip?" His father asked when jarring him. "Yes daddy", his young son cried out. "This will one day be your property and your empire to run – you have to toughen up!" He added with emphasis. Phillip reached for his handkerchief and wiped Robert's tears. "Don't you go and tell Rosie either." Robert shook his head from side to side, and said, "I won't daddy." Phillip cupped his hands around Robert's face for their eyes to meet, and told him, "Son, if you do", he paused to take a deep breath, and then he glared into his eyes adding, "If you tell Rosie, I'll make her disappear- and you will never see her again." "I won't tell anyone, daddy", Robert cried. A satisfied smile came to Phillip's face. "That's my soldier." He gave him a wink and kissed his forehead. "Ok boy, move along now – you've seen enough."

Robert ran to the top of the hill as fast as his thin little legs would take him. As he reached the peak, he heard the echoing blast of a gun and fell into a fetal position in paralyzing fear. As his little body shook he heard the woman screaming and crying. Robert slowly opened his eyes and forced himself to look back down at the woman. She had fallen to her knees as she watched her husband's lifeless body being kicked into the hole that he was forced to dig.

Suddenly, Robert heard a clap of thunder and felt the refreshing and cool raindrops fall on the top of his head, where the sun had baked into his jet black hair only minutes before. He gazed around at his new property as his thoughts were slowly coming back to the present. He looked down at his shaken hand still clenched around his

pistol and trying to slow his heart rate from the dark memories that had haunted him for the past fourteen years, and he knew then that he had to continue trying to change and break the circle of violence and darkness that his father had taught him. But the first thing he needed to do was get the woman he loved back, because without her, nothing else would matter.

Across town, Vivian unlocked the door to her rented room above the general store, and immediately dropped to the floor sobbing. She just could not shake the cold and self-righteous tone of Patsy's confession to her about whom and what kind of man Robert Sterling really was. How could this be happening? She wondered, as her tear-filled eyes roamed the rickety old western style room that she had rented. Despite Patsy's words, Vivian was in disbelief about everything she had heard about the man she had fallen so hard for, the very man she tried to resist since she met him months ago – the same man who literally purchased her from her own father….

1

Minutes after Vivian slumped to the hard wood floor in tears, she managed to pull herself up and wash her face. She had been crying so much, her eyes were swollen and red, but some of the irritation was from the thick dust in the room, and though she was raised in a small shack, she was not accustomed to what she considered to be filth. But this was the only room she could afford and the only one that was available, and because she was again on her own, she had to be able to eat, keep herself clean, and of course, she had to find another job.

Vivian had showered and sat down in her white satin robe at the small round table in the corner of the room, with her brown leather worn journal. She had found the journal in her mother's bureau drawer when playing dress up one day as a child and asked her mother about the empty book of paper with lines. Her mother told her that she received it as a gift, but she never wrote anything in it, and so her mother gave it to her to color and scribble in. Little did she know that Vivian would keep it blank until she became a teenager and lost her mother to Cancer, just days after her fifteenth birthday.

At first not knowing what to write, she just couldn't stop thinking of Robert and wanting to be with him, but she knew she couldn't give in to him after what Patsy had put in her mind about him. She softly drove her hand across the blank page of her journal, and then in her mind, she traveled back to a little over a month ago; to May 8, 1950…

As I shut the car door, I recognized the shiny gray Jaguar as Robert's car in our driveway. Suddenly, I felt ashamed of our badly paint chipped shack and daddy's broken down farming machinery buried in the weeds, and with the barren field as the unattractive back drop of our less than modest living conditions. Funny, I never felt ashamed until that moment."

I walked through the door and saw Robert and that other man standing over daddy. Upon seeing their guns, I slowly and fearfully closed the door. I had seen Robert's gun when he would come into the Steakhouse, but this was different, as I felt threatened in our home.

"Robert", I acknowledged him when swallowing that lump of fear in my drying throat. He gave me that suave smile of his and walked over to me, gently touched my cheek, and softly said, "Hi darlin'". I bit down on my lower lip at the feel of his soft and gentle touch, and then I peeked around to daddy sitting in his wooden rocker that was hanging on by a thread and his eyes looking down at the floor.

"Robert what's going on?" I looked up at him with concern and then looked at his gun. But then I suddenly allowed my eyes to roam over his black button down shirt with the sleeves tightly rolled up, just above his bulging biceps. "I just have some business with your father", he answered softly. The gentle tone of his voice and the soft scent of his cologne were affecting me in a very alluring way; that of which I knew I shouldn't be allowing myself to feel. This man was wearing me down to the point where my legs were feeling as though they were ready to buckle from under me; the same feeling that I had always gotten when waiting on him at the steakhouse. He looked at my dirty brown uniform and gently took my hand. "Come on over and sit down; you look like you've a hard day."

I sat on our love seat that had tea colored stains of what was once a pure white cloth fabric and glanced over at

Robert's henchman standing there before me, dressed in all black clothes and western boots. He gave me a wink through his lewd hazel eyes while Robert made a call on the phone with his back to all of us. I looked over at my father and asked, "Daddy what kind of business do you have with Robert?" This familiar but horrible hired man of Robert's spoke up, and in a mocking tone he said, "Yes daddy, what kind of business is it?" I glared back at him, stood up, and hissed, "You stay out of this!" His smile turned sinister as he grabbed my arm and shouted, "You're the one who will stay out of this - and you will do as you're told!"

My panicked cry sent Robert storming over, knocking this man who smelled of heavy liquor to the floor, as I quickly sat back down. "Enough!" Robert ordered while straddling the man with his gun aimed at this man's head. He shouted, "Don't you ever touch her again!" Noticing the intense and angry look in Robert's eyes, and his gun pressed hard against this man's temple, I didn't know whether I should be frightened or flattered.

The man who attacked me and was ready to do god knows what to me relented in silence with his hands in front of him, as Robert returned the gun to his holster, stood to his feet, and turned back to me – and by then I was shaking and crying hysterically. "Hey", Robert addressed me softly, as he bent down on one knee before me. "Don't cry darlin', everything's going to be alright." He gently stroked my loose blonde curls back from my face and wiped my tears away with the tips of his thumbs. "I have the perfect solution for you to help your father." I finally calmed down to a whimper. "I'm not here to hurt you, Princess." He told me tenderly.

Robert and I reached the bottom of the stairs that would lead to my bedroom. I turned back, looking at him in hopes that he would see my fear and decide to not to force me into taking him to my bedroom. I don't know if it was just my perception or if his eyes really did look hungrier than ever before. But the next thing I know, he gave me a few gentle taps to my rear end and said, "Come on Princess, take me to your bedroom."

As I took each step, my fear overtook me to the point where I fell backwards and into his arms, thankfully he caught me just in time before I hit the steps, and I would have no doubt fallen to the floor, had I been a step or two ahead of him. He gathered me in his arms and carried me the rest of the way. I was shaking and crying all the while holding onto him as he lightly kicked my bedroom door open at the bottom. "Hey now", he said in a quiet and soothing tone. "Take it easy, baby, I'm not here to hurt you."

He approached my bed with me still cradled in his arms, he gently sat me on the side, and then he squatted before me. "Take it easy", he said in his gentle tone. Once again, I began to relax, though I didn't know what to expect from him since I walked into the door of my home. But then he removed my black heels and began slowly massaging my feet – one at a time. My god, his hands were magical, though calloused. I recognized them as a working man's hands, which took me by surprise being he had probably more money than the President of the United States and really didn't have to perform menial labor.

He had me in such a trance with his strong hands massaging my feet, that I hadn't noticed how high he had gotten up one of my legs until his hand was underneath the skirt of my uniform and unfastening my garter belt - and then my stocking came down. As he went for the other leg, I grabbed his hand, stopping him. "Please don't", I begged of him. He took my hand with his free hand and slowly raised it to his lips, kissing it softly. Without saying a word, he removed my other stocking – and like a dummy, I allowed it.

"Robert, I"....Again, he never said a word when he took me by the hands and helped me to my then bare feet. He then he slid his hands down and around to my back, and began unzipping my uniform, as I stood frozen and not knowing what to do. After the zipper was wide open, he pealed the uniform off my body, and let it fall to the floor. And there I stood before him in nothing but my white strapless corset, and as vulnerable as I felt, I may as well had been stark naked. Thinking he would next remove my corset, I crossed my arms in front of my breasts. He gave me a small smile, squatted before me and told me, "Step out of the dress." I did as I was told and he picked the uniform up and tossed it on my bed.

He stood and gazed up and down at my body for what seemed like an eternity, and then he cautiously moved into me, took me by the wrists, gently moving my arms to my sides, and still holding my hands, he guided me into his lap and told me, "You will never wear that brown waitress uniform again." It was then that I realized he didn't bring me to my bedroom to violate me, and taking the uniform off of me was his symbolic way of transitioning me into his world. He never touched me where he shouldn't - well, with the exception of putting his hands underneath my dress to remove my stockings. He kept me in his lap and told me that I would be safe and very well taken care of like the Princess that he felt I was. Safe from what - I had no idea at the time.

Sitting in this man's lap, I wasn't as uncomfortable as I thought I would be, maybe it was because I knew then that his intentions were not to violate me. However, I wasn't about to cozy up to him either. Dressed in nothing but my corset, I was damn near bare and felt his thick cotton pants against my skin, bringing on a very foreign feeling but at the same time, it was a very erotic feeling. Minutes later, he simply stood up with me, tenderly touched my chin and captured my lips with his. His smooth, full lips covered mine and he ever so slowly pulled away savoring it all with his eyes closed. Upon opening his eyes, he softly said, "I will see you tomorrow evening." He picked up what was now my former uniform and walked out the door.

In my room minutes after Robert had left, I felt exhausted and overheated, but not just from the crowd at the steakhouse and the 90 degree weather, but Robert….. I stripped down from my corset and stood in front of the mirror. I observed my one hundred twenty-five pound slender body, knowing I was experiencing some heavy changes; changes I was never told about by my mother. It seems like my body has a mind of its own sometimes, and those changes I would have to learn about as I go.

As I looked into the mirror, I saw my baby blue eyes staring back at me, but I felt as though I were looking at a stranger. I was twenty-one years old, living with my alcoholic, gambling father, and sometimes, I couldn't help but wonder how different life would have been if my father died instead of my mother, and as angry as I was with him, that thought always brought on tears.

I stood in the shower, still reeling from Robert's impromptu visit with that horrible henchman of his; Adam, as I would learn was his name near the end of this visit.

Again, the tears fell down my face, feeling as though I was the bargaining chip between daddy and Robert – and that's exactly what I was. Daddy may as well have placed me on a store shelf and attached a price tag to me. Recalling his words and his gentlest voice, Robert drew me into his lap, and told me, "Come to work for and live with me, and your daddy's debt is paid in full." Now, I knew that Robert was different from anyone I had ever come in contact with, but I guess I didn't expect him to be so bold and forward, and then asking me to lead him to my bedroom –removing my uniform…my God, he could have done anything he wanted to me – and yet, he didn't.

How could daddy owe him five thousand dollars? How could he do this to us? He lost every single dollar of that money on his booze and gambling, while I worked hard outside of the home at the steakhouse only to support his unacceptable lifestyle, while we slowly fell into the deepest level of poverty. It had gotten so bad, that I had to start charging food from the grocery store just to be able to eat. I had racked up such a big bill, that the store manager was becoming impatient and had threatened to cut me off until I pay that hundred dollar bill in full. But of course, there was one evening when he offered to erase my bill if I would have sex with him, so I took the tips I had managed to set aside, paid the debt and I haven't been back to that store since. I continuously wiped my tears as they flowed faster than the never-ending leaky faucet in the kitchen, knowing I had no choice but to give in to Robert's demands, whatever they may be - I was running out of options.

I had turned down every single one of Robert's invitations to dinner since meeting him, but I must admit that I found him extremely handsome. He has a mysterious and intimidating side to him, which frightened me. His dark brown eyes are both alluring and unsettling. He did make it difficult to say *no* to him, because I shamefully confess that though I was saying no, my body screamed yes! But, I didn't dare succumb to his affections. My mother, god bless her soul, raised me to be a devout Catholic, and insisted that I must not enter into intercourse with a man until my wedding night. As much as I didn't trust Robert, I trusted myself even less.

2

May 9, 1950

The morning after Robert's life changing visit, and the last breakfast I would end up cooking for my father, daddy stumbled into the kitchen, hungover as usual and waking to the smell of the bacon cooking. Every morning was routine – I woke at 7am to start cooking breakfast, whether I had to work at the steakhouse or not, and daddy was out the door by 8:30, and he would stumble back in the door, drunk as a skunk late every night. I would have to pour him into bed, where he would pass out the minute his head hit the pillow.

I sat a plate down with two pieces of bacon and three fried eggs in front of him along with the usual bottle of aspirin. And I knew there was no sense in fighting this morning because I was fed up with it all. Due to his drinking and gambling, I was now forced to live with a man I barely knew, and I would be forced to do God knows what for him!

I watched my father's hand shake uncontrollably as he scooped some egg onto his fork. The shaking was due to the excessive alcohol – as told to me by his doctor. I recall my father looking at me as I picked at the eggs on my plate in silence. "I'm sorry I put you in this position little girl", he told me in his usual raspy voice. "But that Sterling fellow seems to be interested in you and…"

I dropped my fork on the plate, making a loud clanking sound. I was livid! I just knew my face was turning red as the heat radiated from my skin and, what's worse, I felt as though he sold me to the highest bidder! I then snapped at him, "And what daddy? He has more money than anyone could ever spend in a lifetime?" My father slammed his fist on the table and shouted, "It's not the worst thing that could happen for you! At least you can have a good life and have someone to care for you in ways that I can't!"

I can only imagine the look I gave him was just as inappropriate as what I hissed at him next. "I hope you're happy with whoring me out just to be able to keep up with your drinking and gambling!" Upon hearing my words, he backhanded me and tipped the table over, scattering the dishes and food all over the entire kitchen, making it look as though a tornado came through. I found myself sitting in the middle of the kitchen floor, holding my hand against my cheek among the mess. I just could not fathom what made me use that tone or language, the only thing I could figure is that I've finally had enough of my father's reckless life that had taken me right along for that awful ride.

After gathering my senses, I slowly pulled myself up off of the floor and watched as my father turned his back on me. "Sterling's driver will be here at five this evening to take you to your new home." He said those words in such a matter of fact tone. And then he walked out of the kitchen door, while I stood there with tears streaming down, as the door swung back and forth, and daddy disappeared from my sight.

***

As scheduled at five that same evening, Robert's driver picked me up in a black Rolls Royce limousine to take to my new residence – the Sterling Ranch, where I was to become a live in personal assistant to Robert Sterling. The title alone shot the fear of God through my veins. As the car pulled away from the home in which I was raised, tears ran down my face as I again wondered how daddy could have allowed this to happen.

As we drove along, the silence in the car was deafening, and I had wondered again what I would be doing for Robert. I had heard what the wealthy men were like, including Robert's deceased father. I've heard the ramblings of the town folk talking about the infamous Sterling Empire, which included hundreds of thousands of dollars in money laundering, illegal poker parties, prostitution, and even murder. But incredibly enough, there wasn't the hard cold evidence to back up the talk, which was why none of Sterling's men ever stayed behind bars for longer than a night or two when they did find a reason to arrest one of them, and that was usually for nothing more than drunken disorderly. Even when there seemed to be a break to catch them at their dirty deeds, at the last minute people stopped cooperating with authorities out of fear of the retaliation that Phillip Sterling and his men was very known for. And now, I was being forced to work for his son, but what would those job duties be?

Despite the fact that Robert agreed to erase daddy's debt in a civil way, the idea still terrified me, and yet, deep down I must admit, there was this attraction I had to him. He's always had a sweet demeanor about him when he spoke to me at the Steakhouse, even when I turned down his dinner dates. And then, I saw firsthand that he wasn't going to let that thug of his hurt me. If I could trust him, time would tell, I figured. People seem to do as Robert Sterling tells them to do – and obviously, I will be expected to do the same. I had no home, no money, and I would be completely dependent on him – from the very minute I enter his world.

***

Fred sat at the bar of the Deadwood Steakhouse shaking as he drank down shot after shot of whiskey, and thinking of the deal he and Robert had made. He had no other alternative with being broke and about to lose the house. He wasn't physically fit to work anymore with his body falling apart, and he felt worse each time he took Vivian's pay, but he was too far gone to stop - even if he wanted to. He reached into his pocket and took out the wad of bills that Robert had given him. He would receive this money every month, provided he never took another dime from Vivian. He counted the bills - five hundred total. And, he thought with a smile, no more nasty visits from the bank. His house was safe – thanks to this arrangement.

***

I was in awe as the chauffer slowly drove through the black iron gates that opened after he spoke through some sort of a speaker, to a sharp and familiar male voice, asking him to identify himself. It was Adam – that dreadful Adam! I had an immediate feeling of being both frightened and a bit intrigued, it was as if I were entering a whole new world inside that gate, and the beauty was indescribable as we slowly drove up the paved drive.

I was touched to the point of tears at the sight of the natural beauty of the Black Hills Spruce trees that were lined in unison on each side of the drive and the sun beams shining through nearly all of them. I had to wonder if I was changing addresses or entering Heaven. I got a small giggle through my tears from the young prairie dogs frolicking with each other, and I thought, how glorious they were, as they showed not a care in the world. In that moment, I had forgotten about my fear, as I took in the sights right before my eyes.

My breath was simply taken away as the car pulled up to the circle drive in front of the house. When I stepped out of the back seat of the car and came face to face with the driver, I had just realized that he reminded me of Abraham Lincoln, given his height and slim body structure, and the only thing missing was the top hat; all of which I hadn't paid any mind to earlier, due to my scattered emotions.

The house was equivalent to a mansion, as I have never seen anything like it; a stunning log cabin home and with stone encircling the entire foundation. And then, what caught my eye out in the distance, was a small pond, surrounded by large rocks and a waterfall flowing from a steep drop off. Off to the side of the waterfall were red rose bushes, lined in unison just as the trees along the drive. In the center of the roses, was a large headstone, with gold writing etched in the middle. The sight brought on such peace and love, and somehow, in that moment, it felt as though God had his arms lovingly around me, reminding me of his love and strength.

"Hello, Vivian." I heard Robert's voice behind me. He gently took my arm, and guided me around to face him. I swallowed the nervous lump in my throat and looked up into his dark brown eyes. His presence was always so intense, he had this mysterious and dangerous persona about him that I just could not shake; and yet, I couldn't bring myself to leave – not that I had a choice in the matter. The smile never left his face, when he said to me, "Welcome home, Vivian."

I was so taken by his gentle demeanor, and not knowing what to say, I stood there in silence as he went up to the driver on the other side of the car, and spoke to him in a low tone. After a moment, Robert approached me, and said, "Follow me to your quarters". Walking through the door in this larger than life home, I could no longer contain my amazement at the breathtaking sight. The decor' was that of something an ordinary person would only see in a magazine – cathedral ceilings made of knotty pine, the shiniest wooden floor throughout, the windows were all open and bare of curtains, and the furniture was a mixture of the old west style and Victorian era, and then I was staring up the most beautiful staircase. I was in such disbelief in thinking that this man who lived in this much luxury dined at the steakhouse, a place where most wealthy people would consider a dive. "My goodness, Robert", I said breathlessly. "This staircase looks as tall and lovely as the one in that picture *Gone with the Wind*." He gave me a small smile, but never said a word.

I continued to follow him down the long hallway made of black marble flooring and filled with plants and modest to large sized statues of safari type animals – lions, tigers and the like. This Hollywood –type, but amazing beauty I have seen since entering the property was overwhelming, as I would never in a million years see this kind of luxury, in fact, I doubt my mind could ever imagine such sights.

"Here we are", he said, motioning me inside. As I walked in, I stood speechless, and then I finally said, "This is like having my own home!" Hearing the tone of my words reminded me of a small child at Christmas after noticing presents under the tree. Never in my life had I seen such beauty that would belong to me, and now this was going to be my home. I was getting so lost in the moment, I had forgotten why I was there. Robert looked over at the driver and said, "Thank you, Paul." "You're welcome Mr. Sterling", I heard the man say in a monotone voice before leaving us alone. I could feel Robert's eyes on me as I strolled around the living quarters that of which seemed big enough to fit my father's entire house in.

The living room area was bright from the sun shining through the bare windows that stood from floor to ceiling, just as it was in his common living room, decorated with rose colored walls and hard wood flooring throughout the entire area. "I can't believe I have my very own kitchen", I told him as I lightly drove my hand across the cherry wood counter of the island bar. Robert smiled and said, "If you prefer to have a table with chairs, I can arrange it." "No please", I replied with a big smile. "It's all so lovely." I then walked over to the double glass doors encased in gold trim. "What a beautiful balcony", I uttered to myself. He then took me by the hand and slowly led me back through the living area furnished with a red velvet Victorian style chair, a matching sofa, and a cherry wood coffee table with matching end tables. "As you can see this is the living room – and the bedroom is over here." Strangely enough in thinking back, his tone he used to introduce the bedroom was a bit emphasized, a tone I don't recall picking up on that day.

My hand broke away from his and I went over to sit on the side of the softest king sized bed I could ever imagine having. I removed my navy blue pumps and as soon as I rose from the bed, my feet sunk into the plushest ivory carpet. I once again felt his eyes on me as he stood in the doorway watching me.

Suddenly, I had that sinking feeling in the pit of my stomach that he was undressing me with his eyes, but I figured that I should get used to that feeling, or pretend not to notice. While searching for a way to shift his focus, I walked into the bathroom, and almost fell on my rear end, as I had not realized that the wood floor had recently been waxed. The bathroom was just as amazing as the rest of the house. The enormous tub and shower was encased with clear glass all the way around it, which didn't leave much privacy if someone were to walk in on a person taking a shower. And in front of me there was this gorgeous black granite countertop that had double basin sinks with brass fixtures, and the biggest mirror I had ever laid my eyes on, covering the entire wall. A fact that I picked up on right away, was that Robert evidently liked wide open spaces, large mirrors, and bare windows. I'm not sure why, but it was an unsettling feeling.

Robert had finally left me alone to finish settling in. Probably about a half an hour later, I was standing on the balcony, overlooking the large swimming pool, and a yard big enough to fit a small city in. Out further were the stables and some other rather large buildings that most ranches would have, I suppose.

***

"Come in", I said when hearing the knock at the door. I heard the door close and then Robert joined me on the balcony. "So do you approve of your accommodations?" he asked with a wide smile. I returned the smile and then walked back inside to the lovely Victorian chair, and sat down. "I admit that you have a lovely home." I tried my best to keep my composure, but I absolutely fell in the love with the place. Robert turned back to the island bar and leaned against it with his elbows and said, "You know, just because you have your own kitchen, doesn't mean you have to eat alone."

I sat in silence, wanting to ask him what duties he had in mind for me as his personal assistant – the title he gave me. I swallowed hard, terrified with what his answer might be. For whatever reason, that label he gave me sent fearful chills throughout my body. Maybe it was because I knew that he had a way of getting what he wanted and people seemed to jump to his commands – as if he had put a spell on them. I had to wonder who would give me all of this luxury without expecting much of anything in return. I knew I couldn't go back home because then daddy would lose everything, so there would be no home to go back to, and then where would I go? I was definitely trapped. My worst fear was that I was arranged to be a kept woman – as people would say, and I would feel the same way about any single woman in my position.

"Vivian." Robert's gentle sounding voice again disrupted my thoughts. I still cannot explain it, but his voice when he talks to me, was and still is very captivating. "Is everything alright?" He sat on the solid coffee table in front of me, as I rung my hands together anxiously and then looked up at him. "Robert, what are your plans for me?" He ran his hand over his smooth, clean shaven face, and said, "Well, Vivian we can discuss that at our first dinner meeting."

He gave me a quiet stare, which prompted me to rise from the chair, and then I walked over to the balcony, immediately changing the subject. "I see you have stables." I said, and pointed off into the distance. He opened the doors and replied, "Let's step out." He nodded toward the pool and told me, "Over there is the pool and club house." He gave me a leering smile, and asked, "Do you swim?" Suddenly becoming anxious, I walked back inside and grasped the top of my white button down blouse, and then I answered, "No, I almost drowned when I was four, and I haven't gone near the water since." He slipped his hands into his black suit pants pockets; following me inside, and telling me in a flirtatious tone, "I would love to teach you how to swim, there's nothing to fear." I recall shooting him quite the sassy look and I strongly emphasized, "You'll never see me in a bathing suit, Mr. Sterling." To which his reply – a silent smile from ear to ear, and the wink of an eye.

***

I had finished freshening up while anxiously waiting for the first dinner meeting with Robert down at the club house, next to the pool. I again stepped out onto the balcony and gazed over the property, and that's when I noticed a tower of some kind – it was as tall as a lighthouse, black in color, and had windows all around it. It was further out in the distance, but I felt I should have noticed it before, and it was unsettling that I hadn't. What on Earth is that and why didn't I see that before? I thought to myself. The more I looked at it, the more I thought of those towers that prisons have, and guards watching every single movement...and there were no curtains or drapes to pull closed to make me feel I would have any privacy.

3

Minutes later in the pool house, near dusk and under dim lighting, Robert and I sat at the wood patio table, which looked to be freshly stained. We talked over glasses of cold lemonade, as it was May ninth and unseasonably hot. The staff of two men wearing white dinner jackets and black ties, stood at attention along the wall of the pool house, made of knotty pine and filled with black leather furniture, a pool table, and a bar off into the corner.

Robert broke the silence, "Vivian, there are plenty of extra bathing suits in here if you would like to slip into one – it may be more comfortable for you." I sat there wringing my hands together and swinging my leg as it rested over the other one. And then I said to him in a sharp tone, "I told you, I don't swim and you will never see me in a bathing suit." Neither one of us mentioned those moments in my bedroom the night before where he nearly stripped me after taking it upon himself to remove my uniform from my body.

He poured another glass of lemonade from the crystal pitcher and replied, "I know what you said, but I just thought you would be more comfortable being it's such a warm evening. Upon hearing his soft tone, I could feel my face turn red with embarrassment and I looked down at the cemented floor in shame. "I didn't mean to snap at you Robert, I'm just not accustomed to sitting around in a bathing suit."

"Listen Vivian, you didn't snap at me, you just wanted to make your position clear and you have. I'm sorry if I pushed you." Hearing the sincerity in his voice, I began to feel my tense muscles relax. "No, Robert, I'm sorry, I have this habit of being suspicious of a person's ulterior motives, and sometimes I have trouble trusting people." And then he rose from his seat and removed his black t-shirt. "It's ok, Vivian, really", he said softly.

Robert dismissed the staff and removed the silver plate covers from the crystal dishes full of fried chicken, mashed potatoes, corn on the cob, and strawberry pie on the side. I couldn't help but notice how his white swim trunks made his deep tan shine. I took special note of those large biceps and his silky smooth chest. I cleared my throat, afraid of my thoughts and how I enjoyed the sight before me; so I began gazing the room in an effort to keep my eyes off of his attractive physique.

I suddenly gave him a smile and asked, "Don't you have a cook?" "Well", he said when wiping his mouth. "I have a maid who cooks for me at the moment, but because she is backed up on cleaning, I decided that I will have you cook for me from now on as part of your duties." I took a sip of my lemonade and asked with sarcasm, "And what makes you think I even know how to boil an egg?" He moved his plate aside, leaned on the table with his arms folded, and smiled when answering, "Your former boss from the steakhouse said you had cooked for them in emergency situations from time to time." "Oh", I said when feeling myself blushing, but I couldn't help but laugh right along with him.

As we went back to eating, I again couldn't help but to gaze over at his smooth looking chest with perspiration glistening down in front of him. And at that moment, I began to feel my temperature rise as well, but I didn't feel right in complaining about the heat and stuffiness when I had asked him to keep our dinner away from the pool after he proposed that we eat outside next to the water. Anyway, I knew deep down that it wasn't only the hot evening affecting me. I was again feeling some things that were very foreign to me – or I should say, my body was really responding to him.

"So", I said, breaking the uncomfortable silence. "Where will I be cooking those meals for you? And as big as this place is, you only have one cleaning woman?" He smiled as he looked up from his plate. "I will be giving you the grand tour of the property after dinner; I wanted to eat first, and I have only limited staff for the time being."
"Oh", I said when driving my spoon through the mashed potatoes. "So I will cook for you until you hire a chef."
"No, you will cook for me permanently; I will have someone cook for the rest of the staff I hire."

Oh boy, another red flag going up. My forehead crinkled into a frown when I said, "I thought I was hired to be your personal assistant." He nodded and said, "You are, but you will be my personal cook as well." He set his spoon down and wiped his mouth. "Look Vivian, you know what I like. You proved that when taking care of me at the steakhouse." The steakhouse – I thought. Yes, every Saturday night, the same table would be reserved for Robert, and I was the only one who was allowed to wait on him. Funny, I never thought of that until right then and there.

His words set off a sense of arrogance for me that I had heard too many times before and had shied away from. Money and power seemed to entitle a man to do what he wanted, no matter who they hurt. But, I didn't want to think that way of Robert Sterling because he had that charm about him, and I was no doubt attracted to him, though I tried hard to dismiss my thoughts; they were there and burning inside of me. How could I be near him without allowing him into my sheltered world?

As he scooped the last piece of food in his mouth, he noticed that I hadn't touched much of my food "Are you not hungry?" He asked when setting his fork down." "I only eat for one person, whereas obviously you eat for two or three", I replied." He grinned from ear to ear and sat back in his chair, showing off his washboard stomach. "I do have a big appetite at times." He must have noticed that my nervous demeanor had returned. "Is there something wrong, Vivian?" He asked, and again in that captivating voice. I sat fidgeting uncomfortably in my seat, and I firmly told him, "I need to know what other duties you expect of me – and why do you require that I live on your property?"

My stomach was in knots as I watched him walk behind the bar to the refrigerator. "Truth be told Vivian", he said. And then he opened the door of the fridge and pulled out a bottle of beer. "Would you like a cold one?" He asked me as he held the bottle up. "No thank you." I answered when swallowing the lump of anticipation in my throat. He twisted the cap off and tossed it in the trash before making his way back to his chair. He sat down, took a long swallow, and let out a loud belch, which caused me to jump anxiously, as I was not expecting the loud rumble coming from his full stomach. "Excuse me", he told me when setting the bottle on the table. "Again, truth be told Vivian", he repeated himself. Obviously he still saw my anxiety, because then he said, "Please relax darlin' – you have my word as a man that I will be a complete gentleman."

He rested his elbows on the table and leaned into me so he could look directly into my eyes, and then he stated in a matter of fact tone, "To answer your question of why I require you to live here – simply put; when I need or want something, I need it or want it immediately." He continued to drink his beer. Upon hearing more of those arrogant words, I folded my arms in a pout, and then I said, "In other words you want me at your beck and call." Amused with my choice of words, he spit a small bit of beer out of his mouth, spilling some on his chin. After coughing and trying to hold back his laughter, he wiped his chin and replied, "Well I would never use those words with you, but…." I stood up in a huff and pointed at him. "You have some dirty ideas!" I then storm trooped to the door while he took off after me. "Vivian", he called my name with urgency. "Don't misunderstand me", he said, and gently took my arm. "Take it easy Princess", he told me softly. "You have this all wrong."

Taking in the soft and sweet tone of his voice when he called me Princess caused weakness in my knees, once again leaving me feeling as though they could buckle from underneath me at any moment. What is it with this man? I thought silently. I literally felt light headed and I began to feel as though he was trying to put me under his spell with the way he looked into my eyes. As I looked up, still dazed by him, I asked in a shaken voice, "What did you call me?" That cool and suave smile came to his face; that same smile that I had become familiar with when waiting on him at the steakhouse. "Princess", he repeated softly. He motioned me back to the table with a draw of his arm and replied, "Just hear me out."

I took a deep breath, adjusted the top of my blouse and cleared my throat in order to gather my senses before returning to my seat. He followed and sat back across from me, letting out what sounded like a sigh of relief. "Vivian, I assure you that I don't have any dirty ideas."

After a moment of silence, I threw my hands up in frustration. "Look at all you're offering me!" I shook my head from side to side in disbelief. And then I started into what was probably more than I wanted to say, but I had lost all self-control. “Really, can’t you understand why I have serious questions here? I come from a different world than you. And then, I come home one day and I’m told that my father owes you money because of an old debt he owed your dead father. On top of that, I have to work for you and live with you to pay it off!” I paused to take a deep breath before starting my rant again. “I don’t get a choice in the matter, otherwise my father and I end up in the streets and penniless!” I leaned across the table and added, “I was raised that I’m to do what I’m told by my father – a man’s word is law, and that’s the way of the world.” I dropped my head and sat back in my chair –feeling defeated. I softly added, “It’s a man’s world and I guess it’s just the way it is.”

After a moment of that god awful silence, I heard him say in a soft voice, “Vivian, please look at me.” Our eyes met and then I noticed his heart pounding so hard that I could see the throbbing in his throat. It was as though he was trying to calm his own nerves when he reached for another drink from his beer. “You and I do have something in common.” He managed to say. “And what would that be?” I asked in a cynical tone. He set his beer down and answered, “I have a hard time trusting people too.” I heard the sincerity in his voice, and sat quietly while he continued. “As you can see, I’m quite wealthy.” He shrugged his shoulders and added, “And sometimes that can bring a lot of people out of the wood work who would do anything to get their hands on my fortune.” He finished his beer and took the empty bottle back to the bar.

I sat watching him rinse the empty bottle under the faucet with a sudden heavy heart. For the first time I heard the loneliness in his tone, and worse yet, I saw it in his face.

I heard my father talk about how different our lives would have been if we were wealthy, and how happy we would be living in the lap of luxury. But, I was seeing it first- hand that having Robert's kind of money wasn't exactly bringing him true happiness.

My eyes followed him back to his seat with another bottle of beer. Though I could feel my heart ache for him, it was more important to find out what he wanted from me. "Robert", I began. "You really need to explain my duties to me. First of all, what line of work are you in?" I guess that question amused him because a smile came to his face. "I own Sterling's Clothing Store and", then came the pause.... I rolled my hands in front of me, motioning for him to continue. "And what?" I asked, rather impatiently. "The gentleman's club here in Keystone", he answered abruptly. I can only imagine the look I gave him, as I wasn't just uncomfortable, but I was downright horrified to say the least! "You mean that place where men pay to see women…" I just couldn't bring myself to finish the question I knew the answer to. Robert gave me a smirk and I could tell he was trying not to laugh. He then asked me in somewhat of a provoking tone, "What's wrong with a man looking at a beautiful woman?"

My heart began to race so fast, I felt as though I was going to pass out. I stared at him sitting there with a sarcastic smile on his face while wearing nothing but his swim trunks, and talking about his disgusting business where men pay to look at naked women! "Women should only show their bodies to their husbands!" I snapped at him. Suddenly he just busted out laughing, making me feel like a fool. "What's so funny?" I hissed. He covered his mouth trying to control his outburst and then he took a few deep breaths. "Vivian", he said in a calm demeanor. "That doesn't leave much fun for the single men."

He gazed over at me quietly as I sat there with my arms folded in disgust, and he went on to add, “Don’t worry - your duties have nothing to do with any of that.” I recall feeling as though my eyes were ready to pop out of my skull as I shook my head up and down in agreement, and told him in a very firm tone, “That’s good for you, because had you asked me to do such a thing, I would have cracked you across the chops!” My words had little influence on him as his smile remained from ear to ear. Then he said, “That’s good to know, I always like a feisty lady.” I waved him off and said, “Never mind all that, please answer my question. “What – are - my duties?” I asked with emphasis. Keeping that wide smile, he told me, “As I said, you are my cook, unless I’m out on the town. In addition, I would like you to oversee the maid staff, those of which I will have you interview and hire. And then, I will have you plan business functions or parties when required, and I will have you accompany me to different functions.” Upon hearing his plans about attending the functions with him, I kept that death stare about me and then asked him, “A man like you can’t find an appropriate woman?” He shrugged his shoulders and answered, “Sure, but I want you to be the one to accompany me.”

I couldn’t understand why but suddenly my stomach began to tighten up in knots again. It was that wealthy and powerful environment; I just didn’t understand it, nor do I fit into it. Their ideas and self-worth is so different from mine, and now, part of my job was to be thrown into that scary and unfamiliar life; that of which I never thought I would be a part of.

“Vivian.” I looked at him upon hearing the sound of his soft voice. “Are you alright? I would never put you on stage for other men, because what you have underneath those clothes will be for my eyes only; when the time is right." Upon hearing those terrifying words, I nervously bit down on my bottom lip. I wanted to run back to the only life I knew, but that was impossible, as there was nothing to run back to. This new life was arranged for me, and that's the way it was. I had no say in the matter. All I could do was trust in what I knew to be right, and that was to trust in the Lord.

"Vivian, are you alright?" he repeated the question he asked several minutes before. "I'm fine", I replied in a firm tone, and I crossed my leg over the other. He nodded and continued, "Good, now let me tell you what you get in return. Besides the living arrangements, you will receive a generous weekly salary and clothing allowance." He gave me that smile that caused me to swoon, and then he asked, "Any questions?" Expecting more of a catch to this whole arrangement, I was taken aback. I shook my head from side to side in amazement and replied, "I don't think so."

4

After the full tour of the house and the property, I plopped down, exhausted on my soft king sized bed, as I struggled to sit up and pull my black shoes off. Boy, was I thankful I wore flats instead of heels! The tour Robert gave me around the property was breathtaking, but quite long as I was introduced to Max, his best friend, two members on the security team, and of course I already knew that awful Adam; who I found out was head of security – of all things! I was told that one of them worked the intercom to the gate. One man roams the fence line of the property and one sits up in a watch tower that oversees most of the property from all angles, just as they do at prisons. Adam made a point to tell me that he was a former prison guard, but given the lewd way he looked at me, I wasn't sure if he shouldn't have been on the other side of those bars.

At that time Robert was too preoccupied with a piece of paper that Adam handed him to notice the way he was eyeing me. I tried to ignore him by looking away, but his eyes were roaming my entire body, as I saw him from the corner of my eye. And then he nodded to the tower while giving me that bone chilling grin. The only difference between Adam and Satan is, that Adam hides his horns. "You see that tower, Vivian?" I can see everything from up there", he told me with the right amount of emphasis to make me feel as though he would be watching every move I made.

Even though he smiled, his eyes were dark and narrow, and he really began to frighten me. But being that he was hired to protect Robert and the property, I wondered if he was trained to be intimidating. He wouldn't dare get out of hand with me though – not after Robert came to my rescue when he got aggressive with me that day at home when Robert was making the arrangements with my father.

My thoughts then turned back to Patsy and how insincere she was in meeting me with that fake smile she had forced. In fact it was so forced, I couldn't tell if she was trying to smile or pass gas, but I knew right away that she was as mad as a wet hen and probably felt that I shouldn't be there in the first place. And the uniform that she was wearing – it looked as though it was painted on her body, and it was apparent she had no problem showing that body off. I thought sure that the top half of her uniform was going to bust open by the way that last button held on for dear life. One wrong move, and that button would no doubt come flying off and someone could get hit with two huge surprises! What was Robert thinking - allowing her to dress that way? Who could clean or doing anything while wearing that uniform? I groaned to myself when putting it together – I think he enjoys looking at her! That's what it is – he likes looking at her!

I had just undressed to soak in the tub when I realized I had forgotten the aspirin was in my kitchen. It had been a long day, my head was pounding from lack of sleep the night before, and the anxiety I have felt all evening long was starting to wear on me. I wandered through my new living area to the kitchen when suddenly this huge bright light came on and shined so bright, that it lit up my entire living area. I was so startled that I dropped the pill bottle, spilling the aspirin all over. I froze in paralyzing fear, all the while showing my naked front directly out toward the balcony. It was only then that I remembered that the only windows that were covered were the bedroom windows! I covered myself as best as I could with my arms and ran into the bedroom crying, I just knew it was Adam, and he was in that tower!

Adam sat in the tower with his feet propped up on the slim ledge of the front window and laughed to himself as though he were a madman and whistled at what he just saw in Vivian's quarters. She was out of sight when he finally pulled the binoculars from his eyes. He slowly pulled his legs from the ledge, and winced as he tried standing up while cupping his stiff manhood through his black jeans. "Damn it", he growled to himself. He reached for the phone and after hearing a voice on the other end, he said, "Patsy get your ass up here in the tower." He never waited for a response, but slammed the phone down. He opened his pants, setting free his bulge and sat back down.

"Well, Vivian", he mumbled to himself. "It's just a matter of time before I get to make you squeal."

***

I finally picked myself up off the floor, collected my nerves and sat in the tub soaking. I felt so violated at what had just taken place in the kitchen, and I just knew that it was Adam who shined that light on me, but there was nothing I could do, and I wanted to forget it – forever. I would be too embarrassed to go to Robert, and I was the one who walked out to the kitchen naked, so it was my fault. Robert's words from dinner came back to me. "What you have underneath those clothes will be for my eyes only - when the time is right." I sat up in the tub, drew my knees to my chest, and gave way to the tears that I had been holding in since I heard those words. He wouldn't come out and say it, but I felt sure that I was arranged to be at his beck and call with everything he wanted, including and especially sex. He was just biding his time, I thought to myself. Finally, I just fell apart and began trembling and crying, not knowing what was next.

5

After a sleepless first night at the Sterling Ranch, I rolled over from my side, looked at the clock, and covered my head after seeing it was five in the morning. But because I couldn't sleep or relax, I figured I would shower quickly, throw on my robe, and go to the main kitchen to begin preparing Robert's breakfast. I felt I had plenty of time, knowing he wouldn't be down to the table until about six-fifteen, giving me plenty of time to prepare the food and get back up to my quarters and dress for the day.

***

When I walked into the kitchen, I once again just had to take in the beauty of it all. And like the rest of the house, the main kitchen had the high beam, knotty pine ceiling that of which matched the floor and the eight foot long table and chairs. I had asked Robert during my tour of the place why he needed the large table for just himself, and he told me that he will have breakfast or dinner meetings from time to time. I was in complete awe of the entire ranch, but particularly with the kitchen. Both the kitchen and the living room was the size of a football field. I drew my hand across the smooth, black granite of the “L” shaped counter top, as I gazed over at the opposite side of the room to the island bar and the built in stove that Robert had designed and built.

I stared out of the window above the deep kitchen sink, which overlooked the pool. Suddenly, my heart started to ache. I turned around and leaned back against the counter and began feeling as though I was allowing myself to betray my life that I had left and I was beginning to get sucked into a whole new world of luxury, even though it’s only been a day; it was that captivating. I love the ranch and the beauty around it, I will have a new wardrobe and a generous salary with no personal bills; with that I’m afraid that it will cause a different attitude about myself. Having the financial security is one thing, but I cannot allow myself to become superficial in any capacity. The last thing I want is to develop an envious and greedy heart like my father.

"Good morning." I heard Robert speak from behind me. I quickly spun around and grasped the top of my white satin robe together. "You're early!" I said in a panic. Naturally, Robert smiled from ear to ear, noticing that I was in a little white robe that of which barely came to my knees. What I was really afraid of though, was that he would notice that I was completely naked underneath. And the way he was smiling, I think he knew right away.

With my hands still clenching the top of the robe, I began making my way to the swinging door that separated the kitchen from the living room and said, "Please excuse me while I go get into something more appropriate." He stopped me with the extension of his arm to my waist. "You're fine just as you are, we'll have the kitchen to ourselves for as long as we need it.

Even in all of my panic, I realized that he was dressed in a suit and tie, instead of his stable clothing. "You must have an early meeting?" He nodded and sat down at the head of the table. "Yes I do, I'm sorry if I didn't mention it, and that's another reason I'm early. We also have our meeting to talk about who you will be hiring for the rest of the staff. I stood before him, vulnerable and fidgeting. "It will only take me five minutes to change, Robert." He sat back in his chair and said in a firm tone, "Once again, you're fine dressed as you are – now, what do we have for breakfast?"

I took a deep breath, knowing that he was insisting on me staying in the robe because he must have known I had nothing on underneath it. Feeling defeated, I said, "Well, I guess I'll just look in the refrigerator." So I opened the door and stood there looking at so much food, one would think I was going to oversee a restaurant.

And then he slipped up behind me. Although he didn't touch me, he was close enough to where I felt his light breath on the back of my neck. "So what do we have here?" He said in a low tone, that of which caused my skin to become goose fleshed – and then, I felt my nipples harden, and it wasn't from the temperature of the refrigerator. I'm not sure I really understand it, but the feeling of vulnerability seemingly caused a stir of arousal in me.

I answered his question, "There's sacon and bausage." Suddenly he busted out laughing. "What's so funny", I asked as I turned to face him. "I think you jumbled your words there a bit, darlin'." Still not realizing what I said, he finally got his laughter under control and told me, "You said sacon and bausage." Upon hearing him repeat what I had said to him, I busted out in an obvious nervous laughter.

The next thing I know, we both arrived to a serious expression across our faces, and neither of us could say a word, until I finally spoke up and told him, "Go ahead and have a seat while I pour you some orange juice. He silently nodded and went to his seat. I turned back to the opened refrigerator and noticed the juice was on the top shelf, and being barefoot, I would struggle to reach it. I turned to Robert and saw that he was reading the paper, so I turned back, and reached the jar by using the tips of my toes to help raise me. I had a hold of the neck of the glass jar, and then Robert asked me, "Do you need help?" His sudden appearance behind me startled me; causing an accidental collision with the jar of orange juice and the whole thing ended up down the front of me, soaking through my robe.

I stood back nearly in tears, drenched and began to feel sticky with the empty jar in my hand. I saw that Robert stood back, eyeing me and up and down, and trying to keep from laughing. "Excuse me, I need to go get out of this wet robe." I began walking away, and once again, he stopped me, this time by grabbing my arm. "No need to do that, just take the robe off here and put it in the dryer." I yanked my arm away from him and told him, "I will not!" He raised an eyebrow and asked, "Are you telling me no?" I pulled the top pf my robe closed, and said, "That's exactly what I'm telling you!"

When he looked down at me, I saw a vein in the middle of his forehead start to form. "Vivian", he addressed me. Though his voice was low and calm, I could see that he was starting to get angry. I know that look from my father, my former boss at the steakhouse, and now Robert. "I don't have time to argue with you", he told me. We have our meeting and then I need to go to the office. Now get the wet robe off and take it to the dryer into the utility room."

I stood frozen and scared to death. Maybe he didn't know I was naked – or maybe he did know, and he was going to make me tell him; then force me to take it off in the end. "Vivian!" Instead of showing my weak, coy side, I finally just had it! "I can't take the robe off!" He clenched his jaw together when he pulled a chair out, he slammed it down, and then sat down, folding his arms. "You tell me why you cannot take that robe off!" I took a deep breath to gather my strength and then I shouted, "Because I'm naked underneath it!" He sat back in his chair stunned while looking at me from top to bottom, with a smile coming to his face.

The silence in those moments as his eyes roamed over my body after knowing I was bare under the soaked robe was terrifying, especially since I knew his reputation with women and how he sees himself as the king of the castle, and he's accustomed to people obeying him. But then he rose from the chair and walked to the other end of the kitchen, and into the utility room without saying a word.

Moments later, I heard his footsteps approach me. I turned around cautiously, almost afraid to move my arms that were still clenching the top of my robe. "Here", he said quietly. He extended his arm to me with a clean white button down shirt. "It's one of my shirts, and it will more than cover you. Get the robe off, use the wet wash cloth at the sink to clean up, and then put the shirt on." He slowly turned around to be a gentleman while I disrobed right there in the kitchen. I laid my robe over the back of the chair, moved over to the sink to wash the juice off the front of me as quickly as I could, and then put his shirt on.

I was looking around to be sure no one was by the windows and doors. It was a frightening thought knowing I was stark naked in the kitchen where anyone could see me; and if Robert decided to turn around before I told him to, all bets were off. Before Robert turned around, I could tell by the expression on his face that he certainly didn't want to turn around, but he did so out of respect for me.

"You can turn around now", I told him coyly, and gave him a small smile. He nodded, took the robe from the back of the chair, and took it to the utility room. As he walked away, he said, "I'll set it aside so you can wash it."

Minutes later, Robert had returned to his chair and went back to reading the paper as I cleaned up the juice. I can't really know for sure, because I didn't catch him, but I felt as though he was slyly taking peaks around that newspaper as my knees met the floor to clean the mess – all in hopes to get a an eye full, should I have a wardrobe mishap. While I was on the floor on all fours scrubbing the sticky juice, I felt a breeze behind me and I realized then that my bare ass was out and facing the kitchen window. Oh please dear lord, I thought to myself, don't let anyone see me through that window.

After I finished cooking his breakfast, we had our meeting. I just could not eat a bite, all the while both of us knowing that I was in my altogether under his shirt that of which came to a rest at the top on my knees – while standing. The sides of the shirt had a high hem in the seams and I forgot to make sure the back flap of the shirt covered me underneath before sitting down, so as luck would have it, I felt the smooth wooden chair against my bare ass, and my hips were showing, as the hem separated some as I sat.

There was no way I would try to fix it, because he was watching so intently. He knew anyway, because he focused on my hips. And even though I was horrified at the thought of him knowing that little tidbit, strangely enough, I also felt a small degree of arousal just from sitting on the chair bare assed. The feeling was indescribable and very new to me, because in our house we were always appropriately covered in the common areas.

Throughout the meeting, Robert seemed as distracted as I was. He was stumbling over his words, squirming in his chair, and he could not keep his eyes from wandering over my body - well, as much as he could see of my body, and not enough of what he wanted to see. I have to give him credit though, knowing that I was completely bare underneath his shirt, we both knew that he could have taken me right then and there, but he chose to be the gentleman he promised he would be, but I could tell he was having a difficult time with his self-control.

There is a backway to the wing where our quarters are located that passes from the door of the utility room through Robert's garage. Because I was worried about running into anyone else dressed as I was, in nothing but his shirt, he graciously accompanied me through that back way.

When we came to the door from the short corridor between the utility room and garage, Robert took me by surprise and scooped me up in his arms, prompting a squeal out of me. "Robert, this not necessary, I can walk." He shook his head in disagreement and told me, "You don't have shoes on, I don't want you to get anything in your feet. "Looking around the garage, the concrete floor was shiny and spotless, and the cars were parked neatly four wide. "The floor is clean", I said with emphasis. "That doesn't mean there aren't some small particles of things lying around", he argued back.

He was certainly taking his time, and we both knew all too well that I wouldn't get anything stuck in my feet, and that this situation was turning him on, knowing my bare ass was completely hanging out, even though he didn't see anything. Thankfully the shirt still covered my front, though it was merely inches from riding up and exposing my innocence. His breathing became rapid and perspiration was running down the side of face, and I just felt the dread that he may be losing his self-control. And I could deny it all I wanted, but the fact is, I was feeling some bit of arousal as well – though I wished like hell I that I wasn't.

As Robert continued to carry me to my quarters, it was clear to me that he was awakening something in me that I have never experienced before. Well, at least I don't recall feeling anything close to what my body was reacting to. I was never able to deny being attracted to Robert, especially when he wore those dark, Italian suits – and the way that he just scooped me up in his arms, reminded me of how Rhett Butler did the same to Scarlet O'Hara and proceeded to carry her up the stairs to have his way with her. The musk scent of his after shave had an effect on me since I met him a few months before, but it was doing a number on me this time because the only thing between us was his shirt that I was wearing.

Robert set me back down to my feet when we arrived at my door. He shoved his hands in his pants pockets and could barely make eye contact with me. I had never seen the man so out of control. Whenever he came into the steakhouse, he was so debonair, but at that moment, it seemed he just didn't know what to do. And then I heard him say in a hurried voice, "Thank you for the breakfast, Vivian – I'm going to be late." And then he nearly sprinted down the hallway and out of sight – leaving me at the door wondering what the hell happened.

***

After leaving Vivian at her door the way he did, Robert was crazed with wanting to have sex with someone, and he just wasn't going to take Vivian against her will, which was the reason he got the hell out of there before he changed his mind. From the time he gave Vivian his shirt, he was hard at the thought of her being stark naked in his kitchen, all the way through cleaning the mess on the floor, cooking his breakfast and sitting through that meeting. He could have let her go up and get dressed, but when he saw her in the robe, he had wanted her to stay that way, and it was incredible.

Robert walked into his quarters, cancelled the meeting until the next day, and sent for Patsy to take care of his needs until he could get Vivian to know and trust him enough for an exclusive relationship with him and to share his bed. He looked at the clock and shook his head, it was eleven-fifteen in the morning and he was ready for a glass of whisky.

For Robert, nothing was worse than wanting to have sex with a woman and not being able to, and Vivian was the first and only woman to have this effect on him, as he was accustomed to the women fawning all over him. He had never been refused when it came to sex. In fact, there were several times in that kitchen with Vivian when he was going to make it mandatory that she meet him down in the kitchen daily wearing nothing, and she would stay that way through preparing and eating breakfast, and through any and all meetings. But because he couldn't bring himself to force her into that, he knew then that it was more than just sexual for him in regards to Vivian. He would just have to get his appetite cured by Patsy or even one of his waitresses at the gentleman's club, until he could have Vivian without force.

Knowing Vivian would be in town running some personal errands, Robert had ordered that Patsy be delivered by Adam to his door naked. He recalled seeing women delivered to his father in the same manner, and it was just one more perk he had that made him feel tremendous in power. In fact, his father always demanded that the woman be carried over the shoulder of the man like a sack of potatoes.

The only difference between Robert and his father, is that Robert only did this to women who were willing, but his father did this to the new women who were taken from their homes and husbands, those of who were in debt to him. When he received every woman, she was completely naked and he would spend hours violating her in every sinister way that he could think of. This was the woman's initiation into the Sterling world, where she would be forced to have sex with strange men to earn the money that her husband borrowed and never paid back. Once in the Sterling organization, they would never be allowed to leave, and would be forced to be money makers for Phillip – all the way up until he died.

Robert opened the door of his quarters and saw Adam standing there with Patsy, she was naked and over his shoulder as ordered. Patsy's bare ass was fully exposed with the lips of her intimate area swollen and ready. He motioned him in with a nod and closed the door.

6

The next morning after breakfast, Robert sat behind his cherry wood desk in his den waiting for Vivian to come in so he could take her into town. She didn't know it yet, but he was going to buy her horseback riding attire.

The ranch was just a few miles South of Keystone, South Dakota, where Robert purchased the 700 hundred acre land, and along with Max, he built his two story log cabin style home that is divided into separate quarters to house the hired help.

Max Andrews grew up with Robert in Keystone since about the age of ten, when Max's father began working for Phillip Sterling as his ranch hand. The young boys became inseparable from the day they met – riding horses, playing baseball, and shooting guns at their handmade targets. And now, Max works for Robert in the same capacity, and resides at his guest house with the understanding that he can come to Robert for anything he needs – there is nothing they won't do for each other, as they're the brothers each had never had.

Robert stood up with a single piece of notebook paper in his hand and paced the room made of cherry wood from floor to ceiling, decorated with his mother's grandfather clock, a glass bar cart, a painting of his ranch, and one of his most prized possessions – the autographed photo of his hero, Lou Gehrig. His father took him to Yankee Stadium on his thirteenth birthday, July 4, 1939, where they witnessed Lou's infamous, *"The luckiest man on the face of the Earth"* speech. He smiled while remembering how he and his father were escorted into the locker room to meet the man in person where he signed his photo and the whole team signed the foul ball that he caught right in the webbing of his glove. That was the fondest memory he had of Phillip Sterling. That trip was all about him and his dad spending time together, for the love of the game - like a real father and son. But, then they arrived home and it was business as usual. And now, he had used one of his father's tactics to get what he wanted – and what he wanted was Vivian. And then he crinkled the piece of paper that he had in his hand while his face reddened, and with gritted teeth he growled to himself, "The same old bullshit threat!"

***

I walked into Robert's den and he was standing by the window, looking lost in thought and holding a picture frame while staring out into the bright sun. I spoke his name softly, "Robert." He didn't respond, and only continued to stare out of that window into the distance. I then walked over to him and gently placed my hand on his shoulder. Suddenly, he jolted away from my touch, and placed his hand on his pistol – nearly removing it from the holster, and whipped around at attention. My heart raced with fear as I ran back to the door. At that moment I couldn't think of anything I have experienced as horrifying as that close call of possibly getting shot. But what I didn't know, was that the most horrifying experiences were yet to come.

Realizing I was the one who had approached him, he removed his hand from his pistol while his facial expression went from guarded to compassionate when seeing how he frightened me, so he placed the picture back on the table and inched toward me carefully. "Vivian", he gently called my name. I was so frightened that I was on the verge of tears. "I'm sorry, Princess", he said softly when he reached for my hand – and taking my trembling hand in his, he kissed it. "I'm sorry", he apologized, and so very sweetly at that.

His gentleness was all encompassing and I was finally able to breathe with ease again. His eyes followed mine as I glanced down at his pistol, hanging in the holster by his side. "I'm ready to take you into town", he told me. But I still found myself unnerved, and I believe Robert saw that as well, and so he added in a soothing tone, "It's okay, baby, I'm not going to hurt you."

***

Minutes later, I was in my quarters, gathering my composure and still thinking about the look on Robert's face as he stared out of the window. He was so deep in thought that he never knew I was there until I touched him. I still cannot describe that look on his face when he whipped around – he was definitely ready to shoot someone, and I couldn't stop shaking all of a sudden. What caused him such anxiety? I'm not much of a drinker, but at that moment, I could have used a shot or two of whisky. But, instead I headed out the door to meet Robert at the limousine out front.

***

Sometime later, Robert and I walked in to the Sterling Department store, he had insisted on buying me some horseback riding attire – much to my distress. I had driven past the store a million times, but never felt comfortable in going inside. And really, there would have been no point, being that the prices were well beyond my budget and the clothes certainly did not fit my lifestyle. I may have the body, but certainly not the means to purchase the clothes, nor was I in the proper class.

Upon walking in with Robert, I observed the bright fluorescent lighting throughout the store shining on the clothing that I could only dream of wearing, those of which included some breathtaking evening gowns. The sight astounded me, as I have always thought of my part of the world as a rural, working class area. Looking around at the glamour of some of the women shopping, I was reminded that not far out of town was the swanky country club, and that I was the one who was out of her element.

Robert excused himself and asked me to have a seat in a small waiting area near what seemed to be a group of fitting rooms. I watched as he went over to another part of the store and began talking with one of the salesmen. As I gazed around, I noticed the far end of the store. There was a long hallway and at first I thought it was the stockroom, but then I saw both women and men, who were customers walking down that hallway – and then they were out of sight. The men were carrying articles of what appeared to be women's undergarments, and the women following behind them and then out of sight.

"Vivian", I heard Robert address me softly. The salesman stood next to him in one of those expensive suits that I have seen Robert in time and time again since meeting him at the steakhouse – and the man had in his arms, a pair of blue denim slacks, a white button down blouse, and white western boots. "Robert took them from the salesman and told me, "Vivian, take this outfit and try it on for me." He extended his arm and said, "There are plenty of fitting rooms and I will be sitting right here waiting to see you in everything." I took the clothes and boots from him and watched as he took a seat on the red velvet chair. I stood there for a moment and just looked at him. "Come on darlin'; I'm waiting", he said while he crossed his leg over the other. I slowly, but anxiously walked into the fitting room and closed the door behind me.

Five minutes later, Robert stood up slowly. "Perfect fit", he said with a look of awe about his face. "How does it all feel to you?" He asked me. "Very nice", I answered him quietly. "I'm just not used to wearing anything like this." He began walking around me from front to back, gazing at the outline of the slacks and how they fit my body like a glove, and I'm sure feeding his imagination with much more clarity – and desire. "Robert?" The sound of my voice disrupted whatever thoughts that were going on in his head. "Very well then, we'll take them", he declared.

***

An hour later, Robert had changed out of his suit and into his denim jeans; a black and white checkered shirt, and his black western boots. He led me to his favorite horse. "Vivian – do you remember Freedom here?" I smiled when walking over to the horse and answered, "Yes I do." He began petting the horse's nose and told me, "She's the one I ride the most. "She looks so much taller now that I'm closer to her!" I told him with concern. Robert smiled and said, "You have nothing to worry about, because I will help you." I backed up a couple of steps and asked him, "Well are you going to catch me if she bucks me off?" He then took my hand, pulled me closer, and guided my hand to pet Freedom's face. "Just get to know her – she's the gentlest horse I have, and any friend of mine is a friend of hers", he told me with the utmost sincerity.

Robert watched as I pet Freedom. I was still very much uneasy of the idea of being on this horse. I love animals, but I have very little experience outside of the normal house pet, and this gorgeous and seemingly gentle horse was huge! Robert apparently saw that I was still apprehensive about getting on this horse and told me, "I have an idea, we can ride her together." I turned around and asked him in disbelief, "Both of us on the same horse?" He laughed softly. "Sure, if that would make you feel safer." To my surprise, my heart leapt at the thought of his strong arms being around me; sheltering me from falling. I wasn't going to show it, so I looked up at him with a dazed smile, forgetting about my earlier feelings of uneasiness; and then I silently agreed; furthermore, it was becoming more obvious that Robert Sterling was awakening some strong emotions inside of me.

I looked back at the horse and told her, "Alright Freedom, I'm new at this so let's walk slowly." Robert laughed as he put the saddle on Freedom's back. "I won't let you fall." Upon hearing the confidence in his voice, I gave him a small smile, and then I looked back at the horse.

"My goodness, Freedom. Your black coat really shines." Robert stroked Freedom's face and asked, "Are you ready to take a walk beautiful girl?"

***

We had been riding for a while and I continued to look around, smiling from ear to ear while Robert's arms remained close around me as we rode down a dirt trail through the enormous Black Hills; filling the air with the scent of his musk aftershave. "Are you feeling more comfortable, Vivian?" He asked me in his soft tone. "Yes, I am – and it's lovely out here. But you better keep your arms around me just in case", I added with urgency. "Trust me", he whispered against my ear. "I won't let you go." Looking back on this moment, I never realized how much he meant what he said about not letting me go.

His words and the way he said them still affects me to this day. His soft tone against my ear has such a calming affect for me – something only Robert Sterling is able to accomplish; even now, despite what has happened to us. The feel of his soft breath against my skin generated a sensation soaring through my body, causing me to shiver with arousal, leaving with me that same twinge of shame I've been experiencing, yet at the same time the feeling made me want to scream from the wonderful sensation.

Trying to direct my mind away from anything inappropriate, I suddenly spoke up. "May I ask why you named her Freedom?" It took him a moment before answering, "Well, it's the feeling she gives me when we ride together; like there isn't a care in the world. I suppose it gives me time alone to decompress and get away from the rest of the world." He laughed quietly and said, "I know – it's corny." I looked back up at him and said, "Not at all. I think you're simply in tune with how nature can touch a person." I thought for a moment and then said, "I think it's a sign that you're also in touch with your spirituality." I'm not sure why it mattered to me, but I had been waiting for the right time to bring up the subject of faith to him, and then I asked him, "Why not accompany me to church sometime?"

"Let's stop here for a bit, shall we?" His suggestion felt a bit urgent and it was as though he wanted to put off any kind of serious conversation. Looking around, I took notice of how deep in the wooded area he had chosen to stop. "Why are we stopping here?" I asked, and again I started to feel a bit anxious. He slid off of Freedom and answered, "I want to show you something. And then he began directing me off of the horse. "Now, Vivian, swing your right leg over so you are sitting sideways and I'll help you down." I slowly did as I was told while he held out his arms to help me down. "It's alright – I've got you." I reached down for him and he placed his hands around my waist, helping me to the ground. When my feet hit the ground, he gazed into my eyes, and he softly said, "I told you I wouldn't let you fall." I held onto his forearms trying to steady myself, as I suddenly felt lightheaded.

"Are you going to answer my question?" I asked him, becoming a bit over-zealous. He gave me a small smile, and replied, "Look Vivian, people can believe in God without having to go to church." Upon hearing those words I asked, "So I can't talk you into going to church with me sometime?" He responded with a shake of his head, and then he answered, "The church is no place for me, Vivian." He paused with an exhale before adding, "I suppose you could say that I'm more spiritual then religious. I'm driven by this land and in my own way I communicate with God through my solitude when I work on this property, and care for his wildlife; such as Freedom here", he added with emphasis and stroking the horse's face.

I looked up at him, unsure if I could see the same through his eyes, and so I asked, "What do you have against the idea of church?" He laughed quietly, seemingly amused with my interrogation. "Where's this coming from all of a sudden?" He asked me. I had silently asked myself the same question – why do I care, really? I stood there stretching my, back as it was tightening up, and then I answered, "Well if I don't ask, I won't know." He exhaled while tying Freedom to a tree. "Alright, I suppose the best way to explain this is that, if I went to church, people would expect me to change too much; and I'm content with the way I am. I love my beer, whiskey; and I really love the women", he emphasized with a wink. I stood there speechless and feeling a bit foolish as he took me by the hand and began to lead me through the trees. "Now – can we change the subject so we can get down to business?" He asked. Not knowing how to take his statement that I found to be crude, I shrugged, and said, "I suppose we should."

After another twenty yards or so, he stopped. "What do you think?" I looked around at the barren land, and asked, "What do I think about what?" He smiled and replied, "I came upon this empty land and I began to think that something is missing." I pointed at him and exclaimed, "I know – you want to build something!" He busted out with a hearty laugh and asked, "How did you know?"

I wandered out further to get a closer look at the surrounding hills and a pond. "Is this considered your property too?" I asked him. He stepped in closer and said, "It is now and if you recall, I had a man out yesterday to see me; this is where I brought him. He happened to be the owner – and well; it won't be a done deal until next week when all the figures and paperwork go through, but yes, it's going to be mine."

I stepped out further and continued to gaze around and then my thoughts went back to our conversation about church. I still couldn't shake the feeling of why I cared at all about his faith or spirituality. What was it about him? Damn it, he is so frustrating; so deliciously frustrating!

Suddenly I felt him walk up behind me. "So, what do you think?" He asked. "Well I"…I paused to choose my words carefully, and then I answered, "It's a lot of land with nothing on it; that's for sure." He stepped beside me and looked right into my eyes. "Is that what you see – nothing?" After a moment of silence, I said, "Tell me Robert; what do you see?" He looked around with inspiration in his eyes, pointed out into the distance and answered, "I see a big cabin with the beautiful scenery of the Black Hills and the pond over there. I'm thinking horseback riding and cooking over an open fire." And then he looked in the other direction and added, "And best yet, I see a baseball diamond over there." He paused for a moment and then looked into my eyes again. "I have decided to look into building a summer camp for kids, but not just for any kids; I want this to be a place for troubled kids, such as orphans – or kids from families who need a place to go but can't afford it."

I looked up at him with a lump in my throat while he stared off into the hills. "Robert that would be wonderful", I replied in astonishment. "You seem surprised", he said with a smile. "I didn't know you had an interest in kids, that's all." He shrugged and said, "I guess it's my way of giving back with all that I have been blessed with, and I want to see kids happy while at the same time teach them to appreciate nature and animals." And then he added with a nod, "God's creation."

Now I knew what he meant about his relationship with God; there was something deeper to this man, who has the power and money of someone like the President of the United States. I felt touched by his plan; I saw a caring and sincere man who could make big things happen, and quite literally by the snap of a finger. That's exactly what it felt like to me, being he brought me into his world literally overnight.

He smiled wide when noticing the look of amazement on my face, and then he continued with his pitch. "I want to show the kids that even though life can knock the wind out of you at times, there are places like this land that we can run to and find some peace and a feeling of safety; I guess it's kind of like feeding the spirit." He looked into my eyes and asked, "Vivian, would you consider helping me with this project?" I looked up at him in awe and smiled. "I would be honored", I told him softly. He cupped my face in his hands and said tenderly, "Thank you; I couldn't do it without you."

His gentle touch sent warm sensations up and down my spine. Seeing just how profound his desire was to build a special camp for kids only fueled my attraction to him on a more personal level. If there was ever a time for him to kiss me, it would have been right then and there. It was at that moment that I caught a glimpse of what was in his heart. He was a big intimidating man who was built like a mountain compared to me, but his heart was even bigger – and that's what did it for me; I thought that maybe, just maybe I could try to trust him – just a little bit; God knows I wanted to.

Robert and I returned to the stables and fed Freedom. "Thank you Robert, I had a lovely day." He led Freedom back to her stall, and said to me with a wide smile, "It was my pleasure, Vivian." He took a seat on the bale of hay next to me, and said, "I like to think we're friends as well as having a business relationship, so I wanted to share my idea with you." I was beaming and I'm sure he could see right through me. I told him, "I'm glad you shared it with me and I'm looking forward to helping you with this project." From the moment he told me his plan, I saw something about him that made me think he rarely showed that gentler side to the rest of the world. It was as if he felt he had to stay with that tough Sterling exterior about him.

I glanced down at his hand covering mine and suddenly I longed to stay in that moment for as long as possible. I wasn't exactly sure why, but I felt a sudden need to fall into his arms and confess that I was thankful to him for extending kindness to my father, and erasing his debt; despite the unconventional way he went about it. I managed to fight the fast approaching tears and rested my head back against the pole, but still keeping my hand in his and listening to the silence between us – and enjoying every single bit of peace. He had taken my hand several times before, but this was different; it felt wonderful and real, because it was unplanned – unlike many of his other moves on me.

"Vivian?" He caught my attention with that soft voice – the voice that I have to admit I was beginning to like very much. "Yes Robert?" I asked while staring off into the distance; with a look of blissful ignorance, I'm sure. "Are you alright? You seem sad all of a sudden." I rose from the bale of hay and glanced off into the horizon through the stall door. "There's just been so much pain since my mother's death", I offered when swallowing back the tears yet again.

I watched as he silently went to the refrigerator and opened a bottle of beer. He slowly walked over to Freedom and began petting her nose as I wondered what his childhood was like. He seemed happy most of the time, and then there was his wealth - and even a bit of arrogance, but today made me see that there was more to him than he showed on the surface.

"What about your mother?" I broke the silence with caution. He sat his bottle down on the wooden stool next to the stable wall, grabbed a brush and began grooming the horse. "She was killed in a car accident when I was three years old." He paused for a deep breath and then added, "I have no memory of her." I went over to him and looking into his eyes, I asked, "So you never really had a mother?" He smiled and answered, "Actually I did. I was a lucky kid because I had Rosie." Relieved to hear that he did indeed have a mother figure, I smiled and asked, "Who's Rosie?" He continued to brush the horse and answered, "She was my nanny and the one who took the place of my mother. My father hired her almost immediately after my mother died." He took a long swig of his beer and added somberly, "Rosie died almost seven months ago." I placed my hand on his, and gently told him, "I'm so sorry, Robert." He noticed the sadness in my eyes, and he seemed as though he was ready to push the boundaries with me by inching further into me – ready to kiss me, but then to my surprise, he backed off. "Hey", he said softly while wiping a tear from under my eye. "Let's not be sad after the nice day we've had."

Hours later, Robert had arranged for a last minute poker game with Max and some business friends and acquaintances. Patsy and I served snacks and drinks the whole time. It was getting to be about ten o'clock when Robert asked me for another drink, and then he pulled me into his lap as soon as I sat his glass of whisky in front of him. Knowing he had several drinks down him, I knew I didn't dare argue with him or embarrass him in front of the other men. The whole time I sat in his lap, Patsy glared at me and it got worse as the night drew on when Robert announced that I was off duty for the rest of the night and would be his companion for the remainder of the party.

There were six men in total, all in business suits. The living room quickly filled with cigar smoke and the stench of whiskey; despite it being the size of Yankee stadium. As I played along with being Robert's companion he held his cards in one hand and caressed my hip with the other. At that final moment, he whispered in my ear with slurred words that he wanted me in his bed that night. That's when I wiggled out of his lap and left the room – with him running after me and begging for my forgiveness.

Minutes later, I approached my quarters and I shut and locked the door behind me just as I heard Robert's quick footsteps approaching closer. "Vivian", he called out my name over and over again, while he pounded on the door in a drunken stupor. I don't think I had ever been so sick of the sound of my own name before that night, the way he kept repeating it over and over trying to get me to open the door.

"Let me in, baby", he said, trying to sound helpless in his tone. "I just want to be with you, I'm not going to hurt you, baby." I leaned back against the door, wanting badly to open it, but I just couldn't trust him, after knowing how intoxicated he was. After he told me about Rosie, his whole demeanor changed to sadness, which I figured was the reason for his drinking so much. I had my hand on the doorknob, but I just couldn't bring myself to turn it, instead I yelled out above his voice. "Robert, I said no; go sleep it off." And with that command, all was finally silent.

7

It was the end of May and I had been working a few weeks for Robert. I stood in the shower allowing the hot water to flow freely over my body and thinking about how I had adjusted very well to my new life thus far, and actually, I found myself enjoying my job working for him and discovered that we have become fast friends. But, I have also discovered that my attraction for him has grown as well, and the one person I was afraid I couldn't trust was myself. Just how much longer can I go on without giving into his flirtations? That question continued to nag at me like a knat at a barbeque.

Robert had called me as I was ready to walk out to meet up with him at the clothing store. He had changed plans and asked me to meet him at the Deadwood Steakhouse instead. I wasn't expecting it, but he had paid for a private lunch. He arranged for the place to be decorated in red carnations after learning it was my favorite flower. Robert had a way of finding out little secrets about me and it almost scared me, but I also had a way of ignoring my fears, and I would justify it away just as quickly as he made his moves.

When I arrived at my former place of employment, the curtains were drawn closed and he had Frank Sinatra playing softly on the hi-fi in the background. At his table was a candle lit centerpiece with red carnations gathered around it. Our conversation was all business until we had finished our lunch. I sat the fork down and gave him a coy smile, though truthfully and secretly, I was bursting at the seams; but I was going to stand my ground for as long as I could.

"Robert, this is lovely, but I can't believe you paid for them to close up for us." He wiped his mouth and shook his head in disagreement. "No, Vivian, not us." He then leaned into me with his elbows on the table and added in that familiar soft tone, "It was all for you." His words touched my heart again. Boy this guy is good, I thought to myself.

"But why?" I asked. Once again, he gave me that look that made me weak in the knees. He laughed quietly and then lightly took his cloth napkin to the corner of my mouth. "You left some salad dressing behind." I shivered at his soft touch when he wiped the dressing from my mouth so sweetly. The man was wearing me down; despite the promise I made to myself to stay aware of everything and everyone around me.

Robert stood up, removed his black suit jacket, and draped it over the back of the chair. "I'll be right back", he told me with a wink. I turned around and watched as he stepped behind the bar and took two glasses and a bottle of wine from the counter. He sat back down, opened the bottle, and proceeded to pour both of the glasses full. He set a glass in front of me and said, "I thought a glass or two of wine would help us relax and get to know each other on a more personal level."

I've never been much of a drinker, so very little alcohol would for sure get me tipsy. My heart pounded to the point of feeling the throbbing in my throat and I thought maybe I could relax after seeing how smooth the last few weeks went. I didn't want to be a prude, but I wanted to stay on my guard at all times too.

"Aren't you going to have a drink?" I heard him ask after he sipped from his glass. "Well, I don't really drink much at all, just a little champagne on special occasions." He sat silently for a moment and then he said, "Well, we can call this a special occasion because we both did well on our first few weeks of our new business relationship." I traced the rim of the wine glass with the tip of my finger, showing off my newly painted red nails, and asked, "Is that all it is?"

He rubbed the back of his neck, and I could tell he was trying to choose his words carefully. "I like to think we have become friends during this time", then he emphasized. "And, it's not as though we were total strangers before you started working for me." I raised an eyebrow with suspicion and asked, "Just friends?" I stood up and paced back and forth in front of the table, and then I continued on. "You rented an entire restaurant, ordered my favorite flowers and candles, and you even have Frank Sinatra playing on the hi-fi, and you claim that you aren't trying to become more than friends?"

We never spoke of his impromptu drunken poker game or the evening he arrived to my father's house and took my uniform right off of me, but those memories shot back through me, which again caused that anxious feeling to return into the pit of my stomach.

After a moment more of listening to me babble on he stood up, took my hand, and guided me back to my seat.

When he knelt beside me he tenderly said, “Vivian, I want to help you to relax and show you a nice time.” I closed my eyes with an exhale as he gently moved a strand of my hair back from the side of my face. “Friends can do nice things for each other, don’t you agree?” I looked down at him with another coy smile coming to my face, and I replied in that shaky voice I tend to get when I can’t control my anxiety. “I suppose you’re right.” He returned the smile and asked, “So will you allow me to show you a nice time and give me a chance to know you more?” I could no longer deny him, his soft voice and gentle demeanor far outweighed his frightening mysterious side, and suddenly, I could feel myself give in just a bit more.

Time had passed while Robert and I continued to talk; I had told him all about my mother and losing her to Cancer. I told him about my Catholic faith and how it was the only thing that had gotten me through my grief and life in general. I quickly came to realize that the wine was making me more open than I had ever intended on being, but it felt good to talk it all out; I felt lighter, and even free somehow.

After a moment of silence between the two of us, Robert asked me with caution, “Vivian, you know who I am, don’t you?” I took another sip from my glass and set it down before asking, “If you mean am I familiar with the Sterling name, then yes.” I nodded and added with a shrug, “I’ve heard stories, but I don’t put much stock into gossip, Robert, and besides, some of it just sounds too farfetched.” At least that’s what I had been telling myself since moving to the ranch, I thought to myself. He reached for my hand and began caressing it with his other hand. “That’s good because gossip is usually just what little old ladies do because they have too much time of their hands.”

I looked down at my hand in his. How smooth his big hands were! My head was beginning to spin some from that wine and I only had a glass and a half. But yet I felt comfortable in talking to him. In fact, I felt safe in asking him that burning and nagging question I had since getting to know him. "Robert if you have that security staff, why do you need to carry a gun everywhere you go?" He looked down at his holster by his side and asked, "This gun bothers you, doesn't it?" I shook my head in agreement and replied, "All guns bother me." I gulped down more of my wine and continued, "The guns are in line with the stories I have heard about the Sterling Empire." He gave me an amused smile and said, "I thought you didn't take much stock in rumors." I shrugged and replied, "I don't."

I knew I was getting a bit too tipsy because I began to feel a bit emotional, and for no apparent reason. And then suddenly, Robert rose from his chair and held out his hand. I looked up at him, not knowing what he had planned next. "May I have this dance?" He asked me with that irresistible smile. I silently placed my hand in his in acceptance of his invitation. His eyes followed mine to the holster on his shoulder, so he released my hand, slowly slid the holster off his rock like shoulders, and laid it on the table. "See - no gun", he replied quietly.

As much as I desired being in his strong arms, my body began trembling as a skittish cat. He held me close with his arms completely around my waist, and a hand caressing the small of my back. Thankfully, I wore my heels, so I was able to lay my head on his shoulder with ease. And then I found myself holding onto him tighter, clinging to him, really. All the emotions of the last few weeks swarming around like bees in my mind finally brought on the tears. I was angry with my father, sorely missing my mother, attracted to Robert, but afraid of his lifestyle at the same time. I had that need to stay true to my mother's wishes, I desired his touch, but yet I didn't want him to touch me, as I had never been touched before; and what if I didn't like it – but worse yet, what if I did like it? What was I supposed to do with this scary rollercoaster of emotions?

And then he slowly pulled away from me, just enough for our eyes to connect. "Hey", he said softly. "Why the tears?" He then gently brushed his thumb tips under my eyes, swiping the tears away. "Oh, Robert, I just don't know your intentions with me." He continued to hold me tight and drove one of his hands down the side of my mid-section to my hip and whispered, "Don't cry, my baby." He lightly brushed his lips against mine, teasing them, wet from my tears. And then he captured all of my mouth, moving in all around - so slow and deep. After our lips separated, and he said breathlessly, "I want you – I want to touch you deep inside." Unsure of what to do or say, I buried my forehead into his chest.

After a brief and silent moment, Robert took my face in his hands and said, "I want you with every fiber of my being, sweetheart. I've wanted you from the moment I saw your beautiful blue eyes." The tug of war match that my heart was playing with my head was exhausting. The way I figure it, despite Robert's denials, I knew he expected me to eventually share his bed, whether we marry or not. He could have taken me a long time ago, so he has been quite the gentleman, but who knows how much longer I will be able to deny him, or how much longer he will tolerate being told no. "Robert", I addressed him as cautiously as I would a wild animal. "I just cannot go against how my mother raised me."

Ten minutes later we were in the back of the limousine heading to the ranch. He told me very politely that he understood, but judging from the silence on the way back to the ranch, I don't think he really did. In fact, he could have been thinking the same thing that I was - that my mother was dead and I'm twenty – one years old, so I should make my own decisions. I think he respected the idea of me wanting to save myself for the man I marry, but it still disappointed him, and may have even angered or frustrated him, given he is used to getting whatever he wanted, and whenever he wanted it. Truth be told, I felt some disappointment too, but I was just so torn.

8

The next evening, Robert had summoned for me to meet him in his den. I was a bit anxious because since our lunch the day before, I felt an uncomfortable distance between us. He had gone out on the town with Max that same night and came home late. I wanted to speak with him, but I really didn't know what to say, and I was afraid that maybe he wasn't alone when he woke up. Not that I really had the right to know anything, or to be upset by it after rejecting his affections, but I didn't like the thought nonetheless.

Upon walking into Robert's den, I found a woman dressed in white loose clothing, a plain top and pants to match. She was a woman of very few words, and was introduced to me as Nurse Mary, except she wasn't a nurse, but a masseuse; and Robert hired her for me! After protesting the idea with him for several minutes, he took me to his quarters where he had set the table up, lit several candles around his living room, and had soft music playing.

Before he left me alone to strip down for my massage, he gently told me, "I want you to relax, Vivian. A massage will do wonders for you, and you deserve the best." I looked around and the ambiance was quite amazing, and then I thought, why not? Soft gentle rain hit the windows and the roof, the only light in the entire living area was from the glow of the flickering candles, and he had the softest, calmest classical type music coming from the other side of the room. Finally, I could breathe a sigh of relief, feeling that he wasn't angry with me or didn't hold anything against me for not succumbing to his affections after lunch the day before.

After Robert had left and I had stripped completely, I got up on the table, with nothing on but a large white towel draping over me loosely. "Just relax, Vivian", the masseuse told me as I laid on my belly "Just close your eyes and enjoy", she said and then she began giving me the most wonderful rub down ever; in fact, I have never had a massage in my life before that moment - and it was amazing.

I don't know how much time had passed, but I had dosed off at some point and I don't even recall her leaving the room. I was lying on my back when I heard footsteps walking toward me again, but I was so relaxed that I didn't even bother opening my eyes. And then suddenly the hands massaging my shoulders felt bigger - and more masculine. I swallowed hard and then cautiously opened my eyes. "Robert!"

I sat up, keeping the towel tight against my naked body. "What are you doing?" I asked him in a panic. "Take it easy, Princess." He said in his soothing tone. "You must relax and just enjoy my touch." He was fully dressed in his suit and tie when he removed his dark suit jacket and then the gun and holster. I recall thinking how I had never felt so vulnerable - well, except that night in my bedroom and the morning in his kitchen. He neatly draped his jacket and holster over the back of the chair. I was wide open in the back, but I was afraid to move to try to cover myself only to accidently show something in the front.

My heart began racing faster and faster as he slowly and cautiously approached me and gently guided me back down on the table by my shoulders. "I'm going to finish the massage." He told me as he rolled his sleeves up. He was in full control and at that point and I knew that the time had come to where he would touch what he wanted and I couldn't stop him. But, as scared as I was, my body also felt a hint of excitement – this, I couldn't deny. Despite what I told him at our lunch about staying with my mother's wishes for me, Robert Sterling was apparently done waiting, and as he told me, he wanted me; so now he shall take me.

To my surprise he didn't immediately remove the towel, which only continued to build my tension in the anticipation of what he was about to do with me. I laid so still with the top of the towel clutched tight in my hands, and barely allowed myself to breathe. He began massaging my neck and shoulders – slow and deep, with his eyes fixated on mine. "Relax, baby", he whispered. And then his lips began gliding down and around my neck to my shoulder blade, his hot and light breath started a chill that flowed throughout my naked body, as if I were receiving a drug through an IV.

I gasped as his hand glided down past my hips to my leg. He continued to lightly stroke the outside of my thigh while he teased the inside of it with his wet lips. And then that moment came, his hand met mine, which was still clutched to the towel. He guided me up into a sitting position, and though he had a soft tone to his voice, he commanded me to remove the towel, as though I was his subordinate; and I guess I was, being I was a paid employee of his. I pleaded in a whisper, "Please, Robert – no." Without saying a word, he guided me to my feet by my shoulders, wrapped his arms around me, and caressed the small of my back.

As frightened as I felt in that moment, the sensations driving through my body were so indescribable, that it drove me to tears. "I'm not ready for this, Robert." He held me close as his hand then swept over my bare ass. And without saying a word, he gently turned me around and pulled the bare side of me against his fully clothed body. He then told me in a seductive tone, while removing the towel from my front, "Let's see if you're ready or not." And then he slid his hand around my waist and down, sticking his thick finger inside of my forbidden intimate area.

"Robert!" I squealed from the shock of his long and thick finger invading my innocence. He gently lifted me off the floor by holding me around my waist and his finger still exploring inside of me as I continued to cry out. The more I cried out, the bigger and harder his bulge continued to grow against my ass, as our bodies remained pressed together. "You're dripping wet", he whispered against my ear when carrying me backwards to the sofa and sat me in the middle of his lap, where he continued to have his way with my vulnerability.

There I was, at his mercy and fully exposed for the first time in his presence. I continued to cry, telling him over and over again, "We shouldn't be doing this." And yet, I never once told him to stop, and even if I had, I don't think he would have been able to. He was ravishing me, but he was also being as gentle as he could, knowing that I had never been touched like this. And then he hit something inside of me that nearly sent me into orbit! I was out of my mind screaming, but this time, it was undeniable pleasure. And dear lord, this feeling was truly out of this world wonderful!

After my explosion, I collapsed back against him exhausted, while he continued to hold me so sweetly and lovingly, driving his lips across my shoulders and the back of my neck. I of course, still felt that bulge against me, which seemed to have grown, making me feel as though I were sitting on a rock. I thought I had an idea of what was to come, but at the same time, I was ignorant of the entire idea, because talking about sex was not something my mother would ever discuss past telling me to wait until marriage. Robert must of have felt me tense up because his embrace became a bit tighter as his caresses were so very gentle and comforting. "Relax, baby", he whispered against my ear.

After a few moments of gathering my senses, I managed to pry myself from his grip and I immediately covered up my body with the towel. He came over to me next to the table and removed the towel from my grip. "Never cover this incredibly sexy body when we're together like this", he told me in a kind way; however, it also sounded as though he was making it a rule.

Before I could respond, he scooped me up in his arms and set me back up on the side of the table. We were almost eye level when he stepped back just enough to where he opened my legs, grabbed my ass, and pulled me so close into him, so that my throbbing womanhood was hanging off the side of the table and level to his belt buckle. He kept his eyes on mine as he hurriedly removed his tie and tore his shirt open, causing the buttons to scatter across the room, along with his shirt. The sultry look in his eyes scared me, but then he inched in closer and ever so tenderly captured my lips with his.

Our kissing soon became hurried and heated as the desperation for each other rose high. Suddenly I gasped as I felt his tongue tracing my hard nipples as he caressed and grasped at the round flesh behind me. My body temperature rose to its peak as he gently kissed and sucked my swollen breasts, but I particularly felt the most tingling as he continued to massage my bare ass. Suddenly, he took my dangled legs and swept them onto the table, lying me down and then sliding his hand down to my most intimate and forbidden area again, which was still quite sensitive from the first time.

"Wait!" I cried out in desperation and broke free from him. I jumped off of the table and headed to the bathroom, but he made a run for me and caught me around my waist, lifting me off the floor before I left the room, and then he gently set me back to my feet. "Come on, baby – don't be so afraid." He told me in that soothing tone; that tone which made me swoon every time. "God help me – I'm attracted to you, but I was raised to be a good girl." I told him very abruptly.

I dropped my head in shame, but then he gently lifted my chin for our eyes to connect. "Vivian, the pleasure your body is feeling is God given – so how can making love be a sin?" I stood in silence and suddenly with my arm across my breasts and a hand covering my womanhood, when remembering I was stark naked before him. He slowly inched closer into me and told me, “Please relax.” And then he gently moved my arms to my sides, and said, “Don’t cover this sexy body of yours.” He cupped his hands around my face. “Baby I’m not trying to sound disrespectful, but your mother is gone; it’s time to live your own life, not hers. Making love is a normal adult function – and a necessary one at that”, he added with emphasis. And with that, he scooped me back up in his arms and carried me back to the table.

He laid me back down on the table and he stood at the end of it like a doctor ready to examine his patient. He then opened my legs, slipped two fingers inside of my folds and began working me as I gripped the sides of the leather cushions, and it was almost immediate when I started to cry out in pleasure. “Oh my, God- I shouldn’t be doing this!” Suddenly – the explosion of my climax brought a loud scream – “Robert!” My legs closed on his hand like a vice as my body jerked and my back arched. He smiled with silent pleasure at his accomplishment when watching me enjoy his touch.

It was a touch I never knew I could enjoy. My mother put so much emphasis on how shameful sex was – especially when it was pre-marital, and the sex was for the man, so it was unheard of for a woman to enjoy or desire anything sexually related. I was terrified on giving into what was actually considered normal, but it wasn’t generally talked about - until one crosses over to the Sterling world, where sex is not just normal, but an expectation and quite literally a lucrative part of their business.

After giving me a chance to gather my senses, Robert once again drew my body into him and being near eye level as before, I reached for him and held onto him tightly with my head on his shoulder. I could tell he was giving me time to take in the feel of our bare chests together. The warmth and sensation from his skin against mine was indescribable. He stood there with his arms wrapped around me and caressing the small of my back until I was ready to go further.

A few moments passed as he held me and then I felt his hand in between us and heard his belt buckle coming loose. Upon feeling me cling to him tighter, he pulled away just enough to look into my eyes. “Don’t be afraid, princess; I’ll be very gentle.”

He slowly scooted my ass to the end of the table and guided me back so I was lying flat on the table. I could tell he was being as gentle as possible when he began to enter me, but as he entered me deeper, I let out an ear splitting scream. Upon filling me up, I began to cry out, “Oh - Robert – that hurts – please stop!” He drove his hands up along the sides of my waist and midsection while speaking softly, “It won’t hurt much longer, baby – just relax, Princess”, he said in a soothing tone.

I cried aloud as I felt the stinging pain of his rock hard manhood slowly tear through me – making me feel as though my skin was ripping apart. He tenderly caressed the outside of my thigh as he continued to make love to me, and then he gently sat me up and gathered me in his arms while still inside of me. I tried not to concentrate on the tightness and pain as he kept his arms around me, and tenderly kissed my neck and shoulders – showing patience and love, as I clung to him and cried into his shoulder.

Robert slowly began moving his hips while still inside me and holding me tight. I still felt some pain, however not as bad, but I began to wish it was almost over, nonetheless. And then he bent my knees up and leaned into me, nearly lifting my ass off of the table, increasing the pressure as he continued to penetrate into me and what seemed to be deeper inside of me, causing me to cry out in more pain. "Please, Robert – it hurts!" He suddenly stopped grinding in and out of me for the moment, and lowered my bottom back to the table, while remaining inside of me. "I'm sorry, baby", he whispered next to me ear. Don't cry, honey." He very sweetly covered my face with kisses that felt as though a butterfly was bouncing against my skin until my cries subsided.

After a few moments passed, Robert pulled out of me, zipped his pants, and asked me to roll over onto my belly. He quietly told me, "I think you need a nice calm rub down." And then he proceeded to gently massage his strong hands into my back muscles. The pain and fear almost immediately slipped away, and I began feeling so relaxed that I had what felt like a floating sensation going on with my body. Never in my life had I experienced such a calm.

I continued to rest in that same spot for several wonderful moments when I felt Robert's hand gently glide down to my ass, as he continued to massage me in a way that I would never imagine allowing anyone to do. But, I was so entranced with his gentle touch that I never moved or said a word, even as he separated my legs a bit and slipped his hand between them, maneuvering his fingers down below my ass to the dripping heat of what was once my innocence. His fingers slowly and almost teasingly massaged my folds, creating a goose-fleshed and tingling sensation soaring through my body.

The tips of his fingers teased the outside of my womanhood, causing me to feel the throbbing of his touch he was creating from my heart to my throat. It was as though he could feel me heating up when he finally entered me with two of his fingers, and began fully exploring me. He never said a word, as I began to moan and cry out his name. The louder my screams of passion became, the faster and more intense his fingers moved inside of me, slapping against the interior walls of my flesh.

As Robert kept working me, he suddenly hit that sweet spot, sending me into the strongest frenzy yet and creating the loudest cries from my lips while my body stiffened through a screaming orgasm. When seeing my reaction to that one motion, he continued to ravish the same spot, as I screamed and cried his name breathlessly, and finally sending my body into what seemed like convulsions.

This was truly the most erotic experience of my life! I never knew such a feeling existed, but when thinking about it in the times of being alone, I cringe at what I allowed – and what's more, I shudder most when knowing that I enjoy that kind of touch.

Robert gave me a few moments to calm down and catch my breath from that incredible release of the sexual tension, and then he positioned me just as he had me before – at the end of the table and my ass hanging over the edge with him preparing to enter me once again. I stared at the ceiling as I heard his zipper coming undone, he removed his western boots, followed by his pants – which he tossed aside.

It still seemed very tight, but now only a bit painful as he slowly and ever so gently slid inside of my wet opening. I did wince some as he began entering me, but as he eased in, there was a lot less pain and I actually felt some pleasure by the time his entry was complete. And then he guided me to a sitting position while still inside of me and held me close. He very carefully moved in and out of me, with his eyes fixated on mine to be sure I was okay. “All better?” He asked with a whisper to my ear. “Yes”, I quietly told him with exhale of relief, as it became much easier.

Suddenly, he laid me back, pulled my ass closer to him, and dove into the center of my mounds, kissing and tracing my hard nipples with his tongue. It felt like a bit of desperation, as if he were afraid that I would disappear right before his eyes. Suddenly his thrusting inside me became more hurried and his eyes showed signs of such focus that I wasn’t sure he knew I was still there. And then came his groans, that’s when I realized what was happening. He quickly and forcefully lifted my ass off of the table, which caused that wonderful awakening inside of me as it did earlier, and once again I thought for sure I would lose my mind! All I could do was scream and I didn’t realize it at the time, but I had dug my nails into his back while I screamed his name, while he held me close and emptied inside of me.

***

Several hours later I found myself lying on top of Robert face down and nuzzling into his neck, while he held me as we clung to each other on the sofa. We were still very naked with just an afghan covering our waists when I drove my hand across his smooth, rock hard chest, contemplating what happened. “Hey babe”, he said quietly. “Are you ok?” I was fighting with my conscience again, that drove me to tears and he had felt those tears hit his chest. “It’s just all so overwhelming.” I told him quietly.

He gently slipped his hand under the afghan and across my ass, and our legs entangled each other comfortably, as we rested in each other's arms. "I know, baby; especially for you, I do understand, but honey, you're an adult who should live her own life, so please don't make this out to be bigger than it needs to be."

I knew what he meant, I had a hang up with sex, thanks to my mother whose dead. I just keep hearing her words to me. *"Sex is for the man, and it's a wifely duty."* After what Robert had done to me and how patient and loving he was with me – well, I just can't believe women saw that as a duty. The man brought out some deep seeded feelings from inside me that I never knew existed. There was no turning back now; I was no longer innocent, as Robert took my virginity and I didn't know it at the time, but this man that I had fallen so hard for would also awaken not just the physical feelings of sex and love, but some deep emotional feelings as well.

9

The next morning, my blurry eyes fluttered open as I saw the clock at seven thirty and smiled when hearing the birds chirping and saw the sun shining through the sheer white curtains. I sat up and saw Robert's side of the bed empty, and then recalled that he kissed me earlier and told me that he was off to the stables.

I rose from the bed, still naked and peeked through the bedroom door. I winced and rubbed my forehead when walking through the living room to the kitchen in search of some aspirin. I was feeling a little sore, even after Robert had lovingly made me a nice hot bath. As I spilled two aspirin out on the palm of my hand, I thought back to my bath the night before…

***

We must have lain in bed for an hour – Robert was holding and caressing me as we rested side by side with our legs intertwined, and quietly and listening to the calm thunderstorm roll through. I was nearly asleep when he rose from the bed and put his pants on to go and start a bubble bath for me. Not long after, he came to me and said my bath was ready and then took my hand and guided me into the tub. And then he did what I hadn't expected – he slowly washed my back – and then my hair – massaging my head with the shampoo, slowly and gently. I knew that I had fallen under his spell with that genius move. He soaped each part of my body and massaged me in the most loving and nurturing capacity. After he dried me off, he had me lay across the bed while he rubbed lotion all over my body. My skin still felt silky smooth at that moment while standing in the kitchen.

After Robert finished rubbing the lotion on me, I went to put my robe on, but he stopped me and asked that I not put it on. He explained how he loved looking at my beautiful body and wanted to feel my soft skin against him all night. Though we had made love, I still felt somewhat awkward with not having clothes on in front of him. But this is what men liked and he was being attentive to me – so I figured, why deny his request? Besides, I knew then that I may as well get used to the idea of wearing very little clothes now that we have crossed that line of no return.

***

After a few hours of running errands, I had made my way back to the ranch and began searching all over for Patsy. After searching the entire house, I walked into the kitchen, but still, there was no sign of her – and then she appeared from the utility room, dressed in Robert's shirt - the one I wore in the kitchen on our first morning…

***

It had been several hours since Vivian stormed out on Robert. He continued to search for Patsy in a fury, but found no trace of her – and strangely enough, Adam was also nowhere to be found, which only fueled his rage; being that he gave Robert a two week notice just as Vivian stormed out the door. Robert tore through the house as though he were on a mission from God, and delegating Max and the other two men on his security staff to search the entire property for both Adam and Patsy.

Just when Robert thought all was lost, his chauffer drove up in the limousine. Robert and Max stood by and watched as the back door flew open with Adam stepping out – and then to their surprise, they saw him drag Patsy out by her hair. He pushed her to the ground right before

Robert's feet. She was intoxicated and still wearing nothing but Robert's shirt. Adam spoke up, "Hey boss, look who I found trying to climb the fence at the South end of your property." Robert kept his darkened eyes on Patsy as he told the driver, "Paul, put the car in the garage for now." The driver nodded and drove away.

As Robert continued to glare at her lying on the ground with her bare ass exposed and her tear filled eyes, he kept his hands balled up to his sides in an attempt to keep his seething rage at bay. Echoes of his father's cold and calculated voice ran through his mind telling him, *"A real man will put a woman in her place by any means necessary!"* He closed his eyes and exhaled, remembering the disdain for his father and his practices, and how he was trying with everything he had in himself to make sure he didn't fall prey once again to doing the same as his father. But, he had to do something to appease his rage….

Patsy screamed as Robert suddenly grabbed her arm and yanked her off the ground, scraping her knees in the process. He ripped his shirt completely off her, exposing her naked body, and tossed the shirt to Max. "Burn this damn shirt!" He growled and turned back to Patsy. "You get your trampy ass in the house." Max and Adam followed them inside as Robert drug Patsy through the front door and into his den. "Simmer down Rob", Max warned him cautiously, while tossing the shirt aside on a chair.

Paying no mind to either man, Robert slammed Patsy down flat on her back on top his desk and then pulled his gun from his holster, aiming it against her temple. "Oh dear God, no - please don't!" She screamed through her sobbing so uncontrollably, that there was no catching her breath. Max hurried over to Robert and began pulling at him. "Come on Robert; you don't want to do this!" Robert shoved him away and shouted. “Get the fuck off me, Max! This bitch needs to be taught a lesson once and for all!” He turned back to Patsy who was still sobbing, grabbed her by the hair and drew himself just inches from her face, shouting, “Shut – the – fuck – up or I will silence you – forever!”

Suddenly the room was quiet as Patsy heeded his threat. She was pinned down on his desk naked, whimpering and trembling. “Please”, she begged quietly. “I’m sorry.” He continued to glare at her with the gun still against her temple. “I could kill you”, he told her with a clenched jaw. “But”, he said with emphasis and then placed the gun back in the holster. “I love Vivian much more than I could ever hate you; you’re not worth it.” And then he grabbed her by the hair, pulled her off the desk, and shoved her to Max’s feet.

Robert told his friend, who appeared to be shaken and drenched in sweat. “Get this crazy bitch out of my sight and on a plane with a one way ticket back home to Texas. His pierced angry eyes cut back to Patsy’s naked body lying on the floor in a fetal position. He glanced at Max, “Get her to her feet.” He watched as his friend helped the shaken woman to her feet. As Max held Patsy from under her arms, Robert then warned her in a chilling and yet calm tone, and stood just inches from her face. “I better not see or hear from you again, and you better pray that Vivian comes back to me, or there won’t be a safe place on this earth for you to hide.”

***

Robert stood over his bed – that same bed that he and Vivian made love in just the night before. He played the moments over in his mind as if he were watching a movie. But then he came to the moment that caused a crushing pain to his chest…

"Vivian." Robert called out her name when arriving to her quarters, only to find her distraught and carrying her suitcase. "Princess", he said softly. "Where are you going?" He asked with urgency when he noticed the sadness in her eyes. "I'm leaving." Her tone told him that her hurt was quickly turning to anger. "Baby", he said softly and began approaching her. She jumped back from him and shouted, "Don't touch me!"

His heart ached when recalling the look of horror on her face, and the tears flowing as uncontrollably as Niagara Falls. "Baby, just tell me what's got you so upset." He said in a raised voice. But all she could do was sob and tell him, "Patsy told me everything." Remembering those words, he still couldn't figure out what Patsy could say to Vivian to make her leave him.

He swallowed back the tears when recalling how much he pleaded with Vivian to stay and talk to him, but that was not be, because then she screamed, "I'm leaving!" And she stopped, turned to him and cried, "I was just another notch on your belt!" He stood still paralyzed and his eyes welling up in tears as she began to run with her suitcase. The sight of her running from him threw his senses into overdrive, causing him to run after her, and shouting with urgency over and over again, "That's not true, baby!"

Vivian continued to run faster than she ever had before and without looking back. She was determined to leave, as she became more distraught. Then at the bottom of the staircase, Max got between both Vivian and Robert, holding Robert back, allowing Vivian to run to the limousine. "Just give her time, Pal!" Max told Robert in an urgent and raised tone. “She’ll be back”, he told him, immediately calm - which finally settled Robert down and he decided not follow her. Robert fought his approaching tears, even now, as he recalled Vivian’s slam of the door behind her.

10

The next day back in Deadwood, Robert stood in front of the old general store that contained a room for rent above it and where Paul had told him he had dropped Vivian off. He was surprised that she hadn’t gone back to her father’s, but then again, maybe she felt she couldn’t because of what had transpired between Fred and Robert. And maybe, just maybe, she herself figured this would only be a temporary separation.

Minutes after staring at the top window and wondering if she was there, Robert found himself standing in front of Vivian’s door. Perspiration flowed down his face with each breath he took. He looked at his shaky and sweaty hand, feeling a twinge of shame knowing he used his money and power to obtain the master key to her room. He had realized the full affect Vivian had on him, because he would never be concerned about any woman he had been with before, and he certainly didn’t care on whether they left his life or not, but with Vivian – he just couldn’t lose her, it was not an option.

There he stood at the white paint chipped door with an inch gap at the bottom, drawing a few nervous breaths and secretly praying that she had the chance to calm down enough in the past twenty –four hours to at least listen to him. After one last deep breath he leaned in against the door quietly to listen for any movements or sounds. Upon a few moments of silence, he quietly inserted the gold key through the loose black door knob and quietly stepped inside.

He slowly and quietly entered the stuffy room - dark from the curtains being drawn closed and he heard nothing but the sound of the worn wood floor creaking underneath his western boots. After not finding Vivian anywhere in the room, he sat at the small desk in the far corner of the room in front of the worn and cracked panel wall.

As his eyes scoped the room, he shook his head in disbelief at the fleabag room in which Vivian was staying. Dingy and dark, a very unsteady looking bed with a rusted brass frame and springs sticking out of the side of the mattress. He glanced at his watch – it was still early afternoon, and he wondered where she could be. It didn't matter though, because he wasn't leaving until he saw her.

A magazine caught Robert's eye and when he lifted it from the desk, he saw Vivian's journal – a more interesting read, he thought, and then he tossed the nature magazine aside and began reading the page of the journal that was open.

Finally, an hour later, Patsy slithered out of the utility room off from the kitchen, wearing Robert's shirt and grasping a near empty whiskey bottle. She glared at me while trying to balance from one foot to the other in her extreme drunkenness. I ignored her condition and said to her, "I've ordered appropriate uniforms and you will wear them – Robert has approved of them." Patsy folded her arms in a pout and turned her back to me, obviously in a snit, but I didn't care, as the uniform she WASN'T wearing was inappropriate. And then she slammed the whiskey bottle on the counter and turned back around to me with her hands on her hips, and wearing a sinister grin. She asked me in her sassy southern drawl, "You think you're the queen of the castle now that the boss has made you squeal?"

I watched in horror as Patsy continued to smile with glee as she took the bottle off the counter and chugged the last of the whiskey down. I stood, almost paralyzed with fear, wondering how she knew about Robert and I – and who else knew. Robert wouldn't talk about something this personal. "You know", she began again with her chatter. "Now that he has gotten you into bed – you're going to get to know the real Robert Sterling. She just laughed and headed for the door. "Wait!" I ordered. "What do you mean the real Robert Sterling?" She had a look of satisfaction when she strutted back to me. "Plain and simple – Robert fucks anything in heels. He uses women for what he wants – just like his old man did!" I shook my head erratically in disagreement. "No, I do not believe you." She glared at me and moved in just inches to my face, and gritted her teeth. "He just had his way with me last week!"

***

Robert's anger grew at the revelation and he slammed the journal on the table. "That fucking tramp!" He yelled. But he knew there was more, because he hadn't even been with Vivian when he had Patsy the last time. He then took the journal in his hand and flipped to the page where he left off.

Robert uses humiliation to discipline his women", Patsy added. "What?" I asked quietly. "Yup, that's right.

The minute you disobey him or piss him off – you've had it!" And then she busted out laughing when she said, "Sometimes it can make a person horny though." I just stared at her in disgust and said, "You obviously want Robert for yourself, and you're trying to cause problems." Patsy shrugged and told me, "Yes I do, and I have had him, but I'm speaking the truth!" I just ran for the door, I didn't care what else Patsy had to tell me; I had heard enough.

***

Suddenly Robert heard the key in the lock, so he quietly and quickly stood along the wall by the door. After Vivian walked in she let the door go shut without looking back and he slowly and quietly slid the lock into place at the top. He watched with a smile as she completely undressed before him, and still without her knowledge as he was standing behind her.

"Vivian." His voice startled her and she whipped around. "Robert!" She hollered and grabbed her silk white robe with urgency, covering the front of her naked body. "Just relax, baby. I'm not here to hurt you, but I'm not leaving until we talk." "What are you doing here – how did you get in?" She asked in a panic. He shrugged and answered, "The key." Her look of concern turned to horror when she asked him, "The owner just handed it over to you?" "Well, it took some convincing, but I made him understand that we just had a small lover's quarrel." She shook her head in disgust and raced to the phone. "I'm calling the police!" As she began dialing, he pulled the cord from the wall and said in a raised tone, "I said I'm not leaving until we talk; and I suggest you dress more appropriately for the ride home." "I'm not going anywhere with you!" She snapped. "Call the police all you want, but most of them were on the Sterling payroll." Vivian tearfully and quickly put her robe on. "You have five minutes."

"Vivian, you were unfair by not hearing me out. Now, I love you, and I want to take you back home with me where you belong", he told her in an authoritative tone. And then he grabbed her brown hard shell suitcase, tossed it on the bed, and began throwing her clothes in it.

She stood watching him take her clothes from the closet and tossing them in that suitcase like a mad man, not sure of what to do now that he professed his love for her. Her first instinct was to run for the door, but what good would that do? Knowing Robert he had one of his men there waiting to catch her. It was evident that he had all the power, which frightened her, and yet, she was completely and utterly flattered by his actions. But she just couldn't let herself get sucked back in.

He finished throwing the last dress into her suitcase, and then asked, "Well, are you going to get dressed or do I take you wearing only the robe?" Her first thought was to snap back at him, but then she thought of that saying about flies and honey.

"Robert", she addressed him carefully and calmly. "We need to talk before you take me anywhere and then I will need time to think." He nodded and paced the room with his hands in his pockets. "Okay", he began. "What Patsy told you is true, but I'm trying to live a different life, and up until I met you I had no idea I wanted to be any different." "How did you know what Patsy told me?" She asked him with a raised brow. He turned back to her and said, "It doesn't matter – this is about us and no one else."

Her silence told him that she must have accepted his answer, and that she wouldn't know that he read her journal. "I've never been in love – until you." He told her softy. "Now, maybe my way of getting you wasn't exactly the most romantic way, but it was effective, was it not?" She bit down on her lower lip and replied in a shaky voice, "Robert, you came in and basically bought me from my father." He began walking toward her and stood just inches before her, and then stroked her hair. "Princess, you weren't giving me a chance by declining my dinner offers. I just wanted to get to know you, and I was ready to court you like a normal man does with a woman."

He then took her hand, sat on the bed, and guided her into his lap. "And then I learned of your father and your family situation." Remembering her father only angered him, and with a low growl, he added, "I needed to take care of you because he wasn't doing his job as a father." He took her hand from her lap and drew it to his lips, kissing it softly. And then he said, "You had me from the moment you first looked into my eyes." She slowly pulled her hand back and rose from his lap, and then stood looking out of the window with her back to him, just then realizing she had the curtains drawn before she left that morning. She took a deep breath with her eyes closed and said, "Robert, I'm afraid of you and the things I have heard you were capable of." He rose from the bed and wrapped his arms around her waist from behind her. "I would never hurt you, baby", he whispered against her ear. "And you make me a better man." She turned around and asked him, "What about Patsy?" He cupped her face in his hands. "I sent her away." Once again she pulled away from him, and asked carefully, "How did you send her away?" He answered abruptly, "That doesn't matter, baby." Suddenly she snapped, "But it does!" He snapped back, "Why? I removed the bitch from the equation – and she never mattered to begin with!"

She backed away upon hearing his tone and seeing the rage in his eyes. "If she never mattered, why did you make love to her just last week?" She cried. "I didn't make love to her – we - had – sex", he said, emphasizing every word. "It meant nothing!" Tears welled up in her eyes when she asked, "How can it mean nothing to be intimate with a woman?" He drew his hand threw his hair with an exhale of frustration. "My god, Vivian, you and I hadn't been together yet – much to my disappointment", he added. She stared at his gun hanging in the holster. "And we can't be together now", she said somberly. She turned away from him after one last glance at his gun.

The room was silent as he scrambled to think of what he could say to change her mind. He just couldn't live without her – it wasn't an option. "I'm not my father, Vivian." Once again she turned to him, and then replied, "Oh no? The money, the women", she paused and then she added, "That awful gentleman's club!" He shook his head in agreement and said, "Yes, and you forgot the clothing store! It's all a part of my income – that's all." She folded her arms in a pout and said, "Well that club is disgusting!" A smirk came to his face when he said, "You know what? I think you're angry with yourself because you're too damn ashamed to admit that you enjoyed me laying down the law with you the other night." Her jaw dropped as she said, "Well, I never!" He gave her a wink and said, "Yes I know, and you laid there dripping wet, and screaming my name", he said in a provoking tone.

She stood there wide-eyed, not knowing what to say in response to his words that seemed incredibly crude to her. He was right, she did enjoy it, but now it seemed like he was making fun of her and making her feel foolish because she was raised to be that good girl. Once again, her eyes filled with tears and then she slapped his face. "I'm not going anywhere with you!" His eyes darkened as he pulled her into his arms and told her, "I love you, Vivian, and I'm not giving up on you!" She began trying to wrestle herself out of his arms that held her like a vice. "Let go of me you big brute!" She screamed and struggled. "I love you, Vivian, and I know you love me just as much!"

***

He drove his lips into mine with that same fire I felt between the two of us. I struggled to break free of his animal grip, but then suddenly I succumbed to him when he ripped my robe open and lifted me off the floor. He then tossed me on the bed and held my wrists above my head with one hand and unbuckled his pants with the other. "We can't do this, Robert!" I screamed and thrashed around, trying to fight him off of me.

Though I was filled with anger and hurt, I couldn't help feeling the heated throbbing between my legs with what was happening. I then realized there was no way to fight him - or myself, as I still felt that raging desire for him, but I wasn't going to admit it to him. My eyes literally rolled back in my head as he kissed my breasts while I continued to squirm, in order to break free from his animal grip.

He straddled me and removed his holster and shirt as if his clothes were on fire and tossed them off to the side on the bed. He then quickly unzipped his pants and entered me with the urgency as if he were racing against time; causing him to exhale in relief, and me screaming as if he were raping me. "No, we can't do this again, Robert – it's wrong!" His arousal was like never before as his thrusting went deeper and faster inside of me while I continued to cry out of how wrong it was, but again, I never once asked him to stop. As he seemed to be close to his arrival, he scooted my ass up into him and off the bed as he released his flood deep inside me.

He collapsed beside me on the bed as I rolled over to my side and I began sobbing. He laid there for a few moments and then wrapped his arms around me. After moments of my continued tears, he slowly sat up and fastened his pants. "Baby", he said softly. "Don't cry – come here", he said as he rested beside me again and gathered me in his arms. I remained with my back to him and curled up. "You can't just barge in here, have sex with me, and expect me to go back home with you." He slowly released me and leaned on his elbow with his body still against mine. He was silent for a moment, listening to me cry. He then gently drew my hair back from the side of my face, and he said quietly, "Well, that's exactly what happened, Princess", he paused, and then added, "And once again, you enjoyed it every bit as much as I did."

After hearing no response, he began caressing my hip and then told me in a calm, but authoritative tone, "If you need it, I will give you a little time to come back to me on your own, but after I give you that time, I will return and beg you to come back to me." He kissed my shoulder, and then he stood up and finished dressing. I slowly sat up and softly admitted, "I love you too." My lips quivered when I added, "But I don't know if love is enough because your lifestyle scares the hell out of me."

The room was silent as I sat and watched him put his holster back around his broad shoulders. Concern swept over me as he had dressed in silence and stoned faced even after my comment. Then he reached for my hand and helped me up. The silence remained and then he slowly took me into his arms, holding my naked body tight.

As he held me, I had to keep myself from giving in and going home with him. I still felt safe in his arms, but yet, I had many questions as to what life would be like if I ended up being his wife one day. And then I heard him say in that smooth tone, "You're mine – I chose you - I claimed you, and I know you'll come back to me." He then pulled back just enough to look into my eyes with his arms still around my waist. "I refuse to give up on us, Vivian." He softly kissed my lips, and then he said, "Living without you isn't an option, and I will be back to take you home where you belong", he added in his arrogant tone before walking out.

I wanted to stop him even as he shut the door behind him; I heard his western boots hit each step while he walking away, but I just couldn't force my body to go after him, so I plopped back down on the bed, rolled over and cried for him; grieving for our new love that would never blossom.

11

June Twentieth - almost three weeks after Robert ravished Vivian in that dumpy room above the general store. He swung fiercely at his punching bag, releasing loud grunts with each powerful swing sending mist from the sweat of his body and hair flying onto the stack of mail he had tossed on his black weight bench next him, just waiting to be opened.

Robert had tried charming Vivian several times after she returned to the Steakhouse to work but, to no avail. She would tearfully tell him to leave her alone every time. It didn't help his cause when he arrived one day and witnessed a drunk trying to put his hand underneath the skirt of Vivian's dress. Robert ended up beating him within an inch of his life, sending the drunk to the hospital with broken ribs, a broken nose, and head contusions; that event just made her fear him even more. He also told the man that she was his woman, and if he even so much as looked at her again then he wouldn't live to see the light of day.

Robert kept a small workout area in his extra-large living room in his private quarters. The living area was identical to Vivian's, when she there with him, with the exception of the stone fireplace and cherry wood mantle. Beside the fireplace were two windows from the floor to the ceiling, measuring twelve feet high by twelve foot wide, side by side. He carefully chose the view to watch the enormous sunsets out in the not so far distance at the most open part of his property. There, he could release tension and receive vigorous workouts, all while enjoying what he considered to be the best of God's natural beauty. It was the best lookout for the biggest moons and the most breathtaking sunsets, not to mention the stars that blanketed the skies, the most at that side of the property.

Running out of breath, Robert stopped drilling his fists into the bag, and although it was a heavy bag, it swayed back and forth as it hung from the ceiling. He glanced over at the mail as his breathing slowed. His tired but relaxed expression turned into a glare as he saw the familiar hand writing on the large manila envelope containing his home address, but as usual it did not have a return address. He knew it was from that coward, but why was the envelope so big this time? What was in there besides that same old note threatening to take everything he had? This envelope was different – bigger – and it wasn't given to him by Adam because he decided to leave only two after Patsy did. Robert's blood turned cold, but he wasn't afraid, he was angry – damn angry! This person was a coward and a menace.

He tossed the black gloves off his hands, and then bent down and picked his white undershirt up from the floor. He gripped it in his hand while keeping his glaring eyes on the envelope, and then he wiped the sweat from his face; immediately tossing the sweat drenched shirt off to the side.

He looked out the window, noticing the faded orange color of the sky slowly blending into the pink sunrise approaching the horizon; immediately calming him. His tense muscles were slowly relaxing as a smile came to his face when he again thought of Vivian and how he knew she would be back in his arms; whether she believed it or not.

Five minutes later, Robert had gulped down two ice cold glasses of water and sat down. He wondered if he should grab a shower before opening that mail but his curiosity got the best of him and he reached down for it. He held the envelope in his hand as he sat there on the red wing back chair; still shirtless and dressed only in his blue undershorts. Suddenly, he ripped it open like a mad man, tossed the envelope aside – and then his heart sank as he saw the photos.

Max looked over at Robert with fear, watching as they rounded the curves with nothing to hold on to as his friend drove faster than he was sure the car was made to go. He swallowed the lump of fear in his throat as they had just missed hitting a farm truck head on after passing a slow moving convertible.

Robert had quickly dressed and then called for Max to accompany him to go get Vivian and bring her back; whether she wanted to or not. Max would be there to assist him in the event she fought him. After seeing the photos of her in the shower he knew whoever was after him had turned their intentions on to her, and he was not about to allow it! The words from the note continued to taunt him. "*Guess what else I'll be taking.*" That's what the entire note said with three photos of a very naked Vivian; and they were taken without her knowledge.

As he drove, Robert focused with a glare straight ahead. Deadwood seemed so far away for the first time. He just couldn't get to her fast enough. It felt like one of those dreams where he was running from danger, but couldn't run fast enough; and would wake up just in time.

Did this sick bastard know where Vivian was? Was he watching her now? And how in the hell did he get in the house with his security staff? Was he known to his men? All of these thoughts raced through his head just as fast as he was driving down that country road in that Jaguar. The worst thought was him wondering what this asshole had planned for his woman; other than the obvious.

***

I quickly and breathlessly rounded the corner that lead back to my room above the general store. I had been on my way back from the doctor's office down the street when I noticed a tall skinny man, wearing all black clothing and following me. When I began walking faster, he did the same. That's when I turned back toward my room, removed my heels, and I began to run as fast as I possibly could.

I trembled when peeking around the corner to see if he was still there, and when seeing no trace of him, I was able to take that big sigh of relief. But then I heard tires squealing to a stop; and as I whipped around to the commotion I saw Robert and Max running toward me. "Robert – what on earth?" Without saying a word, he took me by the arm and led me inside the empty store and up to my room with Max following behind.

Inside the room, Robert slid the lock across the door as I stood there with my arms folded in disapproval. "Robert, I demand to know what you're doing here; and why the urgency?" He began packing my clothes, and told me, "You're coming home, and this time no arguing because I will carry you out of this hell hole if I must." I watched as he finished tossing clothes in the brown suitcase and closed it with Max silently looking on.

Robert walked over to me dressed in his casual white button down short sleeve shirt and his black pants. Of course he had his gun hanging inside that holster. I sighed with disgust. "Robert, I said I'm not going back with you", I argued. "Come on, be a good girl and do as I ask." He then kissed my lips and turned to Max. "Hey, pal, please take her suitcase down to the car, throw it in the trunk, and we'll follow in a minute." Max nodded and did as he was asked.

I threw my hands up and shouted. "I could call the police because you're forcing me to go with you – it's kidnapping!" He shrugged and said, "You could, but half of the damn force was on my father's payroll, so don't expect them to intervene." He eyed me up and down, taking notice of the multicolored floral sundress I was wearing; by giving me a small smile in acknowledgement. "You're coming home where you belong, darlin'." He gently reached for my arm, but I quickly pulled away from him and shouted, “Don’t handle me!” Though I could see by his narrowed eyes that his temper was beginning to surface, he softly warned me, “Don’t sass me.” I stepped back further with my arms crossed; adamant that I wasn’t leaving with him. “Robert, I don’t work for you anymore, so you can’t just order me around as if I did!” “Maybe you don’t work for me, but you’re my woman; and you will do as I ask!” He told me with emphasis.

Five minutes later, Max jumped out of the car after hearing me screaming while Robert had me over his shoulder and carrying me out of the building as though I were a bag of potatoes. “You’re driving Max!” Robert shouted as he gave me a quick slap to my ass. “Stop fighting me, damn it!” People along the sidewalk gawked and mumbled to each other as they watched Robert struggle to control me, and then he managed to wiggle into the passenger seat with me on his lap. Some had looks of horror on their faces; particularly the women while others being men, found it amusing while figuring it was a lover’s quarrel. “Help me!” I shouted as we sped away.

***

A bit later at the Sterling Ranch, Robert got out and guided me out of the car by my arm, and into the house. As I continued to dig my heels, I was slapping at him with my other hand. “Let me go you big brute!” Max put my suitcase down, and told Robert, “I’ll see you later.” Without saying a word to Max, Robert again flung me over his shoulder and carried me up the staircase as Max stood there shaking his head with a wide grin.

I fought Robert all the way up the stairs and inside his quarters by kicking my legs and slapping his back as he kept me over his shoulder. “Vivian”, he addressed me calmly. "Please settle down already." I screamed and continued to kick regardless of his orders – something he wasn't accustomed to and never tolerated from a woman.

Two seconds later, he aggressively set me to my feet, and grabbed me by the shoulders. "Vivian!" He addressed me in a growling tone. "If you proceed to act like a child I will have to treat you as such!" I was so enraged, I pierced my lips together and doubling my fist, I drilled him in the gut; and hurting my hand in the process. "Ouch!" I cried out and held my hand to my chest. "What are you made of, steel?" He gave me an amused grin and took my hand. "Let me see." He looked it over and carefully caressed it; then he slowly drew my injured hand to his lips softly kissing it. A wide smile came to his face when he told me, "I think you'll live, Joe Louis." Suddenly my knees felt as if they would buckle from under me as I tried to hide my pleasure by pouting and then pulling away from him.

His gentle glance turned into that authoritative look with a raise to his eyebrow. "We're going to get something straight right now", he told me in a direct and no nonsense tone. "All you need to know is that I brought you back here to protect you; but mostly because I love you and I can't be without you." I folded my arms in disgust, and began, "But"… "But nothing, Vivian! You're home where you belong because you're my woman, and I don't want you out there alone, and without me to protect you." I stood there listening to him tell me how it was and I then began to feel the sense of desire for him all over again. But, who did he think he was anyway? He was basically laying claim to me as though I were a piece of his property! "Well, you don't have the right to act as though you own me!" I snapped at him.

I watched him and took two steps back as I took notice of his patience dwindling. He took a few deep breaths and ran his hand through his thick hair as he paced and seemed to be searching for a response to give me. "I'm telling you", he said calmly and carefully. "As my woman, whom I will share a bed with; you will walk the line, darlin'." He walked closer in to me, and added, "This means that you will obey me, you won't sass me, and you will not strike me", he told me in that tone of authority.

Upon hearing his words, my jaw dropped and I placed my hands on my hips. "And just what will you do about it?" I asked in a provoking tone; and challenging him. He was about to say something when I began my rant. "For the love of God, you come waltzing in and demand me from my father because he owes your dead father money, you get me into bed, and then I leave you after learning what you're capable of; and then you use your money and power to break into my rented room and once again have sex with me." I paused to take a deep breath and continued, "And even worse, you kidnap me after I told you that I was not coming back!" After I stopped, he asked, "Are you finished?"

I cautiously watched as he removed his gun and holster, placed it on the small table next to the door, and slid the lock across the door. He then walked over toward me and put his foot on top of the cherry wood coffee table; and then without warning, he whipped me across his leg and began spanking me. "Ouch – Robert!" I squealed as he continued on with my punishment; or discipline, as he called it.

Finally, he released me and stood over me with his large arms crossed. "Now", he began in a firm tone. "That's what I will do about it; does that answer your question?" My eyes watered over while I rubbed my sore ass. "Yes, but you didn't have to spank me." I said in a hurt tone. "I'm sorry darlin', but that's exactly what's going to happen when you get out of line; you're to do as I tell you."

Back in Deadwood, Adam stood dressed all in black from head to toe before the grave of Phillip Sterling at the private family plot; that of which was surrounded by a secured fence all around it. But unknown to Robert, now his former boss, Adam had an extra key made. The marker was made of black granite and Phillip's name sculpted in gold. It was a sizable area reserved for future family members with enormous Black Hills Spruce and Aspin Burch trees surrounding the area. The humidity was growing very thick in the early afternoon air, and dark clouds began rolling through; somehow fitting for the dark presence of Adam lingering about.

He inhaled deep with his eyes closed for a quick moment, and then he glared back down at the marker. He began to speak with a clenched jaw. "I bet you thought your dirty little secret would stay buried right along with you – well, thanks to you, I was left with nothing!" He hissed with his face turning beet red and his veins bulging from his temples. "My mother may have been just another whore to you, but you should have been a real man and taken care of me; the same as you did for him! You threw me away as if I were trash. Why, because I came from one of your filthy whores? A whore you put to work for your own gain! What was so special about Robert?" He paused to take a deep breath again, and shouted while pounding his chest. "I was your flesh and blood too; you rotten, gutless son of a bitch!"

Adam's hand shook as he pulled the torn journal page from his black suit pants; the piece of paper that revealed Phillip Sterling as his father, and written in the words of his mother; dead, no doubt in his mind by the hands of Sterling and his clan, but he had no solid proof. She wrote that she lived in fear of her life after her revelation to Phillip about their unborn child; and forcing her to leave for parts unknown until she could give birth safely. *"We have nowhere to go as my family has disowned me, so I must go to Phillip and beg for his help.*

Adam took a long deep breath and placed the paper back in his pocket. He then glared back down at the marker, and with a vile tone he said, "Now you can rot in Hell and watch your golden boy Robert pay the consequences of your sins!"

12

Robert had refused to tell Vivian why he felt he needed to go to such lengths to protect her. All he told her was that she just needed to trust him and obey all his orders. She was not to leave the house without him, and that included when simply walking around the exterior of the property. All of those demands began to frighten her, making it obvious that something or someone was a threat to her – or him – or both. He also mentioned that part of protecting her was not telling her what had happened. She now feared that she was about to see what his world was all about.

I stood over at the windows in the living room next to Robert's weight equipment and punching bag. Dark clouds had been hovering over off and on for the last few hours, so we were sure to get a heavy storm sooner, rather than later.

I thought back to after Robert had spanked me and suddenly I felt that I may have deserved it with the tantrum and then hitting him – which didn't seem to faze him; amazingly enough. I was sure his gut was made of steel, but then he proved that his heart wasn't because after he scolded me, I began to cry, and he took me into his arms. Then minutes later I had succumbed to his affections again. I wanted to say no but, he was wonderful, and gentle. I really wanted to give him rules; my rules! But then he nuzzled my neck; kissed my earlobe, and before I knew it, I was completely naked before him, and in front of the windows; the windows that were as bare - naked as I was. He then took me right there in the living room. There was no stopping him; and if I was being at all honest with myself, I'd have to admit that I didn't want him to stop.

After we had made love, I had drifted off to sleep right there on the sofa while Robert took a quick shower and dressed. I had been so emotionally drained and now physically. I just couldn't stay awake as he held me; making me feel safe and comfortable.

My eyes fluttered open as he kissed my cheek softly. He was dressed in one of his many dark suits. My god, when he dressed in a suit, he looked like a normal business man; and so very handsome. He silently took me by the hand, leading me to the door; and then he took my very naked body back in his arms. He softly explained that he had to meet with what was left of his security team and that he expected me to stay put just as he asked. When I agreed, he gave me a smile and a few gentle taps to my ass, and said, "That's my girl." He softly kissed my lips and whispered, "I love you, my baby."

Tears ran down my face as I kept playing his words in my head over and over. They were happy tears, but I was still scared of what the future held. I knew he loved me, and though he was rather rough around the edges, he was very delicate with me; outside of the spanking of course. If only I could get him to live a normal life and sell his gentlemen's club; I rolled my eyes at the thought of him running such a business. And of course he was eyeing all the women there too. Could I ever be enough for him? I had asked myself that question since our first time of making love.

Robert and Max had just walked into the den after meeting with the two men he had left guarding his property. The decision was made that Max would step in to help with security until Robert could hire more men. The bodyguard he had at the club assured him that he would be fine running the place without him since they hired another man to help keep the women safe.

Robert had finished pouring himself and Max a glass of whiskey and then he sat behind his desk while Max sat across from him as usual. "So", Max broke in. "We didn't have a chance to talk about it, but I assume that things are better between you and Vivian?" Robert took a long swig from his glass and answered with a smile coming to his face, "And how my friend." Max raised his glass to him, and replied, "Glad to hear it."

There was a moment of silence between the two as Robert swished his whiskey around and stared into the glass. "You look deep in thought, pal", Max said; grabbing his attention. "I just hope we can figure out whose fucking with me so I never have to tell Vivian about any of this shit. I just don't want her frightened." Max nodded and took a drink from his glass. "You may have to tell her before it's over; I mean, you can't keep her under lock and key forever." Robert sat back in his swivel chair, looking up at the ceiling. He exhaled and said, "Yeah, I know."

Adam sat in the dark room, the same room that Vivian had above the store. He saw Robert carry her out that day and then after his visit to the cemetery he went and rented the very same room. He sat in the hard wooden chair in the corner with the lights dim and drinking from the whiskey bottle, thinking of what he wanted to do with Vivian; thinking how to get to her, even when knowing that Robert would never let her out of his sight. He sat there in a drunken stupor with his pants unzipped and staring at the beautiful naked blonde in the bed. A sinister grin came to his unshaven face of stubble as he recalled the night before….

Adam gazed the room of the tavern in search of a woman to satisfy his lustful and angry needs, but none of the women were alone. But then he saw *her* walking in; a dead ringer for Vivian! Blonde hair, blue eyes, and that sexy hour glass figure. Not only did she look just like Vivian, she had her style of dressing; wearing a dress that came down below her knees and the top well covered; which only aroused him more. With the level of her beauty, he was quite surprised that she walked in without a man by her side.

He reached into his black suit pocket and with discretion he pulled out a small plastic bag full of a powdery substance, and then quickly shoved it back into the pocket. He carried it around in case he needed it at a moment's notice. After observing she had ordered a glass of wine, he told the waitress he wanted to take it to the poor lonely lady and keep her company. After the waitress set the glass in front of him, he gazed around the busy tavern and quickly slipped some of the powdery substance in her glass; stirring it with his finger. Less than an hour later he was helping her out of the tavern and into his truck. A few eyes were on them on the way out the door, so he convinced them that he was a friend, and she was not feeling well. Too easy, he thought and laughed to himself.

When getting back to the store where Adam had rented the room, he sat the woman down at a corner table while he locked the door and put the *On Vacation* sign in the window to keep people from wondering where the dead owner was. Adam had to kill him after the man asked for more money for the room; and then he threatened to call the police after seeing him put food into his pockets without paying for it.

When Adam got the woman to the room, she had her eyes half open, but she was unable to move. It seemed to him that she was trying to stay awake because she knew that she was in trouble. Some mumbling sounds came from her, almost as if she was trying to cry out as he was cutting her clothing off with his hunter's knife. He gazed at the well-trimmed hair on her womanhood and wondered if he may get lucky enough to have a pure fuck.

There she was, naked on the bed and face up. As he focused on her, he began imagining that she was Vivian. It didn't take much imagination when it came to her naked body, he ought to know; as he had taken pictures of Vivian in the shower and again on her bed. As difficult as it was, he had to wait to take her, due to the knock on the door, Because he wasn't going to take any chances of getting caught, he was forced to hide in the closet until the knocking on the door stopped; giving him that chance to sneak out of Vivian's quarters that night.

He looked over at the tarnished brass bedposts at the head of the bed and smiled. He leaned over and whispered in her ear. "You're going to love this." She gave him nothing more than a blank stare, almost comatose like; and yet she had tears streaming from the sides of her eyes.

He went to his suitcase and pulled out two ropes; smiled and set them aside while walking back to her as she was on the side of the bed where he had stripped her. He took her by the wrists, pulling her up to a sitting position and lifted her off the bed, over his shoulder, and around to the other side; tossing her down in the middle of the bed. He took the ropes and pulled them tight with a laugh. "Oh yeah this is going to be fun."

Minutes later he stood at the end of the bed and smiled wide at his accomplishment. He had the woman's legs apart with her ankles tied to the bed posts. Again, he heard her trying to cry out. He just couldn't understand how she wasn't asleep, but that was okay; because he will enjoy it even more this way. He removed his shirt and boots and jumped into the bed from the end. On his knees, he leaned over her and gave her a wink. "I bet you've never been poked before." Finally, her eyes closed. He then unbuckled and unzipped his pants; releasing his hard rod and with a sinister smile, he shoved himself all the way up inside her. He took pride in noticing her eyes growing big and her mouth unable to open all the way, so what would be a screaming sound, came out muffled as if she had a pillow over her head.

He tore inside her as though he were a wild animal; his body slapping against hers, hard and fast to the point of sending the bed posts banging against the paneled wall. He looked at her, lying motionless; and her head off to the side as she remained in a deep sleep. He smiled wider as he felt that explosion approaching and then his eyes rolled back in to his head, as he let out a loud and satisfying groan; and emptied himself inside of her.

He sat there and grew harder as he recalled every moment he pounded inside of her; just like a Sterling, and he smiled with pride at the thought. He had untied her after he finished violating her; now he would wait until the stuff wore off, and she would open her eyes and gather her senses. But until then, he had to figure out how to get back into the Sterling home; as a trusted employee again.

13

The last week of June, Adam sped off in a rage from the Sterling Ranch in his black Nineteen Forty- Five Ford truck. He pounded the steering wheel while cussing Robert's name. "How dare that asshole dismiss me!" He growled. He continued to glare straight ahead as he recalled the moments before.....

Max had escorted Adam into Robert's den where he found Robert on what appeared to be a business call. Robert's eyes cut to Adam and then he promptly told the person on the other end that he would call them back.

He gripped the steering wheel tight; so tight his knuckles were turning white. What the hell was he going to do now? His cash flow was quickly disappearing. He should have never left in the first place, but he didn't know how else to work for Robert and put his plan into action.

Just when he thought Robert was ready to offer him his job back, she walked in – Vivian! There she was dressed in a pure white dress – one of those evening gown type dresses, he figured. She gasped as soon as their eyes locked; and she moved to Robert quickly and held on to him fearfully. And that's when he was told that he could not have his job back; all because of her!

He quickly pulled his pickup truck over to the side of the road and threw it into park while glaring straight ahead as the engine idled. His breathing began to calm as the horizon began to swallow what was left of the sun. One of these days, he thought. I'm going to have what I want; and little brother won't be there to stop me! I will make Vivian pay for making sure Robert didn't hire me back!

Back at the store, Adam glared at the woman. In the two weeks with Adam, she only cried and she always seemed afraid to talk; which was fine with Adam, as he didn't care to listen to any woman talk. In his mind, a woman was good for only one thing; ironic how he was so much like the father he had never known; Phillip died before he could make his way into Robert's life.

At night Adam tied her wrists to the bed posts so she couldn't escape. He figured she wouldn't try to escape, considering he destroyed her clothes. She was right there naked and ready for him whenever he needed to curb his appetite; and until he could get to Vivian. Vivian would be his best bread winner too. The first thing he would do is make certain she couldn't have babies. No, he thought, no babies! Once a woman have babies they get fat and lazy – and he would not allow that for Vivian or any other woman he puts in his business! He laughed to himself when thinking of gathering any men that were still around from Phillip's organization so he could recreate what he should have had; and best of all, he'll take everything from Robert!

***

I stared out of the window at the darkness from Robert's living room quarters at the approaching storm, as he made his way around the kitchen to fix me some hot tea to help soothe my nauseated stomach. A few days ago I had become sick and had felt nauseated off and on ever since. I blew it off as nerves and lack of rest.

"You should drink this and relax", he told me. I walked back over to him and said, "Robert, I want to know what is going on. I've been back here for several weeks and nothing has happened." He set the cup on the island bar and calmly replied, "You just have to trust me when I say this is all to protect you." I rolled my eyes and gazed over at a picture that had caught my eye; a picture I hadn't noticed before.

The picture was encased in a gold frame and in the color photo was a small boy standing next to a thin, beautiful woman sitting in a chair. I was struck by her beauty from her silky dark complexion, to her ice blue eyes and jet black hair. As I looked closer, I saw what seemed to be a man's hand on the boy's shoulder and the photo looked to be folded back on one side. Robert walked up behind me, took hold of the picture, and smiled. "I actually remember sitting for this picture. I was five years old." I gave him a small smile, and replied, "This must be Rosie." He smiled with admiration, and answered softly, "Yes, this is Rosie; I Felt I was finally able to bring it back out and decided to do so just this morning."

As I watched him look at the photo with a reminiscent smile, I took it from him, and pointed to the man's hand. "And this must be your father's hand?" His smile disappeared as he took the photo back from me and set it back down on the end table. "It's not important." He made his way back to the kitchen and asked, "Are you hungry?" I looked back at the photo, and said, "Robert, let's talk about this. Why did you fold your father out of the picture?"

He seemed to be getting angry and wasn't responding to my words at all. His back was to me as he poured himself a glass of whiskey when he suddenly heard me address him. "Robert, aren't you going to say anything?" His hand shook as though he was fighting his fast approaching anger, and then he suddenly whipped around and shouted, "Damn it, Vivian! If you must know, he was a rotten son of a bitch and he never deserved Rosie; or any other woman!" He then threw his glass against the balcony door, shattering it into what seemed like a hundred tiny pieces.

His darkened eyes cut back to me. I stood paralyzed with fear and my arms clasped against my chest. He hurried over to me and took me in his arms. "I'm sorry, baby", he told me softly. "I didn't mean to lose my temper and frighten you." As he held me, I told him in my shaky voice, "I'm just trying…to help you." And then I began to cry. "I know, baby; I'm sorry", he whispered to me gently and gathered me tighter into his arms.

He held me until my crying subsided and then he slowly released me; and gently swiped away the tears from my eyes with the tips of his thumbs. He moved in closer to me and cupped his hands around my face. "Always remember that despite my temper I would never hurt you." And as crazy as it seems, I believed him.

***

The next morning I laid in Robert's bed, naked and trying my best to stay awake. I was feeling exhausted as I have felt for the last few weeks or so. I had attributed it to Robert's strong sexual appetite; that of which made me wonder if I could continue the way we have. This was no time to be tired though, as I had the finishing arrangements of Robert's big Fourth of July birthday party to complete; which was only three days away. I couldn't cancel it because he had me send out the formal invitations a few weeks ago, soon after my return. In addition, I had the food ordered with the catering company and I hired extra staff for the serving of appetizers and cocktails. And lastly, I had tried to complete the interior decorating of the cabins out at the campsite, but I just couldn't focus.

I had managed to roll out of bed at nine so I could get a shower and meet Robert down in the main kitchen for breakfast. That has been something we began doing when he brought me back home. My aching muscles began to relax as the hot water gently blanketed my body. I closed my eyes thinking back to last night after Robert's tantrum that frightened me so. I was taken aback by how he immediately softened when seeing how scared I was with his explosion. It was after comforting me that he told me about the brutal way his father treated Rosie; the woman he loved as his mama.

He became emotional as he told me about the time he told Rosie that his father taught him what a man does to a woman while forcing him to watch him have sex with one of his prostitutes. This was the first and only time he witnessed Rosie standing up to Phillip when she angrily confronted him about the boy watching such adult acts. Rosie had felt so strongly about her beliefs that she took a severe and humiliating beating in front of Robert after being given the option of apologizing to Phillip for the disrespect and interference of raising his boy as a man.

The tears welled up in his eyes while he described their horror. He fought back in letting those tears fall by clenching his jaw together. I began to cry again when remembering his details as I began drying myself off.

Phillip had forced them both up to his quarters, which he shared with Rosie. It was a large room, entirely made of cherry wood from floor to ceiling and furniture to match. The beige curtains were always closed as Phillip preferred the darkness due to his sensitive eyes. After they entered the room, Phillip ordered Rosie to strip down completely. "He used the same tactics with all his female employees when they stepped out of line", Robert told me. "And they couldn't do a damn thing about it because he owned them; they had no one to turn to and nowhere else to go", he added in a matter of fact tone. That's when I couldn't help but think that it was eerily similar to my situation, being that I could never depend on daddy; or have a home to go back to.

Phillip turned to his young son and ordered him to watch; and learn what happens when a woman talks back and disobeys her man. Robert told me that he stood so still and frightened that he was afraid to breathe while he watched his father back hand Rosie so hard that the impact sent her body flying halfway across the room. Robert cried as he saw the woman he loved sobbing on the floor; naked and bleeding. Then he watched as his father forced Rosie up to her feet by her hair and shoved her face first into the wall, causing her blood to splatter.

Robert said he remembered looking away for a moment and noticed his father's pistol lying on the bedside table while he continued to beat on Rosie. Robert's eyes cut back to Phillip as he entertained the idea of taking that pistol and blowing his father's head off. But, he just couldn't find the nerve to do it; at that point he had only shot a gun off twice in his life, but shooting at only tin cans. He feared most that he would accidently shoot Rosie instead of his father.

Robert admitted to me that he had never told anyone about what happened that day. As a ten year old boy, he watched in horror as his father whipped, beat and raped his beloved Rosie. He told me that Phillip started on her when the sun was shining and finally stopped when the moon came out. When Phillip finished with her, he told his young son to stop his bawling and call for the doctor; and then he simply walked out as if nothing had happened, while Rosie was left on the floor bleeding and unconscious. I think Robert spared me most of the details, but he admitted in a matter of fact tone, "If I could go back I would've killed the son of a bitch; I just wasn't tough enough back then." And then Robert looked back at me with the coldest look I had seen from him up to that point, uttering the chilling words, "If I had one wish, I would go back to that moment and blow his damn head off with his own gun."

After Robert fell silent, I watched as he sipped on that glass of whiskey and wondered what other kind of hell he witnessed. I closed my eyes and silently asked God to take his pain away and guide him to a new life. As soon as Robert finished his drink, he turned and walked over to me;

and slowly cupped my face in his hands, and whispered, "I have to be with you, Vivian." He drew in and softly met his lips with mine. "You're my saving grace, baby", he said; and then paused to kiss me again. "You're my heart", he said as he glided his smooth lips down my neck and then to my collar bone. "You're my soul", he whispered; as he ripped his shirt off with aggression and yanked me close after ripping my blue dress and bra open.

"Oh God, Robert!" I gasped as he picked me up with one arm while unbuckling his pants with the other hand. "This needs to stop", I cried out. "I must have you right now; I want you every day and every night", he told me with emphasis; as he laid me on the bed and quickly tore the rest of my dress off my body, including my blue lacey panties from one side, as he took me immediately. Once again, I cried, "No", as my body screamed yes.

I was crying with pleasure; shameful pleasure, as he slipped in and out of me like there was no tomorrow. All I could do was lay there screaming and crying with passion; as the headboard banged up against the wall. There was no slowing him down and it seemed endless, as I recall that we were still making love three hours later; with very little breaks in between. In some ways I felt he was raping me; and yet I felt that forbidden desire and ecstasy.

After experiencing the mind blowing orgasms, I had to wonder how my mother felt sex could be just a wifely duty. But, then again – my father was horrible to my mother; maybe not to the extreme as Robert's father, but horrible, nonetheless.

***

I had just finished rubbing lotion all over my body when Robert had called me on the phone and asked me to come down to the main kitchen; and he had specific instructions. I was to wear nothing but that short and silky white robe that he liked, and nothing else. I was to be completely bare, including my feet; he was firm about that. When I protested, he promised we would be alone and no one would disturb us. All he wanted was the usual; for me to cook him breakfast and eat with him. I had five minutes to get down there or he would come and get me.

I appeared downstairs minutes later and at the swinging door that led to the kitchen was Robert – and Max! I heard Robert tell him in a firm tone, "And please make sure we are not disturbed." Upon making eye contact with Max, I quickly gathered the top of my robe and held it close to my chest. "Max", I addressed him in a shaky voice. "I wasn't expecting you." Robert stepped in front of me and told me, "It's okay princess, he was just leaving." And then he gently moved me to the door; softly slapped my ass, and said, "Go on in and I'll be right with you."

I walked through the kitchen door with a knot in the pit of my stomach. Max had to have known what we have been doing all this time and if he didn't, he sure did now, as I was sure that he could tell that I was stark naked underneath this robe. And then Robert; slapping my ass like that in front of him! To make me feel like a hussy in front of his friend - his friend! I frowned as I had just realized that Max was cleaned up and dressed in a nice dark suit. It seemed Robert was sending him out to go somewhere on his behalf, and that was strange because Robert was still dressed in his stable clothing, indicating that he still had work to do.

I whipped around as I heard the door swing back and forth. "How dare you", I snapped. "What do you mean?" He asked quietly. "You said we'd be alone." I stated with tears welling up. He looked around and shrugged. "Baby, we are alone." I folded my arms in a pout. "You know darn well what I'm talking about." He walked over to me and guided me into his lap as he sat down on the kitchen chair. "Princess, if you mean Max being here, that wasn't planned; and you were covered." I looked away and said, "What he must think!" Robert busted out laughing. "For God sakes, darlin', Max knows what grown adults do with each other; it's nothing new!" I jumped off his lap and shouted, "Well it's still new to me!"

He rose from his seat and wrapped his arms around my waist from behind, as I stared out of the window above the sink. He whispered, "I'm sorry if I hurt you in anyway, sweetheart." I wiped my tears and turned around to him, I just couldn't stay angry with him. "I'm sorry I snapped at you." And then I reached up and wrapped my arms around his neck as he lifted me up off my feet with his arms wrapped around my waist. "It's okay baby", he told me quietly.

I rested my head on his shoulder as he held me tight. I clung to him and cried; and I really couldn't understand why. I had been feeling ill off and on, and even though I had seen the doctor before I came back to the ranch, he had never called me so everything must be fine. I'm just being silly, I figured. I felt at home with Robert holding me; I loved being in his arms – his oh so strong arms, and whenever I was in his arms, I felt an immeasurable love; that kind of love that most women only dream of.

Because I had become so emotional, Robert decided not to push me into his original idea of having me cook and eat with him without my robe on. Of course that was the reason he wanted me down in the kitchen with only my robe; just as I was that first morning with him. He explained to me that besides the obvious reason behind his request, it was also to help me adjust to more of an open mind sexually.

***

An hour later, I was clearing dishes from the table when Robert took the plates from me. "Oh no you don't; you leave the cleanup for the staff. You will go up with me while I get ready for my meeting so you can rest." I knew that arguing would do no good as I have learned that what Robert wants, he gets. And really, I felt tired again anyway after that big breakfast I had. Robert was just as surprised as I was at my unusual appetite. I grew anxious as we walked up to his quarters and all because of that meeting he had at that horrible gentleman's club. My God – how I detested that place and the whole idea of women showing off their naked bodies.

Robert opened the door to his quarters and motioned me inside. I was relieved that he had stripped and stepped into the shower without wanting to make love; as I became completely exhausted by this point. I removed my robe and slipped under the covers in the bed – and then my eyes slowly closed.

The phone woke me about ten-thirty after I had drifted off to sleep and I barely remembered Robert kissing me goodbye. It was the doctor; he needed to see me and I wasn't supposed to go anywhere without Robert. But before hanging the phone up, I assured the doctor that I would be there soon.

At the gentleman's club, Robert, Max and Robert's lawyer sat at the round wood table in Robert's office while he signed each and every page of the contract. He had just laid the pen down on top of the contract and slid it toward the man with a dark complexion when they heard a knock at the door. "Come in", Robert hollered.

The three men smiled as a petite, slender woman walked in wearing only black heels and carrying a tray of glasses filled with whiskey. Robert looked over at his young lawyer, dressed in an Italian black suit to match his jet black hair; and a smile wider than he has ever seen on the man who is usually a very sober businessman. Robert gazed at his gold watch and said, "They unlocked the doors about ten minutes ago." The man silently stared at her plump breasts as she slid in between him and Max, and set the drinks in front of them. Max and Robert looked at each other and quietly chuckled at the man's response.

"Will there be anything else, Mr. Sterling?" Her voice was soft, but confident. Robert stood up, removed his suit jacket and hung it on the back of the chair. He moved over to her and took her hand. "Darlin', you've always been a special lady and I want you to be the first of my girls to know." He extended his arm toward Max, and said, "My buddy, Max is your new boss; you remember him, don't you?" Her blue eyes grew sad as she looked up at him. "Yes I do, and nothing against Max, but I was one of your first hires." He gently tucked a strand of her light brown hair behind her ear, and said, "I know darlin', but it's time for me to get out of this business."

The sad young woman looked over at Max and then her eyes cut back to the lawyer. She gave the man a small smile when she saw he was perspiring and loosening his tie as his eyes focused on the lower part of her body. She then turned back to Robert and glided her hand down his black tie. "Vivian's a very lucky lady, but should it not work out; you know where to find me." Robert gave her a wink and said, "Thank you, but Vivian and I have an amazing future together and part of solidifying that future is letting this place go." She looked up at him, nodded, and then reached up and kissed his cheek. "I wish you the best." He wrapped his arms around her waist and pulled her body against his. "We had some nice times", he whispered in her ear. As he held onto her for a moment, the lawyer looked over at Max with a wide smile. "You're one lucky son of a bitch, Max."

Robert released his lady friend and the men watched her walk out the door. Max shook his head from side to side when Robert sat back down across from him. "Now I know you're in love with Vivian." Robert smiled and said, "Yes I am – deeply." Then he looked over at his lawyer who had just finished his drink. "My God Sergio, you act as if you've never laid eyes on a naked woman before!" Sergio removed his suit coat and took Robert's whisky, drinking it in one gulp. "I guess you can say it's been awhile since I had some fun; if you know what I mean." Robert grabbed his empty glass from him and slammed it back down in front of his lawyer. "Get your ass out there and get us more drinks!" Max busted out laughing as Sergio hurried to the door. "Hey Sergio", Robert hollered. "She's single." Robert gave him a smile as the man yanked the door open and rushed out wearing a wide grin across his face.

Max shook his head in disbelief and said, "Now that's one horny man." Robert sat back with a smile, crossed his leg over the other, and told him, "You can't tell me that you didn't enjoy looking at her." Max swallowed his drink down and said, "Of course I enjoyed looking at her, and I will love working with her even more."

Robert chuckled and watched as Max swirled the ice around in his glass. “Listen pal”, Max said, breaking the silence. “I can’t thank you enough for giving this place to me.” He shook his head in disbelief and took the contract in his hand. “I can’t believe you just gave it to me; I mean – I could think of a handful of men in this town who would have been willing to buy this place from you.” Robert leaned on the table with his elbows and said, “Listen pal, besides being my best friend, you’re that brother I never had; and then there’s the fact that you know that I want a predecessor who cares about these girls as much as I do, and that they will be taken care of.” Max nodded over at him and then the phone rang.

“Sterling”, Robert answered the phone. Max watched as Robert’s forehead wrinkled into a frown. “Are you serious?” He heard Robert ask with a clenched jaw. After a pause, he said, “Fine, send them in.” He slammed the phone down and looked over at Max. “You won’t believe who’s here to see me.” And then the door opened….

Max slowly stood up as Adam walked in - with Patsy. Robert glared at the two of them. “To what the hell do I owe this displeasure?” He asked with a sober look on his face. Adam walked over to Robert and told him, “I ran into Patsy, she thought I still worked for you and asked me to bring her to you. And then we were told by the staff that you were here.” Adam looked back over his shoulder and nodded to her. Robert watched as she opened her overcoat and drew her hand across her growing belly. “The baby is yours.” She told Robert with a dark smile.

14

Robert sped off in a rage after the unplanned visit at the club and he just couldn't believe they went to his home first! On the way back to the ranch, he thought of the different ways to tell Vivian that he will possibly be a father to another woman's baby; and not just any woman, but that woman would be Patsy! Of all the times they have had sex and she ends up pregnant now? "Damn it!" He hit the steering wheel and thought, I cannot be the only possible father of her baby; not the way she screws around!

He gripped the steering wheel when thinking of the arrangement he made. Until the baby was born and there was a blood test, it had to be this way – period. Patsy would be back at the ranch, but she would be staying at the guesthouse with Max, under constant supervision, and out of Vivian's way.

He felt a seething rage soar through his body when recalling Patsy's smirk when presenting her bulging belly and claiming she was almost two months along. If she hadn't been carrying an innocent child he could have killed her right then and there. In fact, at this point and time, he was sure that carrying the baby was the only thing that saved her sorry ass. He groaned to himself as he pulled through the gates of the ranch; with dread having to tell Vivian the news.

***

Minutes later, I walked out of the doctor's office feeling the shame of a little girl who had just gotten scolded by her daddy. Doctor Robinson was the one who delivered me and was there for every little sniffle I ever had. He's the same age as my father and though he was a stern man, he always showed concern for his patients; especially for me because I was his daughter's best friend. My best friend, Lucy had been sent to the University of Oxford, and now she and I rarely keep in touch. Oh, how I could have used my best friend at that moment.

Doctor Robinson knew the circumstances of our household and how daddy was with losing money to the cards and the booze. Because of those reasons, I received free checkups and medicines over the years, due to the good doctor's fondness of me and my mother. I wasn't surprised at the tongue lashing I received, and I was reminded of how my mother would have reacted to me being in the family way without being married first. I was heading to the church in tears and in search of guidance.

***

Fifteen minutes had passed since Vivian's phone call sent Robert racing to the church. The fearful tone in her voice made him forget all about his ordering her to never go out alone; or without him. All she told him was that she needed him to meet her at the church.

Robert's tires squealed as he sped into the parking lot of St. Rose. He had barely shut the car door as he tore up the stairs and into the door of the dimly lit and empty church. His eyes raced around as he searched for his sweetheart. And then he saw her; kneeling in the first pew. He raced down the aisle to her and saw that she was praying. His heart beat uncontrollably as he allowed her to finish her prayer.

***

As I completed the sign of the cross, I looked up at Robert with tears streaming down my face. I silently rose to my feet and walked into his arms, sobbing. "Hey", he said breathlessly. "What's wrong, baby?" I clung to him with desperation and replied, "I didn't know where else to go." He pulled away only enough to look at me and asked with urgency, "Did someone hurt you?" I looked up at him shaking my head; and then I answered in a whisper, "No, but I have some news." My voice trembled upon completion of my statement. He stroked my hair as I rested my head upon his chest and then slowly pulled away and wiped my tears. "Let me take you home." I led him into the pew and said, "No, please sit with me."

As we sat in silence for a moment I took his hand in mine, and then I looked up at the giant crucifix; encased against the golden bronze wall at the altar. He looked back over at me and put his arm around my waist. "Honey", he whispered. "What has you so upset?" I looked away from him and clenched my purse. After a short pause I told him, "There's a reason why I've felt ill lately." And then I began weeping again. "What is it, baby?" He asked me gently. "Whatever it is, we'll work it out together."

He softly stroked my hair as I continued to cry. Knowing I had been living against what I was taught was tearing me to shreds and I just didn't know how to tell him that we have made a baby. If that wasn't bad enough, I let my parents down, but worst of all; I felt that I had let God down. I sat there crying and wondering how I would ever walk into the church again.

"If you can't tell me here, let me take you home, honey." Robert's soft, comforting voice caught my attention. "No", I shook my head in disagreement. "I should confess it here", I added with sadness. "Confess what, babe?" I then looked up at him and quietly told him, "It seems we're going to have a baby."

Upon hearing my words I could see the shock on his face; but then tears immediately welled up in his eyes while his smile grew from ear to ear. “We’re having a baby?” He asked me with his voice cracking. I shook my head with confirmation; but with sadness. And then suddenly his smile disappeared and was replaced by one of the most heartbreaking looks I had ever seen. “You’re not happy about this”, he said softly. I closed my eyes tight, pinching the flood of tears out. “It’s not that I don’t love you, but you must understand how I was raised.”

I sat silent as Robert rose from the pew and slowly moved closer to the front of the altar. He took a deep breath while looking up at the crucifix. As his tears fell, I was sure I could hear his heart crumble right there before God. And then I noticed he bowed head and his eyes closed. The church had never seemed quieter as I sat and watched him for several moments, knowing in my heart and soul that he was praying. Robert Sterling - the man who claimed the church was no place for him; who all but told me that he was happy in his own skin and he was too content with his lifestyle of drinking, skirt chasing, and other questionable behavior. He would not so much as entertain the idea of going to church, because sooner or later, he would be expected to change his ways and ideas.

Suddenly he turned back to me and when extending his hand, he softly addressed me, “Princess.” I looked up at him like a helpless child and then I took his hand. I trembled as he helped me to my feet, guided me up to the altar; and in front of the crucifix. He stood me in front of him and wrapped his arms around my waist. He held me in silence as I rested my head back against his hard chest and closed my eyes. He gently began caressing my slim belly and softly told me, “Honey, sometimes life takes us to where we least expect it; and I believe everything happens for a reason." He paused, kissed the top of my head, and then he added, "I also believe that love is what life is all about, so how can it be a sin to show your love in every way?"

I turned to him, resting my hands on his forearms as his hands remained around my hips. "My mother would have been disappointed in me." I looked down at the wood floor beneath us and added, "Doctor Robinson reminded me of that today after telling me about my condition." He lifted my chin for our eyes to meet, and said, "Honey, we are two consenting adults and what we do is our business." "But Robert", I began to speak, and then he put his finger against my lips; silencing me. "Baby, listen to me." He turned me back toward the crucifix and said, "We were given a blessing." He paused and then added, "This baby is a symbol of our love and I refuse to see our baby as anything but a gift."

I stared up at Christ with the nails piercing through his hands and feet; thinking of his sacrifice for the world's sins – my sins. Could I really get past the crushing feeling that I had broken the rules? All I knew is that I had to find a way because we were going to have a baby. I placed my hand over my belly; trying to imagine it growing with a little miracle we had made – with God. And then a small smile came to my face as I continued to feel the love I knew from my heavenly father; the father who loved me no matter what I did – or didn't do. And it was Robert who reminded me of that love; a man who saw unspeakable violence throughout his life, but wanted the love and security as I did.

***

Moments later, Robert sent the driver home and put Vivian in the Jaguar. There was silence during the drive;

which also gave Robert time to remember that he had quite possibly fathered another child, but not just anyone's child….

15

Max helped Patsy out of the limousine and walked up the steps to the porch of the log cabin guesthouse where he resided. She stopped to look at the scenery of the wooded area and observed that they weren't far from the stables. "Just what I love to smell – horse shit." She ranted in her southern drawl. Max shook his head in disbelief and threw the door open. "And just what I like to do – babysit!" He snapped back. "Now if you don't mind, please get your ass in here so I can get you settled in." He watched as she storm trooped up the creaky wooden steps the rest of the way, stomping her feet like a child. She stopped at the door and glared at him. "Well don't just stand there; get my bags!" Max rolled his eyes and met the driver at the bottom of the steps. "Thank you." He told him and reluctantly followed Patsy inside with two large suitcases.

***

Upon returning to the ranch, Robert had felt more at ease after talking to the doctor over the phone. He had set him straight about making Vivian feel ashamed; while reminding him that he is her doctor and it was his job to make sure that they had a healthy baby and nothing more. In addition, Robert told him that if it had nothing to do with the health of Vivian or the baby then his opinion simply didn't count.

I leaned against the back of the tub after Robert bathed me. Once again, he lovingly tended to me in the most delicate way; all the while I thought of how I needed to go to confession. There was no doubt that I was very much in love with Robert and wanted to have his babies, but not before marriage. I was sick with utter shame and angst. He must let me go to confession; case closed, it had to be done.

Robert left Vivian alone to soak in the tub while he sat with a bottle of beer on the balcony watching the full moon move in front of the diminishing clouds. He dreaded the next conversation he must have with her; when would be the right time? If he had a chance of keeping her at all; he had to be honest with her and it had to be very soon.

"Robert", he heard me address him and turned around. "Hi babe." There I stood in my dainty white robe; sat in his lap and said, "Robert, I need to go to confession tomorrow. He took my hand and drew it to his lips. "I'm sorry, but I have something planned for us and I had it planned for a week so we can't cancel." I rose from his lap and began to protest. "But Robert, I need to do this!" I told him with emphasis. He stood up and took me into his arms. "Hey, take it easy." He told me in a soothing voice. "I will get you to the church another day."

We sat back down as we were and after a silent moment, Robert asked me, "Do you want me to take you to see your father?" I rested my head on his shoulder and cuddled closely into his neck. I asked him in a tone of disbelief, "Are you serious?" "I know, I know", he said with a light chuckle. "But he's still your father and you haven't been in touch with him since you left him back in May." I kept my head on his shoulder as he cradled me in his arms; finally replying, I said, "He would just be disappointed when he discovers that I'm going to have a baby." And we never spoke of the possibility of telling him that he was going to be a grandfather from that moment on; it saddens me even now that I made that decision in haste, but at the time, I felt it was the right choice.

Adam made his way to the back of the counter of the store that he had taken over after killing the owner; he grabbed a bottle of whiskey and sat on the stool. He guzzled down almost half of the bottle, set it down on the counter, and reached for a photo out of the back of his denim jeans pocket. A sinister smile came about his face as he recalled the day he took the picture of Vivian….

He knew Robert would be in the stables; he had overheard Vivian telling Robert she would meet him in the stables after her shower. He just couldn't miss this opportunity to get a nicer and closer peak at that luscious ass of hers. It would be easy because the shower doors were clear glass and he had all the master keys for emergencies.

As he stared at her naked body in the picture he grew hard while taking his mind back to that day, so much so; he remembered the sound of the water flowing from the shower and he could feel the steam rolling out of the open door in which he stood; gazing while she soaped her hour glass figure.

His smile grew wide and sly while thinking that she had that innocent virgin look to her ass that he hadn't seen on a woman in several years; and he nearly exploded inside his pants at the thought of poking her. But as he watched her, he knew he would have to wait so she would never know it was him; and then he pulled a plastic bag of crushed white powder from his black suit pants….

Suddenly, Adam's mind returned to the present with his shaft ready to poke out of his pants. There was only one way of getting relief and it was upstairs in his room. This store and the room was his only shelter, and with the vacation sign in the window, no one would miss the old man; he smiled as he made his way up the creaky steps.

He entered the room and looked over at his companion, who seemed to be sleeping, despite being tied to the bed by both her wrists and ankles; and with a handkerchief gagging her mouth. He slammed the door jolting her awake. She was always terrified to look at him and she never said a word. He untied the ropes and sat her up on the side of the bed. "Here, have a few swallows", he told her when putting the bottle of whiskey against her lips. She quickly turned her head in refusal. "I said, take a few swallows!" He bellowed out; and then he yanked her head back to face him. He pulled her hair and forced some in her mouth; a few drops streamed down her chin and throat, angering him further. "Damn it, Vivian!" He shouted and then back handed her across the face, causing an instant welt to her cheek bone.

He had called her Vivian in order to fantasize about her again. But he was unable to focus, so he ripped a pillow out of its case and covered her head. And then to the woman's horror, he flipped her over on her belly and shoved his hard rod into her ass like he was a wild animal. Her screaming only encouraged him to where he pounded inside her faster and more ferocious than before, but he didn't worry because no one would hear her; there was no longer a store owner and the streets were empty.

16

I woke the next morning to find Robert in the den on the phone to all of the contacts I had made for the big Fourth of July party he had me working hard to plan. He hung the phone up slowly and cautiously, as he probably expected me to be angry after all my work in my planning.

"Good morning, darlin'", he said when giving me a nervous grin. I walked over to him with my arms folded, leaned up against his desk, and asked, "Robert, why did you cancel that party? It's your birthday party." His grin became wider as he untied the belt to my silky robe and pulled my exposed body into him. "I don't need a party; our plans have drastically changed."

I pulled myself out of his arms and closed my robe. "Honestly, Robert, don't you ever get enough?" He pulled my robe open again and told me quietly, "I could never get enough of you." I began struggling out of his arms as he was kissing and nuzzling my neck; and then he moved his lips down to my bare breasts. "Robert!" I cried out and continued to try to wrestle away from him. "Robert - for God sakes!" I exclaimed breathlessly. "The door." I shrieked as he lifted me up on the desk. "The door – it's open!" I cried out, as he gently forced me to lay down and holding me down by my wrists. "It's okay baby", he told me quietly. "No one is around today, I gave everyone the day off."

I reluctantly gave into his aggressions while I continuously looked toward the door, fearing that someone would see us; despite his claims that we were alone. There on his desk he had his way with me; all the while with the doors and windows wide open. It was then that I had felt the most vulnerable; and yet so very desired by him. Once again, I was torn between the morals that society had set and those of Robert Sterling's world; where he was giving my body the mad pleasure that I seemed to have needed – and wanted, even if I couldn't admit it to him; or to myself.

***

Several hours later, Robert and I sat in the back of the limousine as Paul drove us down the deserted road. "Robert, I don't mind surprises, but I wish you would tell me where you're taking me." He gave me a wide grin and said, "Patience, darlin'."

As I stared out the window and watched the road pass beneath us, I again thought about our morning in his den and the mixed feelings I was still experiencing, despite the love I felt for him. Maybe if he would just get me to the church for my confession; maybe then I could let it go. And then he reached for me and pulled me close into his arms. "I love you, my baby", he whispered, and then he kissed my forehead. I blissfully rested my head against his shoulder; smiling and feeling that overwhelming love yet again.

Minutes later, Paul pulled into an abandoned drive near a piece of wooded area. I looked around at the barren land and asked Robert, "Where are we?" He silently opened the door, stepped out of the car, and then reached for my hand. "Come with me." He said. I took his hand and stepped out of the car while looking around. "Robert", I said, catching his attention. "We're out in the middle of nowhere; what's going on?" I asked with concern. He smiled and replied, "It's alright, baby just come with me."

He continued to lead me through a small patch of the wooded area until we came to a large, open part of the land. "Mr. Sterling." An older, stocky man dressed in black overalls and a matching undershirt approached him. "As you requested", he said when drawing his hand in the direction of the huge hot air balloon.

Robert led me up to the enormous multicolored balloon. "My lord, Robert", I said in awe. "You don't intend on taking me up in that thing - do you?" He drew me into his arms and softly said, "Princess, I've been up in this balloon before and it's amazing; you trust me, don't you?" I looked back over at the balloon and then back at him, and told him, "Yes I do, but honey – it's a balloon!" I added with emphasis. "Are you ready Mr. Sterling?" The man addressed him from behind. Robert looked into my eyes and said, "It's perfectly safe." His lips tenderly captured mine and then he added, "I want you to experience this." I looked back up at the larger than life balloon and answered with a small and uncertain smile, "And I want to experience it with you."

Robert gave the man a nod and then he helped me inside the basket of the balloon. I trembled and stared up inside the balloon, paying no attention to what was taking place; and then suddenly we left the ground. I leaped into Robert's arms at the roaring sound of the large flames powering the balloon as we continued to rise. He smiled as he held me close and tight in his arms. "Come on, baby – you're safe; just enjoy the view."

As we moved along, we talked back and forth and shared the beauty all around us. Robert did well at pulling my fear from me so quickly. But then suddenly he released me, while we hovered over Mt. Rushmore. He bent down on one knee and pulled a black velvet box out of his suit jacket. "I wanted to do this in style", he told me softly. I stood there with my hands clasped over my chest as he opened the box and I began trembling all over again. Joyful tears formed in my eyes when he asked, “Vivian Martin – will you make me the happiest man on this earth and be my wife?”

I stared down at the diamonds circling half of the gold band and the rock in the middle. Finding it hard to catch my breath, I asked, “Are you asking me because we are having a baby?” He slowly rose to his feet and wiped my tears. “I’m asking you because I love you, Princess; and if you recall, I told you last night that I had this planned for a week.” I smiled from ear to ear upon hearing his reminder. “That’s right – you did.” He nodded and then removed the ring from the box. “So, is that a yes?”

I looked at the ring, recalling how I would dream of this moment as a child; Prince Charming would whisk me away to our own castle in a faraway land, and take me away from all the fear and pain. But I never knew my dreams would come true; never like this, and never while floating on top of the world.

“Yes!” I managed to answer through my tears. He slid the ring on my trembling finger. “It fits perfectly”, he said in amazement. I watched as he drew my hand to his lips and kissed the ring, and then my hand. I was so overcome by wonderful elation all I could do was cry. He cupped his hands around my face and said, “I hope those are happy tears.” I shook my head up and down and said, “Oh yes – the happiest.” He gently drew the tip of his thumbs under my eyes, wiping my tears. “Princess, I love you around the world and back again.” All I could do was throw my arms around him as he lifted me off my feet.

***

An hour later, Paul pulled up to the back of the Sterling Department store, prompting me to question

Robert of why we were there; and why we were parking in the back. He led me up to the back door and unlocked it; stepping aside to let me in, he told me, "I arranged it to where no one would be using the fitting room for the intimate apparel so we could have the area for ourselves."

Upon walking in to the former store room made up into a fitting room and what appeared to be an observation area, I gazed around and noticed a chair made of red velvet and gold trim; resembling a king's chair. Next to the chair was a glass drinking cart filled with liquor. The lighting was dim and romantic with the brightest light coming from the large closet filled with women's sexy intimate apparel.

I gazed at the skimpy material in the closet and then my attention turned back to Robert; who was pouring himself a glass of Brandy. He then went to the door that connected the room and the store; assuring it was locked. "Ok Princess, everything is locked up." He removed his black suit jacket, loosened his matching tie, and sat in the chair with his drink; crossing one leg over the other.

I broke the silence and asked him, "Robert, are you expecting me to try these clothes on while you sit there and watch?" He gave me a wink and set his glass down. "Here", he said when rising from the chair. "Let me get you started." I nervously bit down on my lower lip while he took a small rack of three different sexy outfits from the closet and rolled it out on the cart they were hanging from. "These garments were made just for you", he told me with pride. "Let me introduce to you, a clothing line called - Vivian's Closet."

I looked at the rack of clothes and then back at the king's chair and drink cart. Picking up on my anxiety, Robert said, "Listen baby, I know you're still a bit uptight with sex and anything having to do with the idea of sex, but

I assure you that it's all quite normal." I took one last look at the chair and then looked up at Robert. "Is it normal for a man to sit in a chair made for a king and gawk at a woman changing in and out of sexy apparel?" He smiled wide and said, "Well, the man is the king of his castle." I shook my head in disbelief and just looked at the cement floor. His smile disappeared and he took me into his arms. He quietly told me, "It's just us here, baby, and your beauty inspired me to have this sexy clothing made just for you." He pulled back and lifted my chin for our eyes to meet. "The doors are locked and it's just us." He softly kissed my lips while unzipping the back of my dress and then he went to sit back down.

I looked over at him as he crossed his leg over the other and sipped on his Brandy; while enthusiastically anticipating my little fashion show. "Robert, I wanted to go to confession." Again, he rose from his chair and came back over to me. "I promise I will take you tomorrow, but right now this is what we're doing." He pulled the royal blue satin bustier from the rack with matching panties and garter belts. "You know this is my favorite color, so let's start with this one." He kissed me again and told me, "It's going to be amazing on you."

As he sat there in his chair waiting for the private show, I gazed at the sheer white robe on the rack next to a short red silk nightie with thin straps and a low bust line. I turned around and saw him standing there again. "Should I help you?" He asked me in a seductive tone as he slowly slid my dress off me. Just as he went to unbuckle my bra, I took his hand. "I'll get it". I took a deep breath and then told him, "Go ahead and sit down." He gave me a small smile and went over to sit back down.

As I undressed he kept his eyes on me with a wide smile; as if I was the first woman he ever saw undressing before him. He once told me that he had never experienced a woman protesting his sexual desires as I have done; and it had only added to the excitement during his pursuit of me. I knew that once we were married, I would for sure have to adjust to the most extreme sexually active marriage.

I turned around and modeled the blue bustier and panties in his direction all the while feeling somewhat exploited, and yet, I couldn't help but feel so very loved and desired by him. I was thinking the whole time that as soon as I went to confession, I could make things right with God and maybe relax some. But, how would I tell Robert that after I go to confession I was not going to have sex with him again until after we were married? Could I talk my priest into marrying us in the church privately? No one would have to know, but it would mean everything to me to be married by him; in the church I attended with my mother. Maybe then I could feel some peace with both God and my mother.

17

Robert had left Vivian up at the main house when her best friend Lucy surprised her with a phone call; so she could talk to her in private, he would go check in with Max at the guesthouse.

As he walked along the dirt path leading to the guesthouse, the beautiful bright sun was just beginning to sink. His smile was constant in thinking back to the attractive way of how Vivian acted coy when modeling her new sexy attire. She had expressed concern that it was a waste because she would eventually gain weight from expecting, but he assured her that it was no waste at all and they could all be used again after the baby was born.

Upon reaching the front door to the guesthouse his smile faded, knowing that he still had to tell Vivian about Patsy expecting ; and that he could be the father. But, how would he tell the woman he loves, who has also accepted his marriage proposal; and is having his baby, that he could have fathered another baby by the one woman that temporarily came between them? The last thing he wanted to do was cause her any hurt and distress; especially since he doesn't know if he's the father or not.

Robert walked into the guesthouse; a two story log cabin just as the main house, but much smaller. The inside décor mirrored the same as his main house; knotty pine and cathedral ceilings, a staircase leading to the bedrooms just off of the living room; and a small kitchen in a cozy corner of the house.

He walked in the door and found Max standing by the stone fireplace in the living room; looking at a photo on the mantle. "Max", Robert addressed him. "Hi partner", he said as Robert approached him; and picked up the wooden frame from the mantle with a smile. "Man - I remember that weekend", he told Max. Max smiled wide and said, "I remember it well too, we camped and went on a hiking expedition at Yellowstone Park. The whole weekend of cooking over an open fire, beer drinking, and lustful sex when meeting those two sexy women in that country store." Robert chuckled and said, "It was amazing at how free both girls were with us the entire time." Max chuckled; shaking his head in agreement, and said, "I think I had the most sex that weekend than I have ever had in my life." Amused, Robert laughed.

Upon setting the picture back down on the mantle, Robert smiled and told Max, “She said yes.” Max punched the air and shouted, “Well, alright!” Robert laughed out loud and said, “That’s right, my friend; Vivian is going to be my wife!”

Unbeknownst to the men, Patsy stood at the top of the stairs; out of sight and listening; she touched her growing belly and silently hoped that she was right about Robert being the father as she claimed. In a way it didn’t matter though, because Robert will be the father as far as she was concerned. Her doctor owes her a favor and all he needs to do is confirm it with Robert. A sinister smile came to her face when she whispered to herself, “Robert will have to marry me; goodbye Vivian.”

“She’s going to have my baby too.” Patsy heard Robert say with joy. She felt her heart sink and then she began to feel acid rising to her throat; causing her to run to the bathroom before she got sick all over. The two men heard the door slam. “That sounds like the bathroom door”, Max told Robert. Robert’s smile disappeared and then he said, “That bitch up there is trying to ruin my life.” He turned and looked toward the stairs. “I still don’t know how to tell Vivian about this.” Hoping he could divert his attention, Max headed to the kitchen and told him, “Let’s have a beer to celebrate you and Vivian getting married and having a baby!”

Robert was so focused on Patsy that he never acknowledged Max, but inched his way to the staircase and heard the shower start up. He stood there and felt his blood run cold as he once again became enraged with Patsy and her timing.

“Here bud”, Max said, interrupting his thoughts. “Thanks”, Robert told him and took the bottle of beer from him. “I also came by to talk with Patsy and tell her how this will all play out; under my terms.” Max took a swig from the bottle and asked, “Don’t you think you should tell Vivian right away?” Robert shook his head back and forth and answered, “I tried many times and I just can’t bring myself to tell her.” He took a long drink from his beer and added, “I mean this kid may not even be mine.” Max shook his head in agreement and asked, “So why upset her, right?” Robert gave him a silent nod and then watched Patsy walk down the stairs stark naked.

Robert glared at her as she walked up to him with a wide grin and her body and hair still damp. “So to what do we owe this pleasure of a visit from the great Mr. Sterling?” Robert grabbed her by the arms and shouted, “You can wipe that fucking smile off your face before I do it for you!” Max stood by gawking at her naked body and drank his beer in silence; as Patsy pulled away from Robert and asked with a clenched jaw, “Would you really do that to the mother of your child?”

***

Robert was thankful that he walked to the guesthouse as it gave him time to think. He approached his gun range and started firing shots at the targets; made of silhouettes resembling human figures. He shot several of the targets full of holes while remembering the rules he set for Patsy during his visit to the guesthouse….

He indeed wiped that smile off her face when telling her; “First of all, you will never see Vivian or try to contact her; and secondly, you will do as you’re told by me and Max, and you will be under constant surveillance the whole time you’re on my property.” Patsy immediately began to scream and cry. “You can’t treat me like this; I’m the mother of your child!” Robert grabbed her by her arms and shouted, "We don't know that, and you're damn lucky you're here at all!" Then a smile came to his face when he joyfully informed her, "If this is my baby, after you give birth you will sign this kid off to me and Vivian to raise."

Upon hearing those words, there was complete silence in the room. Patsy's tears fell as she stared at him standing before her with his beastly arms crossed and looking as though he was happily waiting for her reaction. Suddenly she slapped him across the face and screamed. "You're going to raise your kid with me; not her!"

Robert angrily shot off more rounds from his pistol when recalling her fit and disobedience; and he thought to himself; how dare she tell me what I was going to do! And the fact that she's carrying a baby; possibly mine, I knew I had to control my seething rage and be careful in how I handled her…

Robert calmly backed her into the corner without touching her and told her with a clenched jaw, "You will never tell me what I'm going to do; and furthermore, you will never raise my baby with; or without me. I don't want you and I certainly don't love you. If you know what's good for you than you will walk the line and approach me carefully." He gently stroked her face and then without warning he grasped her jaw, turned her head to the side, and whispered in her ear, "You don't want to make more of an enemy out of me; I'm a Sterling, and I have a way of making a person disappear." He released her and then watched her slide to the floor while sobbing.

Robert simply went back to his beer and drank it down while he watched her sob in a fetal position on the floor. He caught Max looking over at him; knowing he probably wondered how he could treat an expectant mother so harshly, but he knew Max understood what was at stake for him.

Max broke his silence and quietly told Robert, "I'll take her back upstairs so she can calm down and rest." He watched as Max stepped behind Patsy and helped her off the floor from under her arms. "I'm the mother of his baby, Max!" She cried, screamed; and punched the air. "You should know better than to test him, Patsy", he told her when extending his arm around her waist. He then scooped her up into his arms and carried her upstairs.

Robert decided to forget about Patsy for the moment and replaced the gun to his holster. As he began walking away; he heard a car come to a screeching stop. "Mr. Sterling!" A large dark man hurried out of the black nineteen-fifty Chevy and jogged up to him. He was near six foot with an athletic build, dressed in black combat attire; and had a pistol strapped to his side. "The police arrived to see Miss Martin; and I'm thinking the news isn't good." As Robert darted to the car, he told the man, "Take me to the main house – now."

18

Robert hurried out of the security vehicle and ran up the stairs of the main house, skipping every other step. When he arrived inside, his eyes frantically traveled the room in search of Vivian; and when his eyes met hers, he paid no mind to the detectives standing next to her as she came running into his arms and sobbed, "Daddy's dead."

Minutes later after Robert had calmed Vivian, he helped her to the den for privacy while he gathered information from the detectives and found that Fred Martin was shot in the head; lying beside him was a suicide note. The police informed Robert that the circumstances surrounding his death was still under investigation due to some loose ends; which led to suspicion of foul play, and everyone who knew him or had dealings with him would be considered a person of interest.

Both detectives sported black suits and were of average height, late forties in age, one being of slim build; and the other stocky and of Mexican descent. The slim man had light brown hair and medium to dark skin with a gash above his right eye that appeared to be from a knife wound.

"So what's your story, Sterling?" The slim cop asked him with a sly smile. Robert clenched his jaw together and replied, "Don't fuck with me, Reynolds; not after your sordid past with working for my old man." The other cop took a step into Robert and said, "Listen, I don't know what the hell you mean by what you just said to my partner, but I suggest you cooperate; given the word on the street about your own life", he added with emphasis. Reynolds put his hand on his partner's shoulder and said in a calm, smooth tone, "I'll take care of Sterling;

Francisco, you check in on Miss Martin and see that she's alright." Robert took a step toward him and started to speak up when Reynolds stepped in front of him, and said, "Relax man, she'll be fine."

The two men watched Francisco walk into the den and shut the door. "Look", Reynolds addressed Robert in a lowered tone. "I think you and I both know that given your background you would be the first suspect." Robert shook his head; removed his black suit jacket and headed over to the glass drink cart in the living room.

The detective's eyes scoured the living room; noticing it was big enough to fit a football field in it and decorated in knotty pine from top to bottom, including a cathedral style ceiling. Robert had poured his drink, walked over to the stone fireplace; and leaned his elbow on top of the mantel while pondering what to say to this former Sterling employee, turned detective.

Reynolds walked up to Robert and smiled. "Well, aren't you going to offer me a drink?" Robert glared at the man and swallowed his drink down. "Just tell me what the hell you want and get the fuck out of my house." The smile on Reynolds face faded as Robert returned to the drink cart. "Fine", he hissed. "I know that Fred Martin owed your old man some money and Phillip dropped dead before he could collect." Robert shrugged and said, "So what, there are a few others out there who owed him money, but they're still breathing."

Reynolds gazed around the bright room filled with a wine colored sectional sofa and matching wing back chairs. "My goodness, Sterling", he whistled. "Your taste is quite different from Phillip's; you like it bright and open." And then a smile came to his face when he added, "But you have your security detail to protect you." Robert's face quickly reddened as his anger approached the threshold, causing him to bellow out, "At least I take care of my own business where as Phillip had you little obedient soldiers to do his dirty work for him!"

Reynolds responded by shoving his hands into his pockets and began walking away. But then he turned around. "I also know that Martin was about to lose his house and low and behold at the eleventh hour; Robert

Sterling comes to the rescue." Both men started at each other for a moment, and then Robert chimed in, "I did it for Vivian", he told him calmly. "The last time I checked, it wasn't unlawful to help someone financially." Reynolds nodded in agreement and replied, "No, of course not. But, what did you get in return?" Just as Robert was about to answer, Vivian walked into the room with Francisco behind her.

Robert hurried over to Vivian and took her in his arms. "How are you doing, princess?" She silently trembled in his arms as the men looked on from across the room. Reynolds looked over at Francisco and shook his head from side to side, indicating that he wasn't finished questioning Robert. "What did you get out of the little woman?" Reynolds asked his partner in a low tone. A small smile came to his face when he answered, "She mentioned a deal that her father and Robert had made, but she didn't go into detail."

Reynolds observed Robert as he continued to hold and comfort Vivian from a distance. A deal? It nagged at him as he tried to get a handle on what kind of deal Robert would make an old gambling drunk who owed money to his father. What the hell could the old man offer him in return? And then he looked over at Francisco with a raised eyebrow and said, "Vivian." And then his eyes shot back to Robert.

The detectives made their way back to Robert and Vivian. Reynolds cleared his throat and spoke up. "So Sterling, you never did mention a deal you made with the old man." Vivian lifted her head from Robert's chest and glared at him. "That old man was my daddy." Reynolds nodded to her and said, "I beg your pardon." And then he looked over at Robert and noticed the rage in his eyes.

"Alright", Robert said in a low tone. "I told the man I would secure his home and excuse his debt to my father as long as he arranged it for Vivian to live with and work for me as my personal assistant."

The two detectives looked at each other in disbelief, and then Francisco spoke up and asked Robert, "Are you telling us that you bought Miss Martin from her father?" Robert looked at Vivian and then released her. "No, I didn't buy her." He then stepped into him and added, "You piece of shit! Her father was taking the money that she earned from working at the Steakhouse to gamble and drink away, and I put a stop to it!" Robert stood mere inches from Francisco's face when Reynolds took a hold of Robert's shoulder and said, "Take it easy, Sterling; you don't want to upset Vivian any more than she already is."

Reynolds pulled Robert aside and spoke in a low tone. "I can see how this happened", he told Robert. "You saw what you wanted and you took it; the old man just made it easy for you." Robert held that cold stare as the man continued. "I can see you love her and I want to help you, but you have to level with me." Robert shook his head in disbelief and said, "Look, I may have gotten Vivian in an unconventional way, but I also got her out of a situation that she shouldn't have been in. Her father wasn't taking care of her as a man should." Reynolds looked back at Vivian wiping her tears and asked, "What about all the money found in his wallet; you know anything about that?" Robert exhaled and answered, "I paid him five hundred every two weeks to keep him from coming to Vivian for money."

Reynolds and Francisco drove out of the Sterling gate when Francisco asked, "So do we have a motive for Sterling?" Reynolds unwrapped the foil to a piece of gum and folded it into his mouth. “I don’t see it”, he replied. And then he looked over at Francisco behind the wheel and asked, “Aren’t you curious as to what Sterling said about me working for his old man?” Francisco glanced over at him and said, “I don’t want to pry, but yes, you could say that.” Reynolds gave him an amused half smile and replied, “I’ll buy you a beer.”

***

I laid curled up in Robert’s arms in bed. “I don’t even know where to bury him”, I somberly told him. He kissed my forehead and caressed the small of my back. “I know baby, but you have time to decide; he can’t be buried until after the investigation anyway.” I began to cry again and he drew me closer, pulling me halfway on top of him. “I need you, Robert”. “I’m here for you, baby”, he told me softly and captured my lips to his. He gently kissed and brushed his lips against mine, and then took all of my mouth in his; as I accepted his advances against the inside of my bare thigh.

I grasped his shirt and pulled the tail of it out of his pants. He immediately sat up on his knees and ripped his shirt off, scattering the buttons. I wanted him to take my pain away however he could. But then I put my arms out, stopping his aggression. “Robert, I need you to be gentle with me – please.” He gazed over my naked body and I could see he wanted me with every fiber if his being, but somehow he knew that it wasn’t what I needed in my time of grief. And he softly told me, “I’ll just hold you tonight.”

***

Reynolds and Francisco arrived at the Deadwood Steakhouse around nine that evening; after leaving the Sterling Ranch, and found a secluded table in the back where they ordered a pitcher of beer between them. Reynolds shoved handfuls of peanuts in his mouth as if he hadn't eaten in days, while Francisco knocked back his beer at the speed of light.

"Well", Francisco said after swallowing his last drop. "What's the story with you and Sterling's old man?" Reynolds took a long exhale as he prepared to tell his partner of just one year his only function with the Sterling Empire. "Look, only one of the other guys know about this and I feel I can trust you; being that we have discussed nearly every damn thing since we've started working together." His partner nodded and told him, "You bet you can trust me, pal." Then he smiled, "Just pretend I'm your neighborhood priest." Reynolds busted out laughing and shook his head. "Yeah sure; okay Father Francisco", he responded with sarcasm. Both men laughed heartily, but then Reynolds lost his smile.

During a silent minute between them, Reynolds ordered another pitcher at the bar and then he sat back down across from his partner. "It's not as bad as you may think", he told him when pouring the beer in each glass. "I'm listening", said Francisco. "No judgment here." Once again Reynolds took another big drink and began his story….

"I was five years into my job on the force when Evelyn and I started drowning in debt; somehow Phillip Sterling knew this and used that knowledge to his benefit." He looked over at his partner and added, "It was just a few times that he called on me for help." He exhaled and shook his head in disbelief before continuing. "We were desperate, our baby was sick and in and out of the hospital. It was draining us and then there were the other bills; and the new house." He was reliving it all to the point of becoming exasperated. His partner placed his hand on his shoulder and said, "Take it easy, pal, it was years ago."

Reynolds took another deep breath and drank half of his beer down. "All I did was some nosing around for him", he paused to blink away the approaching tears in his eyes; and then he said in a trembling, quiet voice, "I led him to young women for his business." Reynolds watched Francisco's shocked reaction and then he said, "And because these certain women I found for him proved to be profitable for him, he took care of my entire debt; we were in the clear and able to start over," he added with emphasis, when trying to get him to understand his reasoning.

During a few deafening silent moments, Francisco sat there stunned and dazed at what he had heard from his partner. He looked over at the broken man and felt empathy for his hardships but, he was wrong; there was judgment. How could he possibly justify sending Phillip Sterling to young women just so he could sell them to the highest bidder? And all for debt that could have been rectified by other resources. Francisco shook his head and told him, "I think we best get out of here."

19

Nine O'clock the next morning Robert had kept his promise to me and was driving us into St. Rose to see my priest. I had reluctantly agreed to his insistence of letting him speak to Father alone before my confession; but nonetheless, I agreed that I would sit and silently pray and spend time with God while I waited. I did, however, warn him that this was my confession and I was to tell Father myself; which he promised he would let me do.

I stayed silent most of the morning, other than some small talk that Robert had initiated. I woke up and insisted on eating only dry toast; due to my feeling of nausea. I then took my shower and slipped into a black dress that dropped well past my knees, and covered me at the top completely. Robert hated that dress; he said it was too dark and plain for me, but I knew it was because it wasn't revealing enough for him. And being that I now viewed myself as what I considered a bad girl, he wasn't exactly surprised in my extreme wardrobe change.

***

Robert and I pulled into the parking lot at St. Rose; he got out of the car and walked around to the other side, extended me his hand, and then we walked hand and hand all the way to the front doors when I stopped him. "Robert, you forgot to leave the gun in the car." He opened the door and stood to the side. "I didn't forget; it's staying with me." I stepped inside while protesting. "But we are in a church, Robert." He removed his sunglasses and put them in the pocket inside of his suit jacket. "Please don't worry about my gun, princess." He motioned me ahead of him and he whispered, "Let's get you comfortable and I'll go meet the priest."

Robert escorted me to the front pew with a nun I didn't know looking on with a stern expression and watching our every move as she stood at the altar. She appeared to be in her late sixties with silver hair and deep set in wrinkles, particularly around the mouth; indicating that she rarely smiled. Her eyes darkened as she stood fixated on Robert and I; to the point where I felt her judgment as he stood next to me.

A sly smile came to his face when he bent down kissing me; and holding his lips to mine, he placed his hand on my knee. Upon straightening up, he gave the crabby nun a wide grin followed by a wink; which caused her to leave in disgust with her nose in the air. He held his laughter until she disappeared through a side exit; and then he looked over at me, giving him quite the frown, as he clearly and so very intentionally had offended the nun.

Robert quickly looked away from me and straightened his tie just as my priest walked in to greet us. He was nearly the same height as Robert, with a stocky build and in his early sixties. He approached me with a very pleasant and warm smile and took my hand. “Vivian, it’s wonderful to see you again”, he told me, with much joy and love in his voice as always. And then he looked over at Robert. “And you must be Mr. Sterling, the young man I spoke with on the phone.” Father approached him; shook his hand, and all the while never losing his infectious smile.

“Father”, Robert nodded. “Listen padre”, he continued in a matter of fact tone, “I would like a few minutes of your time alone before you listen to Vivian’s confession.” Father looked over at me and asked, “Are you alright with this, Vivian?” Just as I was about to answer him, Robert spoke up. “She agreed to it this morning; so padre, why don’t you and I go talk in your office, and then you can talk to Vivian.” Father’s smile faded; which was very unusual with his sense of humor and very kind nature. And then he looked back over at me again; as if he were waiting for me to intervene, and then he said, “Very well, Mr. Sterling, follow me.” I watched as they walked up the two steps, crossing the alter and into another room.

The priest closed the door behind him; causing an echo throughout the empty church and then he sat down on a wooden swivel chair. "Young man, this is highly unconventional." Robert looked around the room filled with cabinets, a photo of Pope Pius XII above a wooden crucifix, and many different garments worn by the priest. "Father, my whole life is unconventional; and this is your office?" The priest motioned for him to sit down and told him, "It's sufficient for privacy; now, what is this all about, Mr. Sterling?" He asked him with great emphasis.

Robert waved the offer of the chair and began to pace while loosening his tie. The priest sat there observing him with a sudden uncomfortable feeling, and then Robert spoke up. "As I told you over the phone, Vivian needed to be here to confess something to you and I insist on addressing some rules to you beforehand." Amused, the priest let out a hearty laugh and asked, "Rules?" Robert stopped in his tracks and told him, "You're nothing I expected, Father." He shook his head in disbelief and added, "I mean I was under the impression you guys barely smiled, let alone, laugh." The priest continued to show his amused smile and said, "I'm one of those happy priests." He then extended his hand to the air. "Enlighten me with your rules, young man."

Robert suddenly began to feel comfortable with this guy as he continued to show a very accepting and loving sort of demeanor; to which he wasn't used to dealing with. "Well, for starters, I want to be sure that Vivian is respected at all times; meaning, I don't want her judged harshly." The priest put his hand up to silence him; again something Robert was not accustomed to. "Let me stop you right there. I care very much for Vivian; I baptized her when she was just a tiny baby, so please do not worry about judgment coming from me, Mr. Sterling." Robert shook his head in agreement and told him, "She thinks a lot of you too and it's important for her that you're the one to marry us in this church, in a private ceremony; no questions asked." The Priest rose from his seat and stood before Robert. "Young man, the Catholic Church has its own rules; and we can't just perform a marriage without going through the proper procedures."

Robert exhaled and removed his suit jacket, revealing his pistol. He tossed the jacket on the chair and told the priest in a firm tone, "You don't understand padre, once you hear Vivian's confession, you need to absolve her; or whatever you holy guys do, and then you will perform our marriage ceremony as soon as I get the license."

The priest kept his eyes on Robert's pistol hanging from his shoulder and turned his back facing the crucifix. "I hope this isn't some kind of threat because as Vivian's priest and friend; I don't want her making any snap decisions; she just lost her father and this isn't exactly a good time for her to take such a big step in her life." Robert stepped in front of him and said in his authoritative tone, "I'm not threatening anyone, but I do have to insist that it be done this way in the next few days; for Vivian's peace of mind and conscience."

The priest folded his arms and then looked toward the door that separated the room from the alter. And then he looked back over at Robert and said, "Son, I know who you are and all about your background; I'm concerned for Vivian", he added when pointing at the gun. Robert exhaled with impatience and replied in an elevated tone, "I love Vivian more than my own life and I'm going to marry her; even if I have to go to the justice of the peace to do so.

Now, if you care for her as much as you say; then you must be the one to help us."

One could hear a pin drop between the two men as Robert paced back and forth while the priest focused on the gun. Suddenly Robert stopped and faced him again. "Look, I see this church is on the older side and could use some work; I will provide all the money you need to complete the work in return for marrying us. If anything, please do it for Vivian", he pleaded.

The priest looked over at the crucifix and thought for a moment. "As I said, Mr. Sterling", he addressed him with emphasis. "I know who you are and I also happen to know that you built yourself quite a nice home and ranch." And then a sly smile came to his face as he told Robert, "I'll make you a deal, you can pay for the materials to fix up this church, but I want to add a stipulation; you do the work yourself."

Minutes later; although it felt like an eternity, Father had called me into the same room and Robert sat in the pew waiting for me. His ear to ear smile gave me a sense of dread, as I wondered what he said to Father.

I sat in the room with my lifetime mentor in silence. "Vivian", Father addressed me gently. "Would you like to go to the confessional for this. I shook my head from side to side and answered, "No Father, I never give my confession that way; I feel part of my penance should be to look you in the eye when I confess my sins." Father shook his head in acknowledgement and said, "It's true that we have that type of relationship, but I wanted to offer it to you just the same." "Thank you, Father."

There was an uncomfortable silence between the two of us; which has never happened in the whole time we have been in each other's lives. I have always thought of him as my father figure; that of which I could never feel about my own father . He had also kept me on the straight and narrow, until about a year ago; when I had to work more to support and care for my father; making it difficult for me to attend church on a regular basis; and then Robert entered the picture.

Father spoke to me gently. "You can start anytime you're ready, Vivian." I nodded, indicating I was ready; and together we made the sign of the cross. "In the name of the Father, the Son and the Holy Spirit – Amen." I repeated, "Amen" and then I began. "Bless me Father, for I have sinned; It's been six months since my last confession."

Tears began to fill my eyes as I removed a tissue from my little black purse; and then I took a deep breath. "It's even harder to confess this to you than I imagined", I told him softly. "You've always been able to tell me everything", he replied with kindness. I smiled through the tears and told him, "I think you have probably figured out what kind of relationship Robert and I have." "Yes, and he insists that you and he must marry right away."

Upon hearing those words, I could tell that he must have an idea of what we have done; so I quickly admitted it, "Father, I'm expecting a baby." I looked away in shame as he took my hand and asked, "Vivian, do you love Robert; and do you really think you're ready for marriage?" I looked up at him and replied, "You don't seem surprised in what I just told you." He shook his head in agreement and told me softly, "I kind of figured the way Robert talked that this is what you wanted to tell me." I quickly spoke up and said, "Father, I do love him; very much, and he did plan on asking me to marry him before we knew about the baby." Again, he nodded in agreement and replied, "I can see he loves you as well; because he's going to great lengths to help you with your reconciliation to God; which makes me feel a bit more at ease." And then he squeezed my hand, and added, "I just want you to be sure that this is what you want because there are other options that I can help you with; and it will all be with discretion." I shook my head vigorously and said, "No Father – I want this baby; and I want to be Robert's wife; I just wanted to make it right with God before moving on."

In the next few minutes, we made small talk about Robert and how him and I came about; the whole truth. He explained to me why he agreed to perform the ceremony and why it was important to keep it between us.

Nearing the end of the confession, I recited the Act of Contrition; and then Father said, "God the Father of Mercies, through the death and resurrection of His Son, has brought forgiveness of sin in the world, through the ministry of the Church; I grant you pardon and absolution for your sin; in the name of the Father, and the Son and the Holy Spirit – Amen." Again, he took my hand and then told me, "Vivian, rather than giving you penance I would love to see you return to church on a regular basis; please consider it." I smiled and told him with a lighter heart, "I will be back full time, Father."

20

Robert and Vivian arrived back home feeling much lighter after the visit with the Priest. As Robert went through the mail in his den, he dropped several envelopes from his hand on to his desk; and then he noticed a certified letter from his attorney. He smiled and ripped it open, knowing that envelope contained the final paperwork regarding the transfer of ownership of the club to Max. This was going to make Vivian very happy, he thought; and then he took off up to the quarters to share the news with his bride to be.

As soon as Robert walked into his quarters to show Vivian the signed paperwork, he found that she was in the shower after becoming sick, so he waited for her while making her some hot tea to help settle her stomach.

***

Robert had just set my tea cup down on the island bar when I appeared from the bedroom, dressed in my tiny white robe. He asked me, "Would you like me to give you a rub down while your tea cools enough for you to drink?" I sat up on the stool and answered, "No thank you." And then I held my head and winced. "I have a terrible headache." He walked around to me and led me to the sofa by my hand. "Here darlin'", let's sit here together and relax."

He removed his suit jacket, pulled the envelope from the inside of the pocket; and sat beside me after tossing the jacket on the chair. "I have some news that I think will make you feel so much better", he told me. And then he removed the paper from the envelope and handed it over to me. I began reading it in silence; and then I looked over at him with a blank stare, followed by a wide grin. "You really unloaded that horrible place?" My excited tone caused a chuckle from him. "It's not a horrible place to me and many, many other men", he told me with emphasis. I playfully slapped the top of his leg. "Oh you!"

I read it again as if I couldn't believe what I was reading; he gave this club up after all of these years, which was quite lucrative to his income. His gesture touched me so much that my eyes welled up in tears as I looked back over at him. "You did this for me; didn't you?" He gave me a small smile and gathered me up in his arms. "Yes I did, baby; I would move heaven and earth to make you happy." I wiped my tears of joy and pulled myself up into his lap; holding on to him tighter than I had since the first time we made love.

***

"Max!" Patsy called out to him from the bathroom. She had been calling him for several minutes and she was growing impatient with every second that passed without a response from him. She sat in the tub, soaking and gathering the suds from the bubble bath to her nose; taking in the floral scent. The room glowed from a set of two candles on the ledge of the foot of the tub and a set along the two corners of the sink. She began to reminisce, as she looked across the room and into the corner at the shower stall where she and Robert had a night of wonderful, lustful sex.

She sat and imagined their silhouettes through the clear doors and then closed her eyes; remembering the incredible feeling he gave her as he thrashed in and out of her with urgency, causing her to scream with passion; which eventually drove her to wonderful tears. Sex with Robert Sterling almost felt as though it were a necessity for her to survive. She just had to have him! He was her obsession; her drug of choice, and she would allow him to fuck her until she was raw. In her mind, there was no way that miss goody two shoes could ever fulfill his sexual animalistic desires!

"Max!" She shouted his name while on the verge of one of her angry meltdowns. "What do you want?" He asked when storming in. "For god sakes I was on the phone!" He scolded her. "Was it Robert?" She asked with hopeful anticipation in her voice. "Yes, it was Robert; and it was nothing that concerns you." Her face grew sad and then she burst into tears. "Max, I'm in love with him." She began crying so hard her shoulders shuttered up and down. "Why can't he admit he feels the same for me?" Max knelt down on the powder blue shag rug beside the tub and gently told her, "Patsy, he's not in love with you; how can you not see that?" She continued to cry to the point of losing her breath.

Max shook his head, wondering how much longer he could put up with her. There was that part of him that sympathized with her being that Robert used her in every way sexually and physically; and now she was expecting a baby – maybe Robert's baby at that. But then she has that nasty side that he has witnessed so many times.

"Patsy", he addressed her softly. "Let's get you out of the tub and I will give you a nice massage to help you relax." She looked over at him with black tears flowing from her mascara and she asked, "You would do that for me?" He stared at her nipples piecing through the suds and replied with a hard swallow, "Yes, I will." She sat straight up and silently waited as he grabbed the white cotton towel off the wooden towel holder. He extended his hand to her and helped her to her feet. "Don't slip now." He told her softly and then wrapped the towel around her shoulders and began drying her off.

As he slowly dried her off he fought like hell to ignore his urges when running the towel between her legs and then across her swollen breasts. It had been several weeks since he had been with a woman. And then she did it; he was hoping she wouldn't – sort of. She wrapped her arms around his shoulders and pressed her freshly bathed body against his. "Do you want to play doctor, Max?" She asked him in her seductive Southern drawl. He agreed to her offer with a nod and then led her to the bedroom.

***

I looked out into the distance at the beautiful sunny summer day and wished I had felt up to working at the campsite with Robert, but the pregnancy was already taking its toll on me; causing me much concern. I was already a bit nervous; as I had no idea of what to expect with pregnancy, and I knew I would have to learn as I go. I continued to wonder to myself; how fat would I get? Would I vomit every day? Could I continue to look beautiful for Robert? Could I adjust to the world where I would have to be under constant security because of Robert's lifestyle; and how would that affect our baby and other future children we may have?

I sat at the cherry wood roll top desk that Robert had put in the bedroom for me. After he found out that I kept a diary, he ran right out to buy the desk. I rolled the top up and found my mother's bible lying there. Though it was old and the brown leather was fading and worn; that bible was one of my most treasured possessions. I didn't feel much like writing in my diary at that moment, so I opened the bible instead; finding the only family photo taken, when I was a baby cradled in my mother's arms.

The picture possessed a cold lonely feeling when looking at the photo; now that both of my parents were gone. I had never noticed it before, but both my mother and father had what seemed to me, were forced smiles on their faces. My father looked at least ten years older than his actual age of thirty, and as beautiful as my mother was, she looked as though she hadn't slept in days; knowing her, she probably hadn't.

As I stared into my mother's beautiful blue eyes and gently ran my fingers along her blond curls, I thought back to recollections of my father and how he treated her. He was a gambling alcoholic who came home and flew into rages because my mother was five minutes late in getting dinner on the table; or the potatoes weren't cooked to his liking. Then there were times when he found out that she had spent their last five dollars on food that she had earned working as a maid outside of the home; preventing him from buying his booze and playing poker; which would then lead to my mother crying and bleeding. And then I would hear mother's cries through their bedroom door nearly every night as my father took what he wanted from her sexually before passing out; which I have come to realize is a central cause of my own sexual hang-ups.

The angry tears streamed down my face when I remembered all the paychecks she handed over to him, only to have him throw it all away on booze, gambling; and even women. And then my thoughts to reverted back to when I had to take my mother's place and work constantly with no time for myself, and sacrificing my time in church; the only place in which I found peace and love.

But now, looking at the photo and into my father's eyes, I have come to the conclusion that he died as he had lived; nothing but an empty soul. I couldn't bear to think of my father being murdered, but the thought of him taking his own life pained me just as much – probably more. Tears flooded my eyes when I recalled the day I moved to the ranch and when daddy hugged me goodbye. I didn't hug him back; nor did I say a word to him before walking out the door of the home I grew up in. This memory is one I'm sure I will never forget; that horrible feeling of emptiness and guilt will always be there.

***

The sun was beginning to set in the distance as I sat outdoors in front of the small pond and water fall. I was in awe of this spot from the first day I had arrived on the ranch, but I never took time to just sit on that large rock and take it all in. I clenched my family photo in my hand and rested my mother's bible in my lap; as I listened to the gently flowing water from the fall spilling into the pond. Upon turning the photo over, I observed the bible verse written in my mother's handwriting; *Philippians 4:13 – I can do all things through Christ, who strengthens me.* This particular verse I knew helped my mother through all of the darkness in her life; especially when it came to fighting her Cancer, though she lost her battle, she remained strong until the end.

Suddenly, something caught the side of my eye. It was the sun beaming off of the gold headstone that sat in between two of the rosebushes. I remembered seeing it the day I arrived, but couldn't make out the writing; it was Rosie's memorial. Rosie Sanchez; her name engraved in black; followed by the words, forever loved and missed.

"Vivian", my thoughts were interrupted by Robert's soft voice. He stood over me in his rugged work clothes. Sweat poured off of his chest as I noticed his checkered black and white shirt was unbuttoned all the way down; and his blue jeans were filthy from sawdust and what appeared to be clay. He came down to one knee before me. “Are you ok, Princess?” He asked me while gently stroking my hair back. “Is it alright that I sit here?” I asked him softly. “I mean with Rosie here…” He placed his lips against mine; silencing me. And then he gave me a smile and told me, “It’s absolutely alright that you sit here.”

He rose from his knee and straddled the rock; sitting behind me and wrapping his arms around my waist. Despite the filth on his clothes and the sweat pouring from his body, I could still smell a hint of his soothing aftershave. “What do you have here?” He asked me as he took a hold of the photo. “That’s our family photo”, I answered with sadness. “It was the only one we had taken and mama kept it in her bible.” He then turned it over and asked, “When was it taken?” I rested my head back against his shoulder and quietly answered, “December nineteen twenty-eight; just seven months after I was born.” He smiled with admiration and said, “Look how tiny you were in your mama’s arms.” He kissed my cheek and added, “I can see the love she had for you.” I gave him a smile and then my tears began to fall. “I miss her so much, Robert.” He held me tighter while rocking me from side to side and he softly said, “I know baby, I know.”

***

An hour later, Robert had showered and changed into one of his dark suits to take me out on the town when we received a call on the phone in the quarters from security; announcing that the two detectives were waiting to speak to me in the main living room. Robert led me by the hand down the staircase to the living room where they were waiting. As Robert stopped before the two men, he slipped his arm around my waist to calm me, as I became rattled after being told they had returned.

Detective Reynolds was holding an envelope with my name on it and then he said, "Miss Martin, it appears that your father did indeed take his own life; and there just wasn't any evidence to suggest foul play after talking to neighbors and all who knew him; or had dealt with him. Furthermore, we have released his body to the funeral home and you can now make arrangements with them for burial." He handed me the envelope and added, "This now belongs to you, and please accept our deepest condolences."

My hand shook as I took the envelope from the detective; my tears began to fall as I looked up into his eyes. "Do you have any questions for us?" He asked me gently. I continued to tremble as I gripped the envelope; afraid to open it. "Was this his letter?" The detective nodded and replied, "Yes ma'am, he left it for you, but we had to keep it until the end of the investigation; and now it's yours."

I took a deep breath, trying to gather my senses; and then I looked back up at him wanting to ask the one question that I have been silently wondering since I heard the news, but I was afraid of the answer, but just couldn't get the words out. "Miss Martin", the detective took my hand in his and said, "There's no way he suffered; as he most likely died immediately." I let out a exhale of relief after he had answered the question I couldn't bring myself to ask.

I thanked both men, Robert saw them to the door while I sat down on the sofa. He slowly moved over to me and sat on the coffee table in front of me. "Are you going to read the letter?" He asked softly while gently swiping a tear from my cheek. "Please read it to me?" I asked him when trying to hand him the letter. He placed his hands on the top of my legs, caressing them, and then he said, "why don't we give it some time, darlin'?" I stared down at the envelope with my name written across it; immediately recognizing it as daddy's scribbling. After a few moments of trying to get the nerve to read it, I handed it to him. "I have to know what it says", but I just cannot bring myself to read his final words. After some reluctance, he removed the letter from the envelope and then he slowly began to read it to me.

My dearest Vivian, I know we haven't been in contact and I can't blame you, considering what I have done to our lives. I do want you to know that I never expected to be the bastard husband and father I had become because I wasn't raised that way. I look back at my life and I still don't know what happened, but all I know is that I put you and your mama through hell. Baby girl, I knew I wasn't going to see you again after we had words that last morning, and I went and hit you. I knew it the minute I held you for the last time and said goodbye, and you didn't hug me back or say one word.

"Baby", Robert addressed me softly and took my hand. "Should I stop?" I attempted to control my rapid breathing, but to no avail; and I continued to weep and shake to the point of becoming hysterical. "This is my fault!" I cried out. "He died…he killed…himself!" I wailed and began hyperventilating. Robert immediately tossed the letter aside and dropped to his knees before I collapsed in his arms and sank with him to the floor. "He died." I tried to talk while gasping. "Thinking I – I hated – him!"

21

My eyes fluttered open to find that Robert wasn't in the bed with me. I winced as I turned over to look at the clock and could barely see through my cloudy eyes that it was seven thirty in the morning, and then I heard the shower running; figuring that was where Robert had disappeared to.

I rolled back over to the middle of the bed, grasping the covers over my naked body and ran my hand across Robert's pillow. The only thing that got me through the night was his love and comfort. And what a horrible night it was. After my meltdown from coming to terms with the nature of my father's death and hearing Robert read his words to me, he had carried me upstairs and immediately took my blue evening gown off; followed by the rest of my clothing and put me to bed. I heard him on the phone with my doctor, but I couldn't recall the words he said as I laid there in bed and sobbed. The next thing I knew, Dr. Robinson was there and giving me a pill that made me sleepy; and then Robert held me as I drifted off.

I recalled having frightful visions of my father aiming a gun to his head and pulling the trigger; and what's worse - he was falling and screaming down a dark and endless tunnel with the most horrific agony that anyone could ever begin to imagine; this is when I woke up screaming and crying for my father. It wasn't until Robert held me tight that I fell asleep and stayed asleep the rest of the night.

I suddenly remembered that Robert was unable to finish reading my father's letter due to my meltdown and I wondered what he had done with it. I got out of bed, slipped my robe on, and went to my roll top desk to look for the letter. And there it was; part of the envelope was stinking out in between the pages of my bible. I took a deep breath and removed the letter from the envelope; so I could finish reading my father's last words.

Vivian, please know that I do love you with all of my heart and I had to let you go because I felt it was the only right thing I could do for you. A better life was right there for your taking. Despite the fact that Robert Sterling is a rough neck, I could see that he was going to take better care of you than I could. He had the means to do what I couldn't; and he was right about the fact that you shouldn't be out there working, but you should be taken care of instead; I'm sorry that I couldn't do that as a daddy should. I woke up one morning and decided that I can't be here anymore as I have nothing left and now, my baby girl; you have someone to take care of you; and somehow I see that he does care for you because he's willing to give you everything. You are finally going to live a life of luxury and for that I'm not sorry. I will always love you. Please forgive me. Love, daddy.

Once again, I trembled upon reading my father's words. Was the dream real; was it a vision of him falling into Hell? How could I live with the memories of the last time we spoke? I never hugged him in return. How could I be so selfish? I wondered silently, as my tears fell; hitting the letter and smearing the ink. I quickly dabbed the paper with a tissue to save more words from fading and set it aside. And then, I took notice that Robert had put the envelope right there with my family photo, lying in the book of Philippians; and Philippians 4:13 was circled in pencil, but not by me. I looked over at the bathroom door; listening as the water continued to run on the other side. I removed my robe, slid back into bed, and continued to cry.

Minutes later, Robert slid on top of the bed next to me with his waist wrapped in a soft white towel; and he took me in his arms from behind with my back to him. “Good morning my baby”, he whispered. “How are you feeling?” I turned over to face him and gathered myself closer into his arms. I savored his warm, damp skin against mine and his strong arms wrapped around me while I rested my head against his chest and clung to him.

***

As he held Vivian in silence, the opened desk top caught his eye along with the opened bible and the letter beside it. He recalled reading the rest of the letter after Vivian had fallen asleep; and then he slipped it in the bible at the page of the verse her mother had written on the back of the photo, and circled it. He felt it was important for Vivian to be reminded of what her mother obviously took comfort in.

***

“I forgot”, I said softly, and looked up at him. “Happy Birthday.” He gave me a small smile and said, “Thank you, Princess.” I wiggled out of his arms and sat up, still covered and with my knees to my chest. “We were supposed to have that party.” I reminded him with disappointment. He sat halfway up, leaning on his arm and then caressed my cheek. “I don’t want you to worry about that; it’s not good for you, or the baby.” He took the covers from me, pulled them back, saying, “Here - lay down.”

I rested flat on my back as he began to gently run his hand across my small belly. At this point, it was too early to tell that I had a baby growing inside of me. “All I want is for you to concentrate on our little miracle inside of you.” He then bent down and tenderly kissed my belly. “I wish we could get married today", I blurted out. He kissed my belly again and then looked into my eyes. "Me too baby, but today isn't just my birthday, it's the Fourth of July, so I doubt your priest can perform the ceremony; and we have to lay your father to rest."

I turned over on my side and pulled the covers back over my body. "I don't know how to do this", I told him. "He's not Catholic, Robert, so he's not entitled to a funeral in church." I gave way to my tears and added, "We just need to lay him to rest quickly, because I can't take much more than this." Robert slid up closer behind me and wrapped his arms around me. "Everything is going to be alright, baby; I'll take care of it all for you."

It was early afternoon and becoming muggy outside when Robert finally talked me into sitting down by the pool with him while he took a dip in the water, and then he would cook hamburgers on the grill for us. He had assured me that he would make my father's burial arrangements the next morning, and then we would see Father about our wedding ceremony.

I watched as Robert walked out to the diving board and dove off. There he was, dressed in those white swim trunks, the ones that brought out that sexy deep tan of his, and yet here I was, reclining on the lawn chair in my white sun dress, brooding. But again, I didn't know how to swim and I feared the water, though at times; I had to admit that it looked like fun.

Robert walked up the steps of the pool and then over to me. "Honey, I wish you would trust me to teach you to swim." He nodded over to the pool house and added, "At least go on in there and put on one of those extra bathing suits in there." I looked up at him with hesitation, and then he said, "Go on, baby." He helped me to my feet and gently slapped my bottom, as usual when giving me an order. "I'm sure there are some bathing suits that will meet your approval", he told me with a wink.

***

Robert watched as Vivian disappeared into the clubhouse while the phone rang. He smiled and walked over to the patio table and answered, "Sterling here." He awaited the response on the other end and then exhaled with a slight growl. "What is it, Adam?" As he listened to him talk, he watched through the window; where he could clearly see Vivian strip down naked and then look through the bathing suits. "What?" Robert asked, sharply. "Alright", he said, and then added, "Look, you can come by at ten in the morning, but don't be late because I will only have thirty minutes; I have business to take care of!" He slammed the phone down and headed to the pool house.

***

I frantically covered myself at the sound of the screen door shutting. "It's just me, Princess, relax." Robert told me. "You know", he began in a seductive tone; while approaching me, "You don't have to wear a suit – it's just us out here." I shook my head frantically, and exclaimed, "Oh no you don't! And, what about your security detail?" He pulled me into his arms and told me in his soothing voice, "Hey, not to worry; they're not in the tower today, and they're only monitoring the gate and walking the property; with the exception of this area." I stood frozen as he began leading me out the door. "Robert", I protested as we stepped outside. He took me back in his arms and said, "Come on Princess, this is our world; and we are the only ones in it."

He led me to the pool in my all together while he was still wearing his swim trunks. I wanted to look around to be sure there was no one there, but I was too terrified to find someone watching us; let alone just thinking about that horrifying idea. With that, I kept my eyes on him; pleading for him to let me go back into the pool house and get a bathing suit. “Robert, please, if you’re wanting to make love; I’ll agree to do so in the pool house.” He gave me a small smile and then he wrapped me up in his towel that was draped over the patio chair. “No, baby, we don’t have to do anything you don’t want to do; go ahead and get dressed in a bathing suit; or in whatever makes you happy.”

I hurried back into the pool house and got dressed in a bathing suit; I figured I should at least try to overcome my fear of the water. As I was about to walk back out, I heard Max’s holler out to Robert. “Hey Robert!”

I stood off to the side of the window behind the white sheer curtain out of sight, watching cautiously at Robert and Max exchanging words; that seemed to be getting quite heated with their hands flying around the air at each other. I just wished I knew what they were saying to each other.

22

Robert had abruptly decided our time at the pool was over for the day and he certainly wasn't going to tell me what happened with Max. Of course, I tried asking him what happened, but all he would say was that I had nothing to worry about; it was just something to do with the stables, and that he and Max disagreed on something. So I left it alone; though I felt Robert was hiding something from me, but I think there was a part of me that didn't want to know.

***

Robert had arranged for a special evening of sitting out at a campfire and watching fireworks at the new campground that he and Max had built. All that was needed to complete the project was the adding of Vivian's interior décor plans. While he waited for Vivian to get a small bag together, Robert stared out into the distance watching the sun begin to set and wondered where Patsy had disappeared to. Max had told him that he came out of the shower and found her and her clothes gone. He had Max and his other two officers out looking for her; he thought he had made it clear that she was to be watched, and if she wasn't with Max while on the property, she was to be taken back to the guest house immediately. He put on his light blue polo shirt while still wearing his white swim trunks and then he grabbed his gun and holster.

***

Because I wasn't feeling well due to my condition and the stress of my father's death, Robert chose to drive us out to the campground in his Jaguar, as opposed to riding the horse. He convinced me to wear that red bikini I had changed into at the pool and the matching bathing robe. As we drove up to the large A-frame log cabins, I just couldn't believe the sight before us. "Robert, this is absolutely beautiful." I gazed around with wonder at how the new cabins complemented the surroundings of the Black Hills Spruce trees, the small pond, and his new baseball diamond he had started.

He helped me out of the car, while I just couldn't take my eyes off the pond and the lovely new landscaping he built around it. The pond was drawn up to be thirty foot in diameter and was outlined in beautiful large rocks with the colors resembling those of the Black Hills metals. Across the middle of the pond, he had built a lovely walkway matching the rocks around the pond, and on the other side of the pond was an intimate looking gazebo made of knotty pine and had red roses wrapped around the pillars. Robert pointed out to the gazebo. "I had a special spot set up just for us while we watch the fireworks." I looked up at him with surprise and asked, "You built that gazebo for us to use for one night?" He laughed softly and answered, "No, Princess, it's for us to use anytime we want to." And then he took me by the hand and led me over to our new romantic spot.

We walked across the walkway and then up the three steps of the gazebo. "Oh Robert", I gasped. "It's beautiful." He had windows and screens in each opening, and on each ledge of the windows were candles. And then I noticed the roof was open so we could gaze at the stars while on the bed; that of which was in the center of the gazebo, and roses strewn all over the white bedspread. "Come on", he said when taking my hand. "I'll show you the cabins; this is for later.

I gazed around the beautiful scenery, thinking it looked so different and so much more beautiful from the day that Robert brought me out on the horse to share his plans with me. Before arriving at the deck of one of the cabins, we passed by the fire pit, outlined in large limestone. As we walked inside the cabin, I immediately looked up at the tall ceilings and observed that the inside was made in knotty pine; just as Robert's home and guesthouse. The kitchen had all stainless steel appliances and black granite counter tops with several cupboards, and an island bar with cushioned stools. At the moment the large living room was empty. In the center of the cabin was a staircase leading up to the two bathrooms and four bedrooms.

I turned to Robert and said, "This place is gorgeous." He smiled when seeing how pleased I was; he tenderly touched my cheek, and told me, "We just need to get your décor ideas, darlin. The other cabin is the same." My smile disappeared when I sadly admitted, "I know, honey, I haven't done very well with this project." "Hey", he said softly. "Don't you worry, baby; we'll likely have to wait until next summer to open the camp, so you have plenty of time."

Suddenly we heard what sounded like something dropping on the floor, causing a loud echo throughout the cabin; and it was coming from upstairs. I clung to Robert. "What was that?" I whispered. He immediately pulled his gun from the holster and whispered, "Stay here." I swallowed hard and began shaking with fear as he inched his way to the stairs. As Robert quietly stepped on the first step with his gun drawn, he glanced back at me; shaking like a leaf and holding my arms in tight against my stomach. And then his eyes cut back to the stairs and he began to carefully and quietly walk up. After a moment, I lost sight of him and then it happened; I heard a struggle and a woman scream; followed by her tumbling down the stairs to the floor.

Robert came rushing down the stairs as I ran to the woman and turned her over on her back. I stood back; stunned to see it was Patsy – and she was unconscious and bleeding from her head. As I gazed over her body, I saw that she was expecting, as she was wearing a white, sheer nightgown. I then looked up at Robert standing over her without emotion. "She attacked me from behind", he told me, when showing me the bloodied knife. I jumped back at the sight of his bloodied shirt and let out a scream so loud; it was enough to wake the dead.

***

An hour later at the County hospital, Robert came out into the waiting room to find me. I tearfully ran up to him and jumped up into his arms "I'm alright, baby", he whispered against my ear as he held me tight. Though I had suspicions and questions, I just couldn't bear to see Robert injured; and his shirt was soaked in blood. At this point I only wanted to stay in his arms because nothing else mattered.

Robert put me back down to my feet and led me over to the sofa in the waiting area. "I want to talk to you about this, but it's private so we will talk when we get home." I put my face in my hands with a sigh and then began rubbing my head. "Robert, I could see that she was expecting, so you can imagine that I have many questions." And then Max walked over to us. "The nurse let me use the phone and I called to postpone your special evening." I looked over at Max. "You knew about Patsy, didn't you?" Max bit down on his bottom lip and glanced at Robert. "Princess", Robert addressed me softly. "I'll answer your questions when we get home."

The ride back to the ranch was silent as Robert thought about the loss of what may have been his child and yet he would never know. He wasn't feeling a real loss because he didn't know one way or the other, and of course there was his resentment toward Patsy; but this child was innocent and now lost. But now and most importantly, came confession time to Vivian. How will she react - and will I lose her? He wondered.

Robert and I reached his quarters and I immediately took off the bathing suit and robe that I had on most of the afternoon and evening. I was horrified after the accident when we arrived at the hospital wearing our bathing attire, but we had no time to change; with having to get Patsy and Robert to the hospital.

I could feel my anger build, but I wasn't sure if I was angry at Robert or Patsy, as it was clear that he wasn't surprised to see her. I looked over at Robert as he removed his shirt and I saw the bandage; relieved that his wound near his shoulder only took about a dozen stitches as the stab wound wasn't as bad as originally expected.

Robert turned to face me as I slipped my bath robe on and folded my arms in a pout waiting for him to explain himself. "She claimed the baby was mine, but we had no proof", he told me in a matter of fact tone. "Did you have her on this property; how long has it been?" I asked him in a sharp tone. He stared at me as I remained in my interrogating stance. "She was at the guesthouse with Max since the first of this month; under Max's supervision, but she took off today and"…..I broke in shouting, "And then she ended up at the campground!" Robert inched in closer to me and calmly told me, "You need to watch your tone with me." All I could do was whip round; turning my back on him.

After what seemed like an eternity, Robert chimed in. "Look, I don't know if I was the father of her kid or not, but until the baby was to be born, I felt obligated to keep her with Max so I could make sure she wasn't going to pull any bullshit with us." I whipped back around and cried, "And when in the hell were you going to mention this to me?" He shot a glare at me. "Oh I see", I said, returning the glare. "What the little woman doesn't know won't hurt her, right?" He grabbed me by the shoulders in a rage, "I couldn't find the right time to tell you; you've been under enough stress!" I pulled away from him in silence and sat at the end of the bed.

I then watched as he began aggressively dressing in his suit and tie and headed for the door when he stopped and told me, "Just so you're aware, I wanted to protect you at all costs, and I felt I shouldn't put any undue stress on you; being we didn't know for sure who the father was." I looked over at him with tears falling down. "Where are you going?" I asked him in a defeated tone. "I'm going out; I have business to take care of", he answered in a cold tone. I curled up in a fetal position and sobbed as he slammed the door.

***

Robert drove around in his Jag reaching top speed and thinking about the hurt he caused Vivian once again. He found himself in the parking lot of his gentleman's club; now Max's club. He turned off the engine and just stared at the entrance; wanting to go in a blow off some steam. But because blowing off steam for him is usually having meaningless sex, he knew he couldn't do that, especially now that he had put a ring on Vivian's finger; he was trying to live differently. Just the mere thought of losing Vivian flooded his eyes over, so he started his car and drove away;

knowing that going in those doors would cost him the only woman he ever loved, and possibly for good.

An hour later, Robert walked into Patsy's hospital room and found Max sitting in a chair by her bed. Max glanced over at her sleeping and then walked over to Robert. "What are you doing here?" He whispered. Robert held his glare over at Patsy and told him, "I have a score to settle." Max pulled him out of the room and said, "I figured you would be home with Vivian trying to explain what the hell happened." Robert began to pace with his hands in his pants pockets and replied, "I did explain, but I had to leave and give us both more time to calm down." Max shook his head in disbelief, and sighed, "I told you to tell her right away." Robert drove his hand through his hair and whipped around; shouting, "I tried, damn it!" Max threw his hands up and asked, "What the hell are you going to do with Patsy; beat the hell out of her?" Just when Robert was about to answer, they heard Patsy call Max's name.

Both men walked into her room and found her holding her belly. She began crying when she saw Robert. "We lost our baby!" She sobbed and reached out to him. Robert began moving her way when Max gave him a look of caution and hollered his name, "Robert!" He stopped, looked over at Max, and said, "Please give the grieving mother and I a few moments alone, Max." When he didn't see Max heading for the door, he gave him a look of authority, and said firmly, "Please, Max." He went over to Robert and touched his shoulder. "Just don't do anything that you'll regret; you have enough to deal with now that Vivian knows, focus on her and how you intend on keeping her."

Robert watched Max walk out the door and then he turned back to Patsy. He watched in silence for a moment as she laid there and cried. She curled up in a fetal position and held her empty belly. “I’m sorry I lost our baby, Robert.” She continued to cry as he inched closer, feeling his blood run cold through his veins. How dare she lie there and cry when she chose to attack me? He thought to himself.

“Patsy”, he addressed her in an eerily calm tone and slowly rolled her over to her back. She looked up at him with her tears black from mascara, while he pulled the covers back and ripped her hospital gown wide open, exposing her naked front. As he gently rubbed his hand across and around her belly that may have housed his unborn child, he noticed that she seemed farther along than she originally told him, but it didn’t matter anymore. “You know”, he began. “At this moment I have to wonder what this baby would have done in his or her life.” Her lips quivered when she asked him, “Do you think we can make another baby, Robert?” He stared at her; his hand still on her belly. She then put her hand on his and began gliding it down her belly to the opening of her folds. He ripped his hand away from hers before his hand made contact with her intimate area, and said, “I’m in love with Vivian, she’s going to be my wife and she’s having my baby.”

The empty look she gave him made him realize just how delusional she had become. And then suddenly his anger began to diminish, as he found himself feeling nothing but empathy for her; thinking he may have been the main cause of all of it. He knew he should’ve handled things better, but he just couldn’t even think of losing Vivian; and Patsy was a threat again. At this moment he decided to withdraw his decision to have her arrested for attacking him; he just wanted to get back to Vivian, and Max was right, focus belonged on Vivian.

He covered her back up and told her quietly, “Just get some rest Patsy; we can talk later.” He began walking toward the door as she started with the begging and crying. “Robert, we have to make another baby; please don’t leave me!” He heard her pleading as he walked out the door.

***

I had written a few paragraphs in my diary after Robert stormed out. He was successful in making his point about not telling me because he didn’t know if he was the father of Patsy’s baby or not. And then it came to me, that with Patsy; anyone could have been the father. I realize this is judgmental, however it’s accurate; and then there’s the fact that he and I weren’t an item the last time they were together. As angry and hurt as I felt, I looked down at my belly and couldn’t imagine losing our baby. Despite Patsy’s nastiness, I felt for her as a woman; and now, as an expectant mother.

***

I smiled when I saw Robert walk in about thirty minutes after he had called. He silently made his way over to me, we embraced and he just continued to hold me tight. “I’m sorry I wasn’t up front with you, baby.” He pulled away, softly pressed his lips against mine, and then looked into my eyes while caressing my cheek. “I just can’t stand the thought of losing you.” I took his hand from my cheek and kissed the inside of his palm. “I understand and I’m not angry anymore; we need to move on.” He smiled and then removed his suit jacket.

I watched him as he made his way over to the door and locked his gun and holster away in the small table drawer. “Would you like me to make you a drink?” I asked him. “That sounds enticing”, he replied when sitting on the bar stool at the island bar. He gazed over at me as I began pouring the drink, just the way he liked it.

"Here you are", I told him when handing him the glass. And then he quickly grabbed me as I was walking away and kissed my lips; slow and deep. I pulled away from him, and replied breathlessly, "My goodness, that was some kind of thank you." He held me close and set his drink on the bar. "Honey", he said softly. "I understand what you were saying about no more sex until after we marry, but that doesn't mean we can't have a little harmless fun; does it?" Before I could answer, he said, "Besides, you said you would agree to make love to me in the pool house." I smiled and felt myself blush when telling him, "That was because I didn't want to make love outside in the open." I could tell he didn't know what to say; even with that amused smile of his, so he took a few sips of his drink.

I stood in between his legs, catching the aroma of his musk cologne; which was awakening my senses; those deep down senses that I have failed to keep dormant. I had nearly broken my own rule the night before with all that was going on…And now, the feel of his strong hand caressing the small of my back through my silky robe was igniting a throbbing sensation between my legs, and causing my body temperature to rise to its peak.

"It's getting warm in here", I told him in a seductive tone while removing my robe and allowing it to fall to the floor. The tired back and forth thoughts of right and wrong when doing the forbidden was beginning to wear on me, and I suddenly found myself aroused at the idea of crossing the lines of the proper young lady.

He pulled my body against his, and asked me in a quiet, but hopeful tone, "Are you sure about this?" Without immediately answering him, I ran my fingers through his hair, brushing it back, and then I replied, “Why don’t you just sit here and relax with the drink I made you while I prepare dinner.” He answered with the widest smile, “I can do that.

***

He sat there on the stool sipping his drink while he intently watched her every move; tracing her entire naked body with his stalking eyes as she prepared his dinner. He took the most pleasure in the idea that she had taken control of the intimacy between them for the first time, and it was obvious that she intended for him to look, but not touch until she wanted him to; and it was one of the most erotic experiences he has had with her thus far.

Robert had noticed that she was becoming more comfortable in disrobing in front of him, and in the middle of his living room; even though there weren’t any window coverings. He was starting to make her trust him, in that he wouldn’t put her in a situation to be seen by his security staff – or anyone, during their private moments together; because as he told her from the start, her naked body was for his eyes only.

***

Robert had just finished his drink and began swirling the ice in his glass when he saw that I couldn’t reach a dish at the top shelf of the cupboard. After a minute of watching me struggle to reach, he slowly made his way to me and softly spoke in my ear, “Let me help you with that.” He then picked me up in his arms; cradling me.

We didn’t even bother with the dish and I tearfully looked into his eyes with growing arousal and immense emotions running rampant through my very soul like never before; causing my heart to flutter to the point of feeling the throbbing in my throat. "I need you", I told him quietly. And then I wrapped my arms around his neck and held onto him as though it would be our last time together.

After sharing a few deep and penetrating kisses, he put me down and went over to the turntable. "I think this calls for a little Frank Sinatra", he told me when starting the music. He then made his way back over to me and once again swept me up in to his arms, and began dancing as he cradled me. I rested my head on his shoulder as he swayed to the soft music. I snuggled closer and tighter to the inside of his neck and whispered, "I'll remember this forever."

As he slowly danced with me, all of the vulnerability I had felt slipped away and I began to feel the erotic pleasure of being with him in that moment; with my whole heart and soul. It no longer mattered that I had broken my mother's rules; or society's rules. I began feeling all of my fear dissolve as he cradled me safe in his arms, while he danced in the kitchen with the beef stew simmering on the stove beside us. I think this is what my friend Lucy referred to as wonderful "make up sex."

Moments later, Robert ended up turning the stove off and carrying me to the shower. I don't mind saying I was concerned as we had never made love in the shower; and I was afraid we might slip and break our necks. But as always, Robert reassured me that we would be safe.

The hot water felt wonderful blanketing my body, as Robert stood behind me; kissing my neck and massaging my breasts. I felt his hard manhood against the small of my back; teasing me as he slowly drove the bar of soap all around the front of me. After fully lathering me, he returned the soap to its spot and massaged the lather into my skin; slowly and deeply, he cupped my breasts, massaging my nipples. He whispered against my ear, “Put your foot up on the edge of the tub; don’t worry, baby, I won’t let you fall.

As I did what he wanted, he slid his hand down my abdomen and then slipped two fingers inside of my folds. He pulled me tighter against his hard arousal as he continued to caress that spot that always sends me. The more he teased me with his fingers circling inside of me; pushing my button, I started coming unglued; grinding up against him and crying out in ecstasy. “Ooh, my baby likes this”, he whispered with seduction against my ear, and sending me closer to that breaking point when he went deeper and faster inside of me. “You like it; don’t you, baby”, he exclaimed with excitement, as I began screaming his name. “Come on, baby; tell me how much you like it,” he mercilessly provoked me as I cried out with my explosion.

Robert wasted no time in lifting me up off of the shower floor, facing him and steading me against the shower wall. He guided himself inside me and slowly began to make love to me. I

clung to him; fearful of falling from his soaked body. He reached underneath and steadied me while he continued to glide in and out of me, while tracing my breasts with his tongue. Finally, he reached the depth of me; triggering my desire. Even as I began crying out to him, he kept his thrust slow; teasing against my arousal.

But then he quickly set me to my feet, repositioning me against his hard manhood. “Lean forward just a bit, baby.” I must have shown some panic in what he was going to do, because he told me, “Relax, baby.” He raised one of my legs as I leaned against the shower wall with my hands; as though I was under arrest. He teased me with the tip of his manhood, searching for my opening. I instinctively leaned into him; my ass pressed against him as though I was sitting on him while he made slow and gentle love to me. With this position, I knew it wouldn't last long because I was already going out of my mind before he changed positions. And then he went back to pushing that favorite button of mine between my folds, as he continued to explore the depth of me with his full length.

He once admitted that he knew when I was ready to have an orgasm and he wanted to prolong the anticipation for me; which intensified my orgasms every time. His thrusting became hurried as soon as I came close to my boiling point; screaming his name once again. As soon as I exploded, deep moans escaped his lips. Suddenly he lifted me off my feet and emptied himself inside of me.

23

Robert sat in his den at nine o'clock the next morning and seething at the note staring him in the face. Once again, the words of a coward! He thought to himself and he slammed his fist down on the desk.

***

"Robert", my soft and concerned voice caught his attention. "What's wrong?" After we made love last night, I reminded him of his promise to never keep anything from me again - nothing!

I stood next to him and then he took my hand that I had rested on his shoulder. "Honey, for many months now I have received a few notes that have rubbed me the wrong way, that's all." I moved in front of him, leaned against the desk, took the note from him, and read it out loud. "*I'm coming for what's mine and soon!*" I looked over at him with much concern and asked, "Do you have any idea as to who is doing this?" He silently shook his head, indicating that he did not know. "We have to call the police!" I exclaimed and took the receiver of the phone off the hook, and was ready to dial the number when he quickly grabbed the receiver from me and hung it up. "No baby, I will take care of this myself – don't you worry about it."

I stared at the phone a moment and then watched as he began loading his pistol with urgency to the point where he was starting to perspire. And then it dawned on me that he said he's been getting these notes for many months! Oh my God – that's what he was protecting me from! "Robert", I addressed him in a sharp tone and took his hand to stop him from loading the gun and focus on me. "This was why you came and got me that day and forced me back here – isn't it?" I asked him in a panicked tone. He looked at me and said nothing, but his silence answered my question. "Oh my God, Robert!" I began to tremble and went on to interrogate him. "What do they want; who are they; what if they are watching us right now?" I was on the verge of hysterics when he pulled me in to his arms and held me close. "Take it easy, baby", he told me in a soothing tone. "You know I won't let any harm come to you." Startled by the doorbell, I leapt closer in his arms, and clung as tight as possible to him.

As Robert continued to hold me, Max stepped in the room with Adam. Robert swayed with me from side to side and then pulled away just enough away to look into my eyes. "Hey", he said softly. "I meant what I said, do not worry about this." And then he tenderly kissed my lips. "Max will take you up to the quarters while I have my meeting with Adam, and then I'll come up to get you when it's time for us to leave." I cautiously looked over at Adam and then turned back to Robert. "Why can't you take me up?" I asked with my voice trembling. He nodded and then looked over at Max. "Please keep Adam company while I take Vivian up to rest, she's had a long night." Max looked over at Adam as if he were a rodent, as Robert and I left the room, and then he said, "Sure, no problem, pal."

***

Adam stared at the door Robert and Vivian had gone through and became unaware of his surroundings as his mind began to wander about his fantasies with Vivian. He heard Max talking but could not make out the words, as he had tuned him out completely. Thoughts flashed before him like scenes from a movie. First, he'd tell Robert that they are brothers and when Robert would refuse to share the wealth, he would beat him within an inch of his life and tie him to a chair. And then Vivian would walk in after hearing the commotion and become hysterical when seeing Robert's broken body. And then when she would try to run for help, Adam would grab her, throw her on Robert's desk face first, rip her clothes off, and shoves his hard rod up in her ass. She screams and cries as he rams her from behind like a savage, while Robert begs him to stop. He finishes Robert off, and then Vivian and everything Sterling is his!

"Adam!" He heard Max shout from just inches from his face. "What the hell is wrong with you?" Max asked him with a look of concern. Adam snapped out of his temporary psychosis and turned his back on him, trying to gather his senses. "I don't know", he said in a calm tone. "I was in an accident a few weeks back, and I get confused and lose my senses now and then." Max looked at him, still with uncertainty as he never really liked Adam, but her never knew exactly why. "Well whatever you want with Robert, just know you better not be planning any monkey business with him", he warned him in a stern tone. "He's the brother I never had."

***

Robert had spent a few moments trying to calm me with his arms around me in bed. "Would you like me to draw you a bath?" He asked me softly, while caressing my hip. Not answering his question, I asked him, "What does Adam want?" He exhaled and told me, "I don't know, baby, he said he didn't want to talk over the phone." He kissed the top of my head as I rested it on his chest. "Let me draw that bath for you to help you relax." He then tapped my bottom and added, "Come on babe, get undressed and I'll go get your bath ready."

Robert turned off the faucet and then looked at his watch as I had stripped down and walked into the bathroom. He wrapped his arms around me and said, "I love you and I'll be back before you know it." He gave me one of his softest kisses yet, and then added, "I'm locking the door as usual, and I will use my key." I acknowledged his words with a nod and then he took my hand and helped me into the tub to be sure that I didn't slip. As soon as I sat down, he bent down and kissed me goodbye again.

Robert walked into the den to find both Max and Adam in silence and standing on opposite sides of the room. Robert looked over at Adam as he sat down behind his desk, and that's when he noticed that he had appeared thinner and more fatigued since he last saw him. "Now, Adam – what was it that you wanted? I will give you no more than fifteen minutes." And then he motioned for the chair across from his desk as Max leaned against the wall.

Adam looked over at Max. He silently thought to himself; look at him –standing there like a self-righteous son of a bitch! "Do I need to ask Max to leave us alone?" Adam heard Robert ask as he watched him remove his suit jacket; reminding him of how big his half-brother really was. "No", he said with a smile. "I know you two are like brothers." He looked back over at Max, who had his arms folded and gave out a penetrating stare.

Wasting no more time Adam pulled out his mother's torn out journal page and handed it to Robert. "You need to see this. I was cleaning out my deceased mothers belongings and came upon this from her journal." Robert took the paper from him while looking over at Max, who was walking over to Robert's desk.

Robert read the paper in silence and then looked up at Adam in disbelief. "What is it?" Max asked Robert. Robert looked over at Max, and then again at Adam, trying to find the words to answer him. And then he replied to Max, "According to this piece of paper, Adam's mother claims that Phillip fathered Adam." Max frowned in disgust and ripped the paper from Robert's hand. "Let me see this bullshit!" Adam charged at Max, shouting, "It's not bullshit!" Robert stood in between them and hollered, "Enough!" Both men went to their respective places in the room and stared at each other in silence.

Robert took the journal page back from Max and read it again, shaking his head. And then he noticed the date of, *June 30, 1926.* Robert looked back over at Adam and asked, "Is this date on this page the date of your birth?" Adam nodded and took the paper from Robert, answering, "Yes." Robert took note that Adam was born just days before he was in the same year, and went to his desk, pulled a pad of paper out, and asked, "What was your mother's name – first and last?" He asked with emphasis. "Caroline Wilson", Adam replied with sadness in his voice. "She died when I was only a few months old, so I didn't know her." Max chimed in, asking, "So how is it that you have her things?" Adam glared at him upon answering, "Her parents raised me."

Robert sat in deep thought, drowning out the other two men talking back and forth. How the hell could this be? He wondered. The man I hired as head of security is my brother? There was someone that may be able to confirm his claim – dad's valet, Mitchell Parker. Robert stopped the two from there bickering. "Enough!" He rose from his seat and stood in the front of his desk with his arms folded. "Adam, I'm sure you understand that I must look into this." Adam kept his rising anger at bay by clenching his jaw together, while he found the words of response. "But, Robert, I have proof right here, on this piece of paper." Robert looked over at Max and said, "Get Mitchell Parker on the phone and tell him I need to see him at once."

***

Robert had gone up to fill Vivian in with what was going on, while Max took Adam to his former quarters to stay until they could get more concrete information from Phillip Sterling's valet. Both Robert and Adam agreed to accept any solid information given to them, followed by a blood test.

"Do you believe that he is your brother?" I asked Robert in a concerned tone. He shrugged and replied, "I have always been open to the idea that I could have siblings out there; I mean my father got around even more than I did." I rolled my eyes and mumbled under my breath, "Yeah and with women like Patsy." Not hearing what I mumbled, he went on to say, "It's just hard to wrap my head around the fact that the man I happened to hire to oversee my security team could be my – brother", he added in disbelief. "God works in mysterious ways, honey", I told him. Robert raised an eyebrow to my statement and said, "Yeah he does; Adam and Patsy seem to be two of his darkest mysteries." I couldn't help but giggle a bit to that response.

He sat down at the island bar and shook his head and seemingly at a loss for words, so I went over to him and stood in between his legs. "What are you going to do if it's true and he is your brother?" He exhaled and slid his arms around to the small of my back and pulled me closer while replying, "First let me ask you how you feel about all of this." I cocked my head to the side and gave him a small smile when answering, "It doesn't matter what I think." He caressed my cheek and told me in a soft tone, "Actually it does matter – you're going to be my wife, and I know he makes you uncomfortable." I looked up into his eyes and nervously bit down on my lip. "I never liked the man", I shook my head in acknowledgement, and added, "I don't know why – okay?" I just couldn't tell him about the first night when Adam shined that bright light into my quarters, seeing me in my altogether.

And then I began walking away when I said, “He frightens me, but if he turns out to be family, you can’t turn your back on him. You already said his rented room is gone because the store burnt to the ground.” I turned back to him with my arms folded as I suddenly felt a cold and uncomfortable sort of chill, and I added, “I still can’t believe Charlie’s store is gone; and he doesn’t even know because he’s on vacation.” As soon as Robert was about to speak, the phone rang; it was Max telling him that Mitchell Parker had arrived.

***

Robert quickly kissed Vivian and departed for the den to meet up with Phillip Sterling’s former valet. The man retired after Phillip’s death, knowing he would receive a generous inheritance for his work and loyalty to Phillip. Robert recalled with Vivian earlier that Mitchell did everything for Phillip, from shaving him to arranging trips, business or otherwise. He was loyal to fault, Robert told her. He was loyal to the point that he personally handed over his own cousin to his employer after he ran because he wasn’t able to pay his debt to him. Phillip had his Hench men beat him severely, however, he gave the order to make sure he survived; as a favor to Mitchell – simply put, Phillip paid loyalty with loyalty, and Robert implemented that into his own life as well.

Robert entered his den and smiled upon seeing Mitchell. The man stood at attention just as he always did with Phillip, and now Robert was receiving the same respect. Mitchell was a man of sixty –two years of age, stood at five foot five and had a stocky build about him; and he still wore the black suits and matching hat to cover his balding head.

Robert went over to him and immediately shook his hand. “Hi kid”, the man said with a wide grin and shaking his hand. “Mitchell”, Robert nodded and returned the smile. He turned to Max and said, “You know Max.” And then he drew his hand across the room, saying, “And this is Adam Wilson; the one who is claiming to be Phillip’s long lost son.”

To look at Mitchell Parker, a person would never know that he would play catch with his employer’s son by day and witness beatings, rapes and murders at night. Robert was always amazed at how well he showed that poker face of his and maintained empathy for others.

“Wilson?” Mitchell asked. “Your last name is Wilson?” Adam gave a slight nod in confirmation. Mitchell looked back at Robert and asked, “Can I see the piece of paper from the woman?” Adam took it out of his pocket and handed it to the man. As he read it in silence, memories began to flash through his mind of a young blond woman pleading with his employer to take care of her and their unborn child.

Mitchell looked over at Adam and asked, “Was your mother’s name Caroline – Caroline Wilson?” Adam and Robert made eye contact, and then Adam swallowed hard, answering, “Yes, her name was Caroline.” Robert looked over at Mitchell and asked him, “How did you know that, Mitch?” The man smiled at Robert and asked, “You don’t recall that I was there with your father for everything?”

Mitchell handed the paper back over to Adam and said, “I recall the second time she had come to him; after he told me to write her a check to get her to go away the first time.” He looked at Robert and said with loud emphasis, “Now look, I know your father is gone, but this information doesn't leave this room!" Robert sat behind his desk and nodded, "I promise, Mitch; it was many years ago." Mitchell shook his head and sat across from him. "But you don't understand kid, this was a start to a whole new ball game with your father and his girls." And then he looked back at Adam. "And you - you may have only been a few months old when your mother died, but do you really want to know what happened to her?" Adam looked at him and asked, "Are you saying what I thought all along, and that Phillip Sterling silenced her?"

Robert sat stoned faced upon hearing those words as he knew what Phillip had done to many people, so nothing was going to shake him. Robert asked Mitchell, "Was Adam fathered by Phillip?" Mitchell shook his head up and down in confirmation, and then proceeded to add, "Phillip had one of his prostitutes for himself." He looked over at Adam and said, "And that former prostitute was your mother. When Phillip chose a woman to be his, she was off limits to everyone else. So yes, Phillip Sterling was your father."

Adam scratched his head and asked, "So why the hell didn't he take care of us?" Mitchell stood up while looking him in the eye, and responded in a firm tone, "Because your mother wasn't satisfied with the first big check, she had to have more; and on top of that, she expected him to commit to her when he was already married!" Adam threw his hands up and hollered, "Fine – but why wouldn't he accept me as his kid and take care of me the same as he did with his other son?"

Robert stood up and shouted at Adam. "Hey, you watch your tone with Mitch! He's only giving us the information; it's not his fault!" Mitch put his hands in front of him to calm Robert. "It's alright, kid. I can't say I blame

Adam for feeling the way he does." He shrugged and asked, "Are you sure you want to hear more about this?" Adam spoke up, "Yes, I do." Robert sat back down, and silently nodded in the direction of Mitch. Max pulled a chair up next to Robert as Mitch sat back down and began talking about the last time he saw Caroline Wilson.

"Phillip had been so angry with Ms. Wilson that he stormed out of his office and as always, I was to follow him for any orders he may have for me. After he explained to me that he just couldn't bring a kid into his home because Mrs. Sterling was about to give birth herself, he was to make a decision as it was clear that Caroline wasn't going to go away; and stay away as he had ordered. You see, Phillip made sure that Caroline and all his girls were protected from pregnancy because the last thing he wanted was a bunch of kids ruining his business; as he figured pregnant women stop producing funds for him. Part of my job was making sure all of the girls had that protection and was using it; with the exception of Caroline, as she was Phillips responsibility."

"Phillip and I went back into his office and he told her because she couldn't stay away as ordered, he would have to make her go away. She of course knew what it meant when Phillip Sterling talked about making someone go away and then she became distraught and promised she would leave; but it was too late, she had already angered him and she was now a liability for him."

"Phillip had a room in the basement where he would take his girls and other female staff members when he had to discipline them. He had shackles on the wall and on the bed, and he would sit in his comfortable chair while his men would carry out the punishments. All the women being disciplined were forced to remove all clothing, and depending on Phillip's mood at the time, he would decide if they were shackled to the wall or the bed. After each beating, they were always forced to endure some type of sexual torture at the hands of both him and his men; which could last anywhere from an hour to two days."

"On this particular day, Ms. Wilson was to find out just how angry she had made him, and she was not going to die without suffering; Phillip wasn't going to allow it! Though she pleaded with him to spare her, he ordered three of his men to escort her down to the basement and shackle her to the table after stripping her. When the boss and I arrived downstairs, one of the men was having his way with her; which wouldn't have been tolerated if Phillip hadn't decided to do away with her, so he allowed him to finish and then he began inflicting his anger on her."

"He had a doctor on the payroll and sent for him to perform a hysterectomy on her; this was to happen without her being sedated, so she could feel the pain all the way through. The hysterectomy was punishment for her pregnancy, as Phillip felt as though she tricked him by not taking her birth control. The screaming that came from her could make ones ears bleed, and by the time the surgery was over she was already knocking on death's door. And even though Phillip no longer wanted her, he made it clear to her that it was her fault that one of his men had sex with her; so he took the hot brander engraved with the Sterling name on it, and shoved it between her legs and nearly up inside her."

"I could tell the more she screamed and cried, the more Phillip became satisfied that she had paid her penalty. That's when he pulled out his revolver and ended her misery. That had to be the most blood I had ever seen and one hell of a mess to clean up. He had ordered me to have it cleaned up, while his men went and disposed of her."

"After that day, Phillip decided that all his working girls would have a hysterectomy, but lucky for them, they wouldn't endure the pain as they would be sedated; his basement became his personal operation room."

24

It was mid - afternoon when Robert took me into town and made arrangements to lay my father to rest. I had decided that I should be the one to take care of everything as I had remembered my parents burial plots were actually paid for. By the grace of God, my mother was able to put that money away without my father missing it; all I needed to do was have him buried.

As I stood there in my black dress and heels, looking at the pile of dirt next to my mother's headstone and recalling our family, I shook my head and looked up at Robert. "I'm not so sure they should have been buried next to each other", I told him in a sad tone. He reached into his black suit jacket pocket and handed me his handkerchief. "Well", he said carefully. "I think your mother thought differently being she bought the joint plots, honey." I looked back at the pile and said, "Goodbye, daddy; I love you and always will." And then I turned and walked back to the car.

Adam walked into the hospital room where Patsy was receiving her sponge bath. Upon seeing him, the nurse quickly covered Patsy and exclaimed, "You aren't allowed in here!" He walked over to her with a smirk on his face and told her with his drunken slur, "Oh please, lady, not only have I seen her naked ass many times, I've fucked it too." She appeared to be shaken as her eyes grew wide; not knowing what to say. Adam pulled the covers right off the bed and said, "Continue with your job."

He took his flask from the inside of his black suit pocket while he watched the nurse's hand shake as she continued to give Patsy her sponge bath. Patsy laid there silent and looking away off to the side the whole time. Adam wasn't sure that she knew he was even there. As far as he could see with Patsy, the lights were on, but no one was home.

The nurse was of average height and in her early to mid-forties, Adam had figured. She had a nice hour glass shape, and a firm looking ass; just like Vivian, including the blonde hairstyle and length.

He smiled to himself and decided to pour on some charm to see if she would bite. "Look", he said softly; grabbing the attention of the nurse. "I can be such a beast at times; I'm sorry." She gave him a look of disgust and went right back to Patsy's bath. "A real gentleman wouldn't stand there and watch a private moment like this", she mumbled. Amused at her words, he began laughing. "Yes, I need some work on that area, but I just haven't found the right woman to teach me how to be that gentleman." She looked back over at him, still giving him that look of disgust, and said, "Well don't look at me, I'm married." He walked over to her and looked into her blue eyes; causing her to back away from him. And she told him in a trembling voice, "Mister, if you lay a hand on me, I will scream so loud your ears will bleed."

Adam stood in place and shoved his hands in his pants pockets, all the while giving her his penetrating look. He fought his inner rage against doing away with her right then and there because people have noticed his presence around that hospital; so he couldn't risk any slip ups. "Just tell me when she will be released", he replied with authority. She shook her head from side to side and answered, "I don't know, doctors are concerned because she hasn't responded to anyone since her loss." He looked back over at Patsy and with a sinister grin he told the woman, "I bet I can make her respond." The nurse shouted, "You leave now!" He snapped his head back in her direction and grabbed her by the shoulders. "You go ahead and scream", he said through his gritted teeth. "I'll fuck you in the ass so hard it will split you half; and I'll be long gone when they find your body." She shook her head from side to side; on the verge of hysterics when she told him, "I'm sorry, please don't hurt me." He released her and said, "I have a way of knowing who tattles, and who doesn't; so you better make sure you keep that beautiful mouth of yours shut!" He slapped her on the ass on the way out, leaving her alone to her hysterics in private; while walking away with his hard rod nearly breaking through his pants.

The nurse stood in place trembling so uncontrollably that her body became wracked with pain and then the acid rose from her stomach; giving her seconds to get herself to the bathroom in Patsy's room. She fell to her knees while she heaved into the toilet and sobbed hysterically; convinced that she had just made eye contact with the devil himself.

Robert and I had returned back to the ranch after burying my Father, and then we started to make arrangements to get married. It was decided that we would be married on Saturday - four days away. This will be a private ceremony with Max as a witness; I had discovered that my best friend Lucy would be unable to leave school, so Max would be the only witness; along with extra security present. Robert and I agreed that it wasn't the most romantic idea to have armed security staff at the wedding, but it was definitely necessary.

Upon returning, Robert had talked me into going out to the gazebo at the campsite, and because it was hot, he insisted that we both wear our bathing attire and take a change of clothes; should we get cool after dark, as we would stay the night out there. I had noticed how preoccupied Robert seemed after the meeting with Adam and Mitchell; and of course, I was concerned.

"So you really believe that Adam is your brother just because of what this man told you?" Robert took my hand as we cuddled on the bed out at the gazebo. "I wasn't sure – at first, but then he was certain of his information. And then I looked over at Adam's face, and from the side, he looked just like my father when he was that age; our father", he corrected himself quietly while stroking my hip.

I rested my head on his bare chest and felt the throbbing of his heartbeat against my cheek. I had to wonder what the details were surrounding Adam's mother and her time working for Phillip, but I didn't dare ask; as deep down I really didn't want to know. There was a calm silence between us as we just rested in each other's arms, while listening to the beautiful sounds of nature. The security detail that now surrounded us as we were to have private time at our new campsite made me feel uneasy, to say the least. Because of those damn notes, the armed guards were just a stone's throw away as we laid there in the center of the gazebo on the bed; awaiting the fireworks that were meant for a few nights before.

"Where did Adam go?" I asked with caution. "He and I both agreed to take some time to think, but he will be back tonight after he replaces his clothing that he lost in the fire." I lifted my head to look at him and asked, "Is he going to live here on the ranch?" He slid his hand down from my back to my bottom; giving me one of his gentle love taps, when answering, "Only until he gets his own home; and he's sure as hell is not entitled to my clothing store either", he added with emphasis. "Do you think…?" Robert placed his finger on my lips, gently silencing me. "Come on baby, I don't want to talk about Adam right now – let's worry about him later and just enjoy the peace." He lifted my chin with his index finger and softly kissed my lips. "I love this – us being here, and just enjoying each other and nature", he told me. Whenever I hear him emphasizing his request, or an order of any kind; I know that I need to drop the subject of the discussion, because there isn't anyone who can talk him out of anything when his mind is made up.

***

Adam's watch had just struck midnight when he saw the nurse walking to her car in a brisk pace and looking around cautiously. He ran across the deserted street and followed her from afar; but she wasn't seeing him, as she had finally slowed her pace and stopped looking behind and around her. He staggered a bit from his whiskey, but he still had most of his senses about him when he caught up to her, parked next to a poorly lit alley; and struggling to find her keys in her oversized black purse.

His mind went back to earlier in the day when he was confirmed as Phillip Sterling's son. The time has come where he will never be denied by anyone ever again! He's a Sterling, and he was going to have the Sterling power and money – he was unstoppable; especially since he left no trace of his female companion at the store after setting it ablaze.

Adam grabbed the unsuspecting nurse from behind; which brought on her screaming. "Shut up!" He hollered as he began delivering blows to the side of her head with his fist; until she went limp and dropped her purse. He then shoved his handkerchief in her mouth, tossed her on top of her car face first, as she made muffled whimpering sounds; but she was unable to move or fight back. He held her down by the back of her head while he lifted the skirt of her uniform dress and ripped her pantyhose and panties away from her body. She began to squirm as the muffled cries became louder. He shoved two of his fingers up inside of her, and whispered in her ear, "I knew you had a virgin ass." She began to cry harder as he shoved them up further inside of her and continued to molest her from behind. Her crying angered him to the point of insanity; provoking him to pull her hair back, lifting her head off the car, and then slamming her face into the hood; causing blood to splatter all over the hood of the car. Though the blow was brutal, she was still half conscious. Unable to control his appetite, he unzipped his pants and shoved his hard rod up inside her; which brought on one last muffled scream from her.

After Adam finished with the nurse, he zipped up and flipped her over on her back; and saw that she was still breathing. "Hey", he said slapping her face. "Wake up, you fucking whore." And then he ripped her uniform wide open from top to bottom and just stared at her in a deep trance as she laid there, exposed.

He couldn't erase the images out of his mind when he again recalled what he heard about his mother's last moments; and how she suffered through that torture with that surgery that mutilated her womanhood. "I got the shitty end of the stick because you were a fucking, rotten whore!" He no longer saw the nurse, but now it was his mother's face. He only knew her from photographs his grandmother had shown him. The rage began seething and his blood ran cold as he began beating the woman as she laid there unresponsive. "You stupid bitch!" He screamed as he delivered blow after blow with his fist to her face and head. And then he took out his jack knife and began gutting her womanhood. "You dirty, rotten good for nothing whoring bitch!"

Adam stood there and looked all around the bloody mess of death and destruction that he had caused. He was exhausted and thirsty; he looked down at his bloodied clothes from head to toe. He knew he couldn't go back to the ranch in that condition, so he went back to his truck and drove off toward the lake so he could wash up and destroy his clothes soaked of the nurse's blood.

25

Robert had sent one of his armed officers into town with Vivian so she could buy her wedding gown; while he was to have a breakfast meeting with Adam and his lawyer, Sal. Robert was under the impression that they had agreed to wait until after the wedding to discuss anything further about their situation, but now Adam insisted that they do business immediately; and although Robert didn't generally respond to orders given by others, he just wanted it all to be over.

The three men sat out at the patio table alongside the pool and Robert put his empty plate on the cart. He sat back down and looked over at Sal, asking, "Just to confirm, I'm under no obligation to give Adam anything, correct?" Sal loosened his tie, relaxed against the back of his chair and nodded, "That's correct, Robert." And then he looked over at Adam who wrinkled his forehead into an angry frown. "I'm sorry, but you were never mentioned in Phillip Sterling's will; so therefore, Robert is under no obligation to give you a penny." Adam slammed his fist down on the table in a rage. "This is horse shit; I'm his son too!" Robert leaned into him and exclaimed, "You can stay here until you find your own home, but you cannot – and you will not live with us permanently!"

Robert took notice of Adam's change in his demeanor as he sat there trembling and wringing his hands together. And then he noticed his hands were bruised and swollen. "What happened to your hands?" Robert asked him. "I got into a scuffle; don't you concern yourself – brother", he said with emphasis. And then he asked Robert, "Are you not allowing me to live here as a Sterling because of Vivian?" Robert took a drink from his orange juice and answered, "That's a big part of it, but it's also because I still can't wrap my head around all of this shit." Robert stood up as his anger began to escalate. "And furthermore, I have worked hard with my business and my ranch so why the hell should I just hand any of it over to you; just because we share the same father?" Before Adam could reply, Robert added, "You were hired as my head of security, so for God sakes; I only knew you on a professional level."

Adam wanted to pull his revolver out and start firing away at him, but no, that wouldn't get him anywhere – yet! He had to play it cool so he didn't get kicked off the ranch. Adam took a deep breath and swallowed his anger away for the moment, "Alright, I understand", he told him calmly. "But you must understand that I'm jobless at the moment – and homeless; so I'm a bit crazy right now." He shrugged and said, "Look, I just want to get to know you – as my brother", he emphasized. "It was hard hearing what took place with my mother all of those years ago, and to know that our father did that...."

Robert shook his head from side to side, knowing the man had a point. "Look, I'll make a few phone calls to get you a lucrative job in your field; and I suppose I can help you out with some cash until you get on your feet." Adam gave him a wide smile and said in an elated tone, "I would really appreciate it." And then Adam offered his hand. "So we can really try?" Robert extended his hand and nodded in agreement, "We can try." Adam continued to smile as they shook hands. "Thank you, brother."

"Hey, pal", Robert heard Max address him from behind. Just the sight of Max nearly caused Adam to lose control of his temper again. But, he watched and listened intensely to what Max said to Robert. "Look my brother, why not sign the gentleman's club to Adam." Robert wrinkled his forehead and was about to say something, but Max put his hand up; stopping him. "Hear me out." He looked over at Adam and then back to Robert. "I really appreciate you giving me that club, but it's not for me; I'm more of an outdoor kind of guy. Adam is your brother and he needs to earn a living"....Adam forced himself to keep his elation to himself and waited for Robert's response.

Robert was silent for a moment and then asked Max, "Are you sure about this?" Max gave him a nod and then answered, "If Adam took ownership of the club, he would have a place to live too; with that extra office space that can renovated into his private living quarters." A smile came to Robert's face when he said, "Kill two birds with one stone." Then his eyes cut back to Adam. "What do say; do we have a deal? You take complete ownership of the club and make it your home until you can buy a house; or continue to make it your home for as long as you want."

Adam stood by, stunned at what he was hearing. Just like that, he thought. I have a place for my business, and for free; I can have a piece of ass anytime and make money off the whores. "Adam?" Robert addressed him; interrupting his thoughts. "Well, I guess I would be an idiot to say no", he answered with a wide grin. Robert nodded to his attorney. "Sal, draw up the new papers."

***

Robert had just hung up the phone with Lucy, Vivian's friend. He had arranged to fly her in the day before the wedding so she could attend and surprise Vivian. He just couldn't stand the idea of Vivian having no one there for her special day, as Max would be there for him. Because it was a private ceremony, there would be no one from the church there to support her, and they probably wouldn't be there even if they were invited.

Adam hurried into Deadwood to cash the check that Robert had given him. Five thousand dollars was acceptable at the moment, he thought. And then of course, there was just a small wait for the transfer of club ownership. Boy, that Max guy isn't too much of a dope after all, he thought; and then laughed like a madman.

His smile never disappeared, knowing it was only the beginning, and he had his partner in crime waiting in the truck for him; Patsy - stupid whore, he said to himself. He had convinced the doctors that he was going to be her caretaker. Thankfully, Robert had already arranged for them to bill him for her stay, but he left no instructions to be notified of her departure; so they had no reason to keep her.

After cashing the check, Adam hopped back in his truck and looked over at Patsy in the passenger's seat. She was finally responding, but not quite herself. She looked over at him and said, "Take me to Robert." He shook his from side to side and answered, "Not yet – we have a plan to work out first." And then he drove off in the direction of a place to hide Patsy.

26

I stood alone in the church dressing room and unzipped the garment bag that held my wedding gown while I waited on my bridesmaid Lucy. The room was small, but very bright with the shades wide open and the sun shining through the entire room that held only a set of folding chairs and a three way mirror. I smiled upon remembering the moment I saw Lucy walk through our door yesterday. Though it had been several years, I immediately recognized my best friend. We embraced each other and cried with happiness. It was a wonderful surprise that Robert had arranged for me and I would never forget it; as it made my day complete.

Lucy had just walked in, wearing a satin royal blue off the shoulder bridesmaid dress and matching heels to add to her already five foot five inch thin frame. She stood in place with a warm smile as I stood in front of the mirror wearing only my white lace corset and inspecting my body. I ran my hand over my belly and asked Lucy, "Do you think I look almost two months along?" Lucy came over to me, putting her arm around my shoulder; and in reassuring voice, she answered, "You're only about a month and a half along, and no; you do not look like you're almost two months along." I looked at her through the mirror and we both busted out laughing.

***

Robert paced as he waited for Max to show up with the rings. The priest stood in the doorway, amused at the nervous, but handsome groom dressed in his black tuxedo and his matching patent leather shoes. "How are we doing today, young man?" Robert whipped around upon hearing the priest's soft tone. "Well", Robert began as he rung his hands together. "I will feel better when that best man of mine gets here with the rings." The priest gave out a hearty laugh and said, "Patience, my friend." Robert began to pace again and then looked out of the window at the parking lot, looking for Max's car. He turned back to the priest and asked, "Father, can we talk?" The man drew his hand to the chairs where they had their first conversation and said, "Have a seat."

Robert sat beside him, loosening his tie, and exhaled. "Look Father, I don't have to tell you how important you are to Vivian, and I know that you care about her as well." He paused to look over at him as if he were waiting for a response. "This is true, Robert, I care very deeply for Vivian, and I know that even though this is a special day in her life; she is most likely missing both of her parents today. I'm thrilled that you surprised her by bringing Lucy home to attend her big day." Robert nodded and said, "I was happy to do it, but Father"... Robert paused, not sure of what to say next. "But what, Robert?" The priest asked with a concerned tone. "Well, I was wondering if you would check in with Vivian since she doesn't have her dad here today." Father touched Robert's shoulder and softly told him, "I would be honored."

***

Lucy had stepped out of the room at the request of Father. He smiled and shook his head in disbelief as he gazed over at me, dressed in my wedding gown, made with shimmering jewels along the strapless top, complete with a sheer wrap for my shoulders. "You look absolutely beautiful." I gave him a small smile and hugged him as I usually did whenever I paid him a visit. "Thank you, Father. It means the world to me that you agreed to perform the ceremony for me and Robert." He released me from his embrace and softly told me, "It's an honor, Vivian." And then he nodded over at the two folding chairs in the corner and asked, "Shall we talk?"

We sat down and he took my hand. "I know that you're happy, but I also know you must be missing your parents today. How are you doing with that?" I leaned over and gave him another hug. "Thank you for checking on me, but really, Father; I'm doing very well." He squeezed my hand and said, "I just want to remind you how special you are to me, and though I'm still concerned about a few things, I can see that Robert loves you very much, and I would have never agreed to perform this ceremony had I thought otherwise." Tears welled up in my eyes when then I told him, "Thank you, Father, and you know you are just as precious to me as I make this journey in my life."

Just as he was about to speak, he was interrupted by a knock at the door. "Vivian." We heard Lucy's voice from the other side of the door. "Come on in", I hollered. "It's about time, Viv", Lucy announced with a wide grin. Father helped me to my feet and gave me one last hug. "I love you, kid." I looked up at him filled with complete joy and answered, "I love you too, Father."

***

Minutes later, I stood at the end of the aisle looking over at Robert standing at the altar wearing a wide smile with Max on the other side of him. I never took my eyes off of him as my bridesmaid walked down the aisle ahead of me.

There would be no wedding march, as the church was empty; with the exception of the photographer and the armed men stationed at each door. And then I headed down to meet the love of my life in the very church I had been baptized as a baby. I was about to become Mrs. Robert Sterling in this same church I loved, and by the same priest who baptized me. It was the perfect wedding day, despite my parents not being present. But, I could not dwell on that fact; I just wanted to live in the moment.

Father smiled as I stopped at the front of the altar, and then Robert and I turned to gaze into each other's eyes as Father said, "Please join each other's hands." I handed my bouquet of red Carnations off to Lucy, standing behind me, and then I put my trembling hands in Robert's.

"Dearly beloved, we are gathered her in the sign of God and in the face of this company to join this man and this woman in holy matrimony. If any person should show just cause why they may not be joined together; let them speak now or forever hold their peace." I broke in, saying, "I need to say something." I immediately saw that look of concern come to Robert's face, and he was likely fearful that I had changed my mind. "Go on, Viv," Father told me.

I could tell that he suddenly expressed concern as well when raising an eyebrow.

"Robert, today I stand before you – the man who proved to me that love is indeed patient and kind. We have both endured much pain and fear in our lives, but I do believe that the combination of the two is what has drawn us together. Despite our past obstacles, my faith speaks to my heart; that God's will brings us together to love as one." I took a deep breath and continued, "You have taught me that to love someone as profound as our love is for one another, it's never sinful to show each other that love; through body and soul."

I paused as my happy tears bean to fall. "I have never in my sweetest dreams believed that I could ever receive this incredible and powerful love from another human being; let alone feel this intense and magical love I feel for you. Robert Sterling, I love you around the world and back again; and then so much more." I took a deep breath, trying to calm my heart rate as he whispered, "I love you too." I took a deep breath again and added, "Though we've had trying times, one thing is for sure - my favorite place to be is in your arms; where I also feel at home. And from this moment on, I look forward to sharing this journey in life together. Whatever may come to us, I will work it out with you; forever – as your wife."

"Wow!" Robert exclaimed while trying to hold back the tears flooding his eyes. "There isn't a strong enough word to describe how I'm feeling at this moment – or really, at any moment when I look into your beautiful blue eyes; or when I think of you when we aren't together." He took a deep breath and gently squeezed my hands.

"You've seen me at my best and at my worst, but yet here you stand before me; agreeing to be my wife. My love for you is immeasurable, as I again cannot find the words. You taught me that it's okay for a man to be strong and gentle at the same time. And being honest and patient definitely brings on more desirable results; even though patience has never been my strong suit", he added with emphasis; and creating a bit of laughter among all of us.

Robert's smile disappeared into his serious expression as he ran his thumbs over the tops of my hands. "It wasn't until I first looked into your heavenly blue eyes that I believed in love at first sight – and from that moment on, I was - and I remain under your spell; and very deeply in love with you."

He smiled with a light chuckle. "I know I may never convince you of this, but it was your eyes that captured my soul with the innocent and helpless way you would look up at me; and the coy way you always tried to pretend that you weren't attracted to me in the beginning. And the feistiness; which by the way, I find incredibly sexy."

"Robert", I whispered, and then looked over at Father; who was of course laughing – his laughter always reminded me to never take life so seriously that I stop laughing.

Robert cleared his throat when looking over at Father and said, "I'm sorry." Father nodded with a chuckle, and said, "Please, I love to laugh, and I especially like the sound of laughter from others. And then, Robert turned his eyes back to me with a wide smile on his face. "I lose control of my senses even now." And then in his very Robert – like charm, he said, "Honey, you must forgive me – we are in a church after all." I just couldn't help but crack a wide smile with that statement, and I teasingly told him, "Well alright, but just this once!"

After the laughter subsided, he caressed my trembling hands in his and with his smile slowly fading again, as he became serious. "Vivian, you're my princess, and as we grow older throughout the years that will never change. And just know that my love for you will burn in my soul long after we depart this Earth." I smiled through my falling tears, as he gently wiped them away from underneath my eyes. And after a moment of a silent gaze, he looked over at Father and said, "We're ready to proceed."

***

I write this as I look up at the photo that so beautifully captured our first kiss after Father pronounced us man and wife, knowing in my heart that it was meant to be for us. But what Robert and I didn't know, was that something darker was just around the corner for us; and we would need our faith and each more than ever.

27

Robert and I had agreed to postpone the honeymoon until after the baby was born so that I could better enjoy our time without the feeling of being nauseated as the morning sickness had increased as of late.

A week after the wedding, I had one of my harsh days of fatigue and nausea, and I had begun feeling a bit chilled, but I didn't want to stay in bed, so Robert tucked a sheet inside the cushions of the sofa, and fluffed two pillows against the armrest.

As I walked out of the bedroom with a book in hand, he noticed I was wearing my heavy white cloth robe. "Thank you very much for taking care of me", I told him, and then I removed my robe, revealing pink flannel pajamas. A look of horror came to his face. "What's this?" He asked when pointing to my sleeping attire. "My new pajamas – I bought them yesterday. "Don't you like them?" He shook his head in disbelief and answered in that firm tone of his, "No, I do not." I looked down at them and asked, "Well, what on earth is wrong with them?" He threw his hands in the air and raised his voice. "My grandmother wore flannel pajamas for God sakes! And I don't want you covering up that beautiful body."

I watched in disbelief as he went over and drew our new curtains closed to keep the light out of my eyes. And then I asked, "What do you care if my body is covered? You're going back to work at the campground." He shrugged and answered, "I don't want to it to become habit." "What?" I asked him with a confused frown. "Look", he said when walking over to me. "I don't want my wife to dress like my grandmother; even when she becomes a grandmother one day", he added with emphasis. "I'm not dressed like a grandmother, I'm dressed for comfort", I argued. "Oh – alright", he said with a long drawn out groan, which brought on my giggling. "But", he emphasized. "I absolutely don't want you coming to bed to me wearing those old pajamas – I forbid it!" As I watched him become adamant over a trivial subject as flannel pajamas, I broke up with a hearty laugh. "Vivian", he addressed me with a serious tone. "I mean it – no – flannel – pajamas!" I covered my mouth when trying to keep my laughter in control as he stood there with his hands on his hips in his authoritative stance, and waiting for me to agree. He shook his head in disbelief while eyeing me up and down as I moved closer into him. "You hate these pajamas that much that you are seriously forbidding me to wear them in your presence?"

"Vivian", he addressed me when showing signs of laughter that he was do desperately trying to hold back. "I want to burn them in the fireplace." "Well!" I exclaimed when moving over to the sofa and covering up with the afghan. "You just make sure you stay away from my pajamas, mister!" I added in a playful tone. I looked over at him with a smile and I began to read my book.

A wide smile came to his face and then he came over to me and said, with a groan, "You win." I nodded in satisfaction, but he just couldn't help himself. He fell to his knees and playfully nuzzled his stubbly face into my neck, causing me to scream out. "Robert, that tickles!" After hearing my laugh as never before and causing me to start coughing, he stopped, and looked into my eyes. "I love you, Princess", he told me in the most serious tone. I brushed his hair back and said, "I love you too." After a smile and a lingering moment, I asked him, "I'll see you in a few hours?" He drew in and caught my partially opened mouth with his lips. "In a few hours", he answered gently.

After that soft kiss, I found it hard to catch my breath, as it took me back to our first kiss. "Wow", I said softly as my heart began to race. Still smiling, he asked me, "You do know I was teasing you about those pajamas – don't you?" I nodded with a smile and bit down on my lip to keep from laughing again, and then I answered, "Yes, honey, I know you were teasing." He drew a piece of my hair back and added, "Princess, I want you to know that you look beautiful in everything you wear – or don't wear", he emphasized with a flirtatious smile.

Though he was smiling, I saw the sincerity in his eyes and it nearly drove me to tears. He took my hand and kissed it without taking his eyes off of mine. "You are the most beautiful sight I have ever laid my eyes on", he told me softly." There was something in his voice that seemed different and though I knew he had always been sincere, it seemed more so than ever, and I was so touched by him in that moment, that I could no longer hold in the tears. "Don't cry", he said gently, while caressing my cheek. "You have this way of making me feel like the most loved and cherished woman in the world", I told him. He drew in a gently and kissed me again. "You changed my whole world, Princess", he said, in the softest of his tones.

After a few more tender kisses, he slowly lifted my pajama top, stopping just under my breast bone, and he gently drew his large hand over my belly and abdomen. "I think I finally see a bump here", he told me with a smile of amazement. I silently took notice of his desire to bond with the baby we had made, as he continued to caress my belly all around while just staring in awe. His touch relaxed me to the point of nearly putting me to sleep. "Get some rest, Princess", I heard him whisper as I closed my eyes. I then felt his tender lips touch my bare belly as I began drifting off to sleep.

***

A few hours after leaving Vivian's side, Robert closed the tool box after completing the plumbing in the bathroom in the girl's cabin. He then stood next to Max and looked up at the sky through the bay windows. "This weather has gone from one extreme to the other; look at that dark sky", he told Max. "Yeah, it looks like we're in for a hell of a storm", Max replied. And then he looked at his watch, and added, "You know, we're ahead of schedule, so maybe we ought to call it a day." Robert shook his head in agreement and said, "Maybe you're right, I do want to check on Vivian; and I told her that I would take her shopping if she felt up to it."

The two men began putting all the tools away when suddenly Robert said, "I have a surprise for Vivian – well, two actually." Max tossed a hammer in the tool box and asked, "Yeah; what would that be?" Robert wiped his dripping wet forehead off with his shirt and answered with a smile, "I'm putting the store in her name for an extra wedding present; and I'm working on acquiring a baby line with clothes and other accessories." Max gave him a wide smile and exclaimed, "That's great, Rob!"

I woke to a splitting headache and my body wracked with such pain, it hurt me to just breathe. Barely able to open my eyes from the sting, I saw two blurry figures in the distance of a dark, dingy room that smelled of mold. My breathing became short and rapid when hearing a man's monotone voice. He sounded familiar, but I couldn't quite remember. And then I heard him tell someone in a growling tone, "You'll get Vivian back when you pay for her!" More pain shot through my body as I heard what sounded like a phone being slammed down on the receiver.

Next, I heard the familiar voice of a woman shouting at him, "You forgot to tell him that the other part of that deal was that he would be marrying me!" I felt my heart drop when I realized it was Patsy; and that I was tied to a bed – naked! I shivered and began shaking as though I were experiencing convulsions when discovering that I had been stripped of my pajamas, and I was lying in a dark and filthy room, naked with Adam present – I had just remembered his voice! I tried to cry out from under the strong tape across my mouth, but my cries were muffled. The panic ripping through my body overtook me as I became short of breath and feeling as though the walls were closing in on me.

Suddenly, he was standing over me – Adam! My vision was still a bit blurred and I couldn't make out the details of his face, but I knew that horrible raspy and evil voice. I was terribly sleepy; and yet, I was also too terrified to close my eyes. I then felt his fingers run up from my foot and along my leg – slowly and seductively. "You have beautiful silky legs", he told me in that vile tone; that of which made me want to crawl out of my skin, as I knew what he was going to do to me.

. Fear shot through the core of me, as I silently began to pray like never before. God, please protect me – I need Robert! I screamed from within myself. And just then, I felt my legs being pulled apart; and my ankles being tied to the bedposts. I thrashed my head from side to side in desperation as I felt his large hand sliding up in between my legs. My screams were muffled from the tape over my mouth, as he shoved his entre fist up inside of me, penetrating me deep inside, as far as he was able to go.

All I could do was close my eyes and turn my head to the side, crying as he continued to molest me with his fist, and praying with every breath that Robert would get to me before he went all the way with me. And then suddenly, I heard a gun going off. Adam pulled his hand out of me and whipped around. "What the hell is wrong with you, bitch?" He snapped at Patsy, who held the gun to him. "You can fuck her later; right now you don't touch her, because I don't care to see it!" Patsy raged at him. And then he stepped into her and shouted, "Give me that damn gun, you stupid bitch!" She shoved the gun in his face and exclaimed, "You get over there where I can see you – I'm in charge now!" Adam stood still and glared at Patsy. "I'm going to kill you!" He shouted. Patsy cocked the gun and said, "I will pull the trigger if you don't get your ass over to the other side of the room and watch for my husband to be!"

I watched as Adam did as he was told, and then I turned my eyes on Patsy as she stood in front of me and wearing a wedding dress. "Robert will be here soon", Patsy told me with a wide and vile smile. She tore the tape from my mouth and said, "Now you can watch Adam, and if he starts coming for me – you tell me." I shook my head up and down in agreement and then Patsy told me in a cold tone, "Because if you fail to warn me, "I will not only allow him to have his way with you, but I will shove your ass right over to him!" I swallowed that hard lump of fear, and told her, "I promise - I will warn you."

Patsy continued to glare down at me, and then I said quietly, "Patsy, thank you for getting him away from me." Patsy gritted her teeth and said, "I didn't do it to help you; I stopped him so Robert will be happy with me, because now that I'm in charge, I'll save his money and property."

I knew my only chance of not getting raped was to stay on Patsy's good side, so I continued to push my rage down, when I noticed Patsy had removed my wedding ring and put it on her finger. "Patsy", I addressed her carefully. "Could you please find me some clothes – or even a blanket?" Patsy shook her head from side to side and shouted, "No! You are being sent away after you witness my marriage to Robert, and you will be sent away with how you came into Robert's life; with nothing!"

Robert and Max sat in the back of the limousine on the ride over to the address that Adam had given him. Robert stared ahead and told Max, "She's having our baby." His lips began to quiver as he said, "I shouldn't have left her alone." "Don't do this, Rob. We'll get her back, and she will be just fine; and the baby will be fine too." Max told him while grasping his shoulder in comfort. Robert turned to him and asked, "You remember the plan, right? I mean we can't mess this up, and Adam can't know you're with me", he added in an urgent voice. "Don't worry, pal – I'll be there every step of the way, and neither Adam, nor Patsy will know what hit them." Max told him as he loaded his pistol.

Robert stared out his window and watched as the pavement rolled under the car. He finally realized who was behind those damn notes. His driver sped up each time he asked him to do so, but it still felt like they were crawling. It had only been thirty minutes, and they still had at least another thirty minutes before they would start looking for the address.

Robert's mind wandered back to just hours earlier and the flannel pajamas Vivian was wearing – but the pajamas were on the floor in a pile in front of the sofa where he had left her. The tears fell down his face as he thought about her laughter while he nuzzled her with his light whiskers. He then ran his hand through his face, noticing the whiskers were stronger since now. He smiled through his tears when remembering the incredible love he felt as he kissed Vivian's belly with their baby growing inside of her.

Patsy stared down at the street and saw Robert exit the vehicle. Adam smiled and thought, Good – you did as I told you for a change. And then he stared at Patsy, knowing he just had to bide his time with her too.

Patsy turned to me and raved. "Prince Charming is here, and I'll soon be his wife." She walked over to me, sat on the bed, and held my ring in front of my face – flaunting it on her finger. "You know, this ring should have been mine to begin with." Although Robert was there, I didn't want to push my luck, so I simply looked away, and then there was the knock at the door.

Patsy and Adam both greeted Robert at the door. Upon seeing him, Patsy threw herself in his arms. "You're finally here!" She exclaimed. As he reluctantly wrapped his arms around her, he felt the acid rise from his stomach, but somehow he was able to keep from vomiting, as he knew he had to play along in order to get Vivian home safely. She released him and led him inside with the gun in hand and around the corner to the bed where Vivian laid, still tied up, and naked.

Robert clenched his jaw together in anger when seeing the woman he loved laying there naked, battered and bruised all over her body. God only knows what Adam did to her! He thought to himself. The rage ran rampant through his body and all he wanted to do was run over and rescue her, but again, he knew he had to play whatever game he had to in order to get her out of there.

Robert looked over at Adam and saw that he wasn't armed and then noticed the gun Patsy had was Adam's. "Patsy grabbed Robert's attention when she told him with her seductive southern drawl, "Alright lover, time to focus on me. This is what is going to happen, you and I will be married right here in front of Vivian and Adam. And once they sign this license I drew up then we will send them both away."

Robert cleared his throat, trying to remain calm while he waited for Max to appear through the fire escape window of the abandoned building. It looked like someone could have been living in this trap, but they wasn't home, or they disappeared – at the hands of Adam and Patsy, of course. Just like the room above the general store, everything was one room with the exception of the bathroom; and as bad as that room above the store was, this whole building should be condemned. He just had to get his wife out of that hole!

Robert addressed Patsy carefully even though he wanted to take her and throw her rotten ass right out of the window. "Patsy, we will be married, but first I have business with Adam." He observed how Patsy was the one who obviously took control over Adam, and decided he would use her against him, and from there he could take control. And then he saw Max appear at the fire escape. He had to be slow and quiet, so Robert was ready to take the reins when Adam shoved a contract into Robert's rock hard chest and shouted, "If you want Vivian back – you will sign over every damn penny, including the ranch and the store!" Patsy jumped in between the men and shoved the gun in Adam's face. "He doesn't want Vivian, so you're shit out of luck!"

Robert gently pulled Patsy away from Adam and said, "Come on now – take it easy. I noticed you have a lot of rope over there by that chair. Let me tie the son of a bitch up and gag him, because I'm tired of hearing his fucking voice." She gave Robert a smile and stroked his face. "I like that, and then we can leave him and Vivian here tied up until they become a rotten smell", she added with emphasis.

Robert pushed Adam into the wooden chair and grabbed the robe. “If you move”, Robert told him with clenched jaw. “I will rip your manhood off with my bare hands.” Adam glared at Patsy the whole time and desperately tried to think of a way to get Robert to side with him. Robert snapped a piece of duct tape off the roll and gave Adam a sinister smile as he saw Max waiting to come through the window.

As Robert taped Adam’s mouth shut, Patsy ripped his contract in half and tossed it to his feet. “Fuck you”, she told him, and then began laughing as though she were insane. Robert looked over at Vivian and saw her sobbing. He knew he had to distract Patsy so Max could get in the window. “Come here”, he told Patsy. “I want you to hear me tell Vivian it’s over between us.”

He turned to Patsy when they reached the bed and asked, “But Patsy, why is she naked? Why did you two strip her of her clothing? I just need to know.” Patsy gave him a look of disgust and answered, “Because she is leaving your life as she came – with nothing!” Robert gently took her by the shoulders, and though his rage was at the boiling point, he calmly said, “Relax, I was just curious.” His heart leapt when he saw that Max had made it inside. Adam was trying to wiggle enough to get Patsy’s attention, but to no avail, as Robert had her full attention and began to speak to Vivian; and prayed that she knew he didn’t mean anything he was about to say.

***

“Vivian”, Robert addressed me carefully. “Patsy is correct; I will be with her now.” He then pulled Patsy toward him as her back remained against the sight of Max. “Please give me the gun so we don’t have to say our vows with it between us.” He reached for it, and then she yanked it away. "No – I'm in charge!" He slowly pulled her in his arms and said, "Ok, I understand, just take it easy." He saw Max nod, indicating he was ready. Robert eased Patsy back and sat her down on a black leather worn foot stool. "Patsy – I owe you for having endured all the pain in losing our baby, and because people should always get what they deserve; I'm happily going to give you what you deserve."

I watched from the side as Robert knelt down and softly said, "I'm very sorry for what I put you through." He slowly grasped the gun and she tried to hang onto it. "It's ok, please trust me", he said gently. I turned away as Robert gently spoke to Patsy, while caressing her face. And then I caught Max's eye in the distance, all this while wishing I was covered, knowing everything was about to explode.

I laid there praying and then suddenly I saw Patsy turn the gun over to Robert. "That's it", he said softly, and then rose to his feet. "Time to make it up to you." She gave him and smile and said, "I knew you would come to your senses. "You bet I have", I heard him say. When he turned toward me, he suddenly whipped back around, kicking Patsy in the face with his western boot; sending her flying across the room from us.

As Max ran to an unconscious Patsy, Robert quickly began untying me. "You're safe now, baby', he told me as he untied the last knot. "Robert!" I cried in pain and reached out for him. "I've got you", he softly told me and took me into his arms. I sobbed in his arms as Max stood guard over Patsy's sleeping body. "We have to get you to a hospital", Robert told me.

As Robert gathered the sheet off the bed and wrapped me up in it, I stared at the approaching sunset into the distance. Despite the horror of the day, I saw God's grace and beauty as the sun began to sink into the bright orange and pink sky. He then scooped me up in his arms and began carrying me to the door. I cuddled tight against his neck as he faced Adam sitting bound and gagged in the chair and Patsy's sleeping body on the floor. "Max, you wait here for Mitchell." He looked directly at Adam, and said, "Soon we will find out who the true Sterling is." Adam continued to stare as Robert told him, "Just you wait until I return." And then he rushed out the door with me safe in his arms.

28

Later at the hospital, the doctor had sedated Vivian after telling her that their baby was gone. Robert laid there holding her as she slept and thought back to the sight he came back home to after working at the campground.

The minute he and Max walked into the main kitchen he saw the cook and one of the maids out cold, and lying in puddles of blood from being hit over the head with an iron skillet. The master key to their quarters was missing from the maid's key ring. Robert had immediately gotten that sick feeling and charged up to their quarters to find that Vivian was gone without a trace – but her flannel pajamas were lying in a pile right where he left her. He knew then whoever took her, knew the place inside and out because they got past the security team.

A few hours later, the full moon shined through the dirty old room where Robert had returned – with his dark side re-emerging, as he walked through the door. Upon walking in, he saw Mitchell, and stepped aside to speak with him privately. "Are you sure we're set with the arrangements?" Robert asked with concern. "I promise", his old friend assured him. "You do what you need to do, but make sure they're alive at the end – and when you're through with them, Max and I will deliver them to their new location where they will be under lock and key, and they will never be seen or heard from again." Robert gave him a nod and said, "And then after you return you can just add to the retirement that my father provided for you.

Robert looked over at both Adam and Patsy sitting side by side - both bound and gagged. And then he looked over at the bed where his sweet Vivian was held prisoner for hours, battered and naked. He turned to Max as he walked over to him, and Max softly asked him, "How's Vivian?" Robert glared at the two people responsible for their loss, and then he answered, "She lost the baby, and because she will be under sedation all night, I was able to leave her long enough to settle the score."

Max looked over at Mitchell and then went over to stand next to him on the other side of the room, as Robert stood over Adam and Patsy. He ripped the tape from both of their mouths and then leaned into them. "Time to pay for your sins." He looked directly into Patsy's eyes, those of which were swollen and black and had dried blood all around her face, from his kick with his western boot. He gave her a look of contempt and said to her with a clenched jaw, "You're the one who is going to leave my life with nothing!" After saying those words, he ripped her dress open, untied her and continued to strip the wedding dress off of her like a savage, as she sobbed. He never heard a word she was screaming through his rage, as he shredded that dress – and stripped her completely.

Though he couldn't make out what she was ranting through her tears, he grew angry and tired of her noise, causing him to send the back of his hand sailing into her face. "Shut the fuck up – you crazy bitch!" He glared at her, noticing the instant welt on her cheek from the slap and matching the rest of her facial wounds.

He felt the rage build back up as moments of his beloved Vivian lying on that filthy bed beaten and bruised came back to haunt him. His heart nearly pounded out of his chest when he suddenly grabbed Patsy by the throat and shoved her into the wall. "I can't tell you how much I hate you!" And then he slammed her face into the wall, as she let out a blood curdling scream, and then he whipped her around. "Congratulations, bitch, you're the first woman I have beat the hell out of." He continued to glare at her as the blood poured from her nose and mouth. He pulled her by the hair to force her to make eye contact with him. "You helped that sadistic mother fucker kill our baby – and now you will pay!"

Upon ending that statement he saw the hand written marriage license that she had prepared for them and he crinkled it up as she sobbed. "This shows how delusional you really are – to think you could marry me when I'm already married!" He leaned in, just an inch from her face and he told her in a vile tone, "I wouldn't have married you if you were the last damn woman on the Earth." She started sobbing uncontrollably once again and slid to the filthy cement floor. "Get your pathetic ass back up here", he ranted when pulling her up by her hair, and then he drilled his fist into her abdomen, causing her to gasp for air and fall back to the floor.

He once again forced her to her feet by her hair, put the crinkled license rolled up into a tight ball in her face, and said with emphasis, "I'm going to take this license and shove it right up your ass, so maybe you'll finally get the message!"

She began screaming as though he was murdering her when he dragged her to the bed and forced her ass side up, and over the rusted brass bar of the foot of the bed. He slapped her bare ass so hard, he left an instant welt and shouted, "Oh come on, Patsy – you've always enjoyed it like this!" And then he yelled for Max. "You hold her there!" Max came over and held her down in place by the small of her back, while standing aside. Robert ripped the leg off of her wooden chair, placed the wadded paper in between her cheeks, and viciously began shoving it up her ass with the leg of the chair, that of which caused her to scream loud enough to make ones ears bleed.

Robert continued to molest her with the wooden leg even as he saw blood begin to drip from her. Max swallowed hard and his eyes grew big as he noticed she was losing consciousness. He released her and shouted, "She's had enough, Rob!" But Robert wouldn't stop and as he kept going, he hollered with more rage then Max had ever heard and seen from him. "This bitch hurt my wife and killed our baby!"

Max then grabbed him and began pulling him away from her. "I know man, but she's had enough! Remember, you love Vivian more than you hate Patsy!" Robert stopped fighting him and stood staring at what he had done, as he tried to catch his breath; his glare gazed over to the stick remaining inside of her and blood streaming down her and to the floor. Max looked over at Mitchell who only stood by with a stone face.

Max then turned back to his best friend, despite his actions. He then told him, "Vivian needs you, Rob." Robert took his eyes off of Patsy and looked over at Max. "Tie her up – just like they did with Vivian." Max watched as his friend went over to Adam, and then Robert gave him a nod and ordered him with emphasis, "Tie – her- up, Max!" Robert watched as Max gently helped a nearly unconscious Patsy over to the side of the bed.

And then his eyes cut back to Adam, giving him such an intensely dark stare, that he had drowned out every voice and movement around him. "So brother", Robert addressed him with emphasis. "You think you can rape my wife and get away with it?" Adam shook his head from side to side and shouted with fear, "I didn't rape her!" Robert immediately grabbed him by his shirt collar and yelled in his face as though he were a drill Sargent. "Oh you don't consider ramming your fist up inside my wife rape?" Robert untied him and immediately whipped his leg around and kicked him in the face; which sent him flying out of the chair and backwards into the wall.

"Let's see if your man enough to take the beating you having coming", Robert growled, and then picked him up off the floor by the back of his belt and his shirt, and then tossed him over the broken down wooden desk that held only the phone. Adam was trying to pull himself up by using his hands and knees when Robert casually walked over and kicked him in the ribs, sending him a few feet away. "Please – stop", Adam pleaded, and was only able to lean up against the wall. "You raped my wife – and now our baby is gone!" Robert raged, and then delivered a side kick to his face, causing blood to splatter the area.

Adam laid on the floor crying in pain and spitting out several teeth. After taking a moment to catch his breath, Robert rolled him onto his back and proceeded to stomp on his manhood; causing him to give out a high pitched scream while he laid in agony and choking on his blood.

Robert glared down at him, watching this nasty and mean drunk, cry like a baby. But then, as he looked at him, Robert suddenly saw his father's face. Becoming lost in the past, it took him back to when he was forced to helplessly watch his father torture Rosie all of those years ago.

Robert slowly became unaware of his surroundings as he stepped back in time and began to savagely kick Adam in the abdomen, and then back to his manhood. His rage completely took over as he began shouting as though he were beating on Phillip. "You gutless, rotten son of bitch – this is for Rosie!" He continued to work him over, sending blows and kicks to his entire body. Upon watching Robert savagely continue to beat and kick Adam within an inch of his life, both Mitchell and Max ran over and pulled Robert off of him. "Come on Rob!" Max shouted to get his attention. "He's had enough! We have to get them out of here," he added when helping Mitchell pull him away, as Robert continued trying to kicking him. "We have to get them out of here, son", Mitchell told him in a raised tone. "It's time for us to go." The sound of his father's loyal partner from all of those years ago somehow caught Robert's attention, and it was only then that he finally relented.

***

Twenty minutes later, Robert sat mentally spent in Adam's chair just staring at the bed where they had Vivian tied up and exposed. Max and Mitchell had carried both Adam and Patsy to the vehicle they had parked in the alley behind the building, and were preparing to take them away. Before they moved them, Max got Robert settled down, and asked him to stay put until they got everything ready and under control.

Robert was alone for a few moments as his best friend and the man who formally belonged to his father's team took care of business. He looked down at his blood soaked shirt; that was once white, and then his bruised knuckles. He had never in his life gone that crazy. Now that the anger was out, he began sobbing over the loss of his first unborn baby. The woman he loved most in this world was violated, so he just had to get justice –in his mind he had no choice!

He could have killed the both of them, but then their suffering would end and that can't happen. It would serve him well to know that they are far away and will live in darkness until they take their last breath. He had never in his life inflicted that kind of pain on another human being, but what they did to Vivian and their unborn baby was unacceptable and unforgivable! Phillip was correct, he thought. Knowledge is power - and power is everything; the power to send people away to parts unknown, all in the name of keeping the love of his life safe.

***

After having gone home to shower and change into his fresh clothes, Robert drove into the parking lot of St. Rose and walked in, wearing a white polo shirt and khaki pants, but for once; he wasn't wearing his gun. As he stared up the aisle, he recalled the day when Vivian told him that they had made a baby. He was on top of the world and Vivian had finally come to terms with conceiving their baby out of wedlock after going to confession – all to make it right with God.

He stood at the altar with tears rolling down and as he looked up at the crucifix, he asked, "Why – why did you take our baby?" His voice echoed throughout the empty church. He then began to feel the rage well up inside him once again. "You should have come after me; not our baby, and not Vivian – me!" He shouted, while pounding at his chest. "I did this; It's the way I live my life – isn't it?" The crushing despair he was enduring brought him to his knees, sobbing. "I'm sorry", he cried out. "Please – God", he paused to catch his breath, and then he repeated, "Please – God – I'm sorry!"

As Robert continued to weep, he felt a gentle hand on his shoulder. He looked up to see Father holding out his other hand out to him. "Come with me, son." Robert took his hand as the priest helped him to his feet, and motioned for him to sit in the first pew.

As Robert sat there with Father, he suddenly began to feel a bit lighter as the priest rested his hand on his shoulder. At that moment he felt like a child who had fallen down in the dark and couldn't find his way out. But then he was picked up and led back into the light by this man, who seemed to be larger than life – and ironically, it was what he had felt about his own father, Phillip, when he was a young child; before he knew the truth.

"Talk to me", Father told him gently. "Tell me what's on your heart." Robert looked up at the cross – calm, but still with a feeling of defeat and loss. And then he looked over at the priest and said, "I need your help, Father – I'm lost."

29

August 1, 1950

I rested in bed a few days after being released from the hospital as Robert walked in from the bathroom after taking a shower. I looked over at him and asked, "Do you feel better?" "Yes, I do", he answered me quietly.

I watched as he tossed the towel aside and slipped into his tan trousers and his white button down short sleeve shirt. I had tried not to think of how distant he had become since losing the baby, but I began wondering if he blamed me. He did manage to comfort me when I would wake up screaming from nightmares of that horrific day that I was held captive, but he wouldn't talk about that day, or the baby – and he never showed any emotion over our loss. Father had encouraged me to be patient, and he assured me that Robert would come around – in his way, and in his time; but I only wanted to grieve for our baby together.

"Robert?" I caught his attention with my soft voice and tears filling up in my eyes. "Yeah, baby?" He asked and sat next to me on the bed. "Can I get you something?" My eyes cut back to the padlocked door on the other side of the room. "I want to see the nursery you made for our baby." He quickly rose from the bed and I could tell it was still devastating for him, and he would search for yet another excuse to keep me from entering the other side of that door.

Robert started fixing up the nursery in secret as soon as I told him about the baby, and to keep the surprise, he moved into my quarters with me, so he could fix up the extra room just off from his bedroom without my knowledge. I had stared at that nursery door from the very moment I arrived back home. I would lay in a fetal position and just cry over and over again, "I want my baby."

Robert turned around upon feeling my hand on his shoulder. "Honey", I said when looking into his eyes. "We both need to say goodbye to our baby – and I don't know how else to do it." He cupped my face in his hands and softly kissed my quivering lips. "Are you sure you can do this?" He asked me somberly. "No", I said when shaking my head from side to side. "But I have to." I added with tears falling.

He exhaled and looked away; for the first time, I could tell he was unsure of what to do; and then I gently guided his face back to me. "Honey, we both need this, so we can let the pain out and start to heal – please, I can't do this without you." I gave him an affectionate smile and added, "I know you think that it's your duty as a man is to be strong and shelter me from hurt and danger, but it's not fair for you to have to endure this horrible tragedy by keeping the pain inside; you have a right to show your sadness."

Upon hearing my words, his tears began to fall, as he pulled me into his arms. "I'm so sorry – about everything", he said with his voice cracking. "I promised to protect you." He held me tight and cried into my shoulder. "I'm sorry I wasn't there to protect you, or the baby." I stepped up on the tips of my toes and wrapped my arms around his neck. "Honey", I said while stroking the back of his head. "This wasn't your fault!" I emphasized. "It was my lifestyle that caused all of this"…he trailed off. "I failed you." "Oh, God no!" I said when pulling away to look at him. "You never failed me!" I exclaimed, as I continued to cry. "Don't ever say that again." "But", he said. And then I stopped him by putting my finger against his lips, "But nothing, Robert", I chimed in gently. "It was all Adam and Patsy." I paused to take a deep breath before adding, "And as horrible as it was to endure, it was all their doing." I wiped his tears as he had done for me so many times. And then I continued, "I'm thankful you handled it the way you did." I shook my head from side to side in disbelief and added, "It was a horrible and frightening ordeal – our baby is gone, but we're not, and we need each other now more than ever." His lips gently touched mine, as we slowly swayed from side to side. When cupping my face, he rubbed his thumbs along my cheekbones and softly asked, "Do you really feel this way?" He asked while looking at me in awe. "Yes I do – you'll always be my knight and shining amour." I told him, smiling through my tears.

He turned toward the nursery door and asked, "Should I really open the door, honey?" "I know", I chimed in. "It's tragic, but…" once again, I released more tears. "We need this, and besides", I swallowed back that lump in my throat and continued, "The doctor said we can have more babies, so we have that to be thankful for, right?" "That's right", he whispered, when gazing into my eyes. "We'll have all the babies you want, Princess."

Upon walking into the room, I gazed around at the unique work the artist had done. While Robert designed the nursery himself, he elected to hire an artist to complete the décor. I tearfully went over to Robert's old baby crib that he had refurbished, and ran my hand along the cherry wood railing while looking down at the empty mattress. Painted on the wall above the crib was a star-filled sky and a full moon with squirrels, deer, dogs, and cats sleeping under Black Hills Spruce trees.

I then walked over to the other side of the room to the wall painted in a clear blue and sunny sky, and surrounded by the Black Hills forest were animals frolicking around the rocking chair where I would hold and rock our baby. In the corner was Robert's homemade cherry wood shelves that held books, stuffed animals, and a copy of our wedding photo. I made my way across the plush ivory carpet to the closet filled with clothes we had purchased for both genders; and then I reached for my old baptismal gown. Touched by the gesture of him adding it to the baby's clothes, I held it against my chest and began sobbing. Robert walked over to me and took me in his arms. "Honey, I think this is too much for you", he said quietly. All I could do was continue to cry into his chest while grasping the gown in my hand.

After a few moments of silence and my cries had settled down, Robert carried me back to bed. As he laid me down, I looked up at him and quietly said, "I need you." He sat beside me and softly told me, "I'm here, baby, and I'm not going anywhere. I took his hand and guided it to my heart and said, "I need you to make love to me." He slowly untied my robe and gently ran his hand over my belly where our baby used to be.

"The doctor said we can go back to making love", I told him. "I know", he said, and then he asked me, "Are you sure you're ready for this after…." He just couldn't finish saying those ugly words that I knew was on his mind. "You mean after Adam did what he did to me?" I asked, carefully. He nodded in confirmation. "That's why I need you to help me get through this – you're my husband, and I don't want love making to become an issue because I was violated."

After he gazed over my body in silence, I took his hand and asked, "Do you blame me for what he did?" He pulled me closer into his arms and kissed me ever so sweetly, and then he answered, "Oh baby, I could never blame you for what he did; I just want to be sure that it's not too soon for you – and I don't want to hurt you." I then guided his hand to my womanhood. "I love you and I trust you", I whispered. He slowly began touching me as he held me close. "Please stop me if you need me to", he whispered.

***

Later that night, Robert held Vivian as she slept after waking from another nightmare about that miserable day. As he laid there exhausted, he recalled how she told him that she was thankful for how he handled the frightening experience that day, but she still didn't know what he had done after he left the hospital – and she will never know; he decided.

As far as she was concerned, Adam and Patsy were locked up and she was safe from now on. Despite what she went through, she would have never condoned what he did – especially what he did to Patsy. Even he found it difficult to believe he let it go as far as beating and basically raping a woman with an object; and all in the name of the Sterling brand of justice and revenge. Now that he had told Father everything, he had to start to let it go and move on. Vivian's priest became his friend that night, and the man told him that if he wanted to transform his life it would take time; literally one day at a time, and sometimes, maybe even one hour at a time.

Father had made it clear to Robert that he did the right thing by coming to the church and making things right with God that night. And though he should really consider turning himself in to the authorities, confessing all to God and changing the way he lives his life is what really matters. “Keep following Jesus”, Robert continuously heard the words of Father over and over again.

30

December 23, 1950

Robert walked in the door late evening from working at the department store. Though he put the store in Vivian’s name, he was the one who ran the business. Exhausted, he tossed his black suit jacket onto the sofa of the main living room, loosened his tie, and plopped down on his new easy chair.

“Honey”, Robert called out to me and asked, “How about some sugar?” I peeked out of the kitchen door and saw him sitting in his favorite chair, resting his head back. “Just a minute, honey”, I replied. “With the help out for the holidays, I’m scrambling to get dinner ready.” “Please fix me a drink, honey – I’ve had a long hard day with trying to help a bunch of crazy women at that store.” “I’ll be with you in a quick minute, honey”, I told him, and slipped back behind the door. “Ah, baby – please”, I heard him plead. “I need that drink now – please don’t make me get up.”

He continued to rest his head back with his eyes closed, and as he heard me fixing that drink, he mumbled, “That’s my girl.” I walked behind the chair and handed his drink to him. “Here you are, honey.” “Thank you, babe”, he said and then took a long swig from his glass. When reaching behind for me, he said, “Hey, come and sit in my lap for a few minutes and talk to me." I immediately began rubbing his shoulders, and then asked him, "How about I help relax you first?"

He moaned with pleasure, so I could tell his tension was slipping away immediately. "Ohhh", he let out an extended moan. "My baby knows what I need." He took another drink and asked me, "So everyone left today?" "Yes, honey it's just us", I told him. "My goodness", I said as I continued to rub his shoulders. "You're quite tense – maybe I should have worked with you today." He shook his head in disagreement, and said, "Now come on, Princess, you know how I feel about you working outside of the home." "Yes, but you can't keep working there until we find a new manager with everything else you have to do." "Baby", he said with exasperation. "I have no choice with having only one salesperson."

There was a few moments of silence as I continued to rub his shoulders when he put his glass down and said, "Hey, you never gave me that sweet kiss of yours." I stopped massaging him and nervously said, "I will in a minute – but I have to go check dinner." He grabbed my hand as I tried walking away. "Vivian – baby, I'm not in the mood for games. Now please give me that kiss", he ordered.

Knowing I stalled long enough, I slowly walked around in front of him; dressed in a tiny low cut, ruby red corset designed with a black Santa belt and white ruffles – complete with black stockings and heels. A wide smile came to his face as he stood to his feet and gazed at me from head to toe. "Well hello, darlin'", he said with a whistle. "When was I going to be able to see this lovely sight?" I bit down on my lower lip, still a nervous habit of mine. "I wanted to wait until I was ready to serve you dinner – and then you asked for a drink; and well"…I tapered off, just as he took me into his arms. "This is very nice to come home to", he told me in his seductive tone.

I savored the feeling of being in his arms in the middle of the living room where it was private at that moment, but we would usually have staff walking through. There I was - in a tiny and seductive outfit, making me feel somewhat silly; and even a little dirty, but it lifted my husband's spirits, and that's all that mattered.

He nuzzled my neck and stroked my naked round flesh. "I think you're missing something back here", he said in a teasing tone. "So this is what Mrs. Claus really dresses like", he added with a growing arousal. I let out a nervous laugh, and then I pulled away. "Ok buster, before we go any further – dinner is ready." He sighed with a smile and said, "Well, I have quite the sight while I eat." I took his hand and led him into the kitchen with that feel of excitement of what was on the horizon – for I had a plan, and it was sure to be the highlight of our holidays.

"Sit down", I playfully ordered him. He was already about to explode, judging from the growing bulge in his pants at the sight and anticipation of what was to come; so I knew I shouldn't make him wait too long. And no doubt that I surprised him, because I was still coy about wearing such things; especially if it's outside of our bedroom door. One thing for sure is that Robert has slowly but surely pulled me out of my preconceived attitude in regards to sex, and as a result, I have become more open as time goes on; making this surprise all the more important, as there was no urging from him.

He watched as I served his dinner and then I took it a step further and sat in his lap. He looked down at the bulge in his pants and then asked me, "Can we skip dinner and go right for the desert?" I gave him a small smile and said, "No." He exhaled and looked over where my plate would be, and asked, "You're not eating?" I ran my fingers through his hair, and then wrapped my arms around his neck. "We're going to share a plate tonight", I said with a hint of seduction in my voice.

As he held me in his lap, he caressed my bare flesh; triggering that feeling of my warm and wet sensation seep through to his pants. In all of this seduction, he finally noticed the small wrapped gift off to the side of the table where I would normally sit when we ate. "What's in that little red box over there?" He asked as I scooped up his favorite mashed potatoes and held the spoon to his hungry mouth. "Open up", I told him without answering his question. "We do nothing else until after dinner", I said in a firm but seductive tone.

As he took the last bite of his dinner, he sat there perspiring. I could tell that he was ready to throw the dishes clean off of the table and make love to me right then and there; so I reached for the little red box. "You need to open this now", I told him. "It's not Christmas yet", he replied. "You will understand when you open it", I answered with tears filling my eyes, and I rested my head on his shoulder as he opened the box.

"What's this?" He asked with a confused look on his face. I lifted my head off his shoulder and gave him a wide smile. "Don't you know?" I asked. "They look like baby booties made into a bronze figurine of some sort", he replied; still with a puzzled look – and then a smile came to his face. "What on earth?" I smiled through my tears and said, "Turn it over." He looked at the bottom and read aloud the engraved writing, "Baby Sterling – Nineteen Fifty-One." He laughed and smiled with the same joy I saw from him when I told him about our first baby, while in church not so long ago. "We're having a baby?" He asked me in disbelief. "Yes", I confirmed as my own tears of joy rolled down my face.

After discovering the blissful news, he seemed to be having a hard time catching his breath, as he began to cry with joy along with me. He rested his head against my chest and took it all in. This time we would have our baby – nothing and no one would stop us. And I told him in the most sensual and loving way I could.

Moments later after the tears dried and holding each other while rejoicing, he looked up at me and asked, "Can I have that desert now?" I giggled softly and asked, "By desert, I'm guessing you don't mean the strawberry pie?" "That would be correct", he answered while he rose to his feet with me cradled in his arms. "Where are you taking me?" I asked.

He didn't say a word with that handsome smile still plastered across his face, as he carried me into the living room and stopped right before our twelve foot brightly lit Christmas tree in front of our bay window. He gently set me down to my feet and strolled over to the hi-fi, so tall and proud. One would never know that just twenty minutes ago, he was ready for a long winter's nap.

He turned off the light switch, so that the only lights that were on was from our tree and the flickering glow from the fireplace we had going in full force. I turned to look behind me, and as always our largest window in the front of the house was just as bare as I was about to become. Robert didn't like curtains or any window coverings except for the bedroom and the living room in the quarters; that of which he added only to appease me. He always told me that if he wanted privacy outside of his quarters, he simply dismisses his staff at the time.

The sweet instrumental sounds of Christmas began playing through the room as my handsome and hardworking husband moved slowly toward me; with his smile seemingly wider than ever, if that was possible. He untied his tie, letting it hang freely as he began swaying to the music with me wrapped tightly in his arms. And as usual when we danced, I rested my head against his shoulder blade with one arm around him and the other grasping the opening of his shirt. He whispered against my ear, "are you warm enough, darlin'?" I looked up at him with a small smile crossing my face and whispered, "Yes."

As we danced, I continued to think of that wide open window right behind us, and I knew that we were all alone on that property. Even Max was visiting Lucy, as they had become closer. But, it was just the idea, I suppose. Sometimes I still felt as though someone was lurking, and with that feeling, I held onto him a bit tighter; prompting him to ask me, "Are you ok, baby?" I smiled back up at him, and nodded silently. I didn't want to take away not even the smallest amount of pleasure, knowing he enjoys making love to me anytime - and anywhere.

His hand slid right down to my round bare flesh and his other hand quickly unzipped the back of my corset. I allowed him to take complete control, as he turned me around facing that big open window. With only the tree lights on, I was able to see our reflection and I watched through the window as he pealed the front of my corset top down, revealing my aroused mounds. He pressed my bare seat against his hard middle; and then tore my outfit clean off of me. All that was left was my stockings, that were nearly falling down due to the straps being snapped that were once holding them in place and my heels.

And then suddenly, he whipped me back around to face him and dropped to one knee; slowly gliding his fingers up one of my legs, ripping the stocking off. My entire body became goose fleshed while griping my ass in one hand, and then he slid two of his fingers inside of my wet desire. I squealed with delight as one of his fingers flickered up against my sweet spot, as his other finger continued to ravish inside of me so much so, that I nearly passed out. I wildly drove my hands through his thick hair and began screaming for mercy; as I was about to lose control.

Keeping his finger inside of me and one arm around me, he lifted me off the floor from behind and sat on the stool of the sectional sofa. With my lower body laying elevated and across his lap, and the top of my body lying on the sofa, he continued to tease the inside of me with his thick middle finger. I felt his eyes on me as he watched me grip parts of the sofa while screaming in pleasure. After bringing me to three screaming climax's he removed his shirt and opened his pants as though he was racing against time. Kneeling over me, he lifted my hips into him and he let out a loud groan of relief as he entered and began thrusting inside of me; while he held me at the hips.

I can always tell when he's at his breaking point – his thrusting slows down, which always prolongs the experience for both of us. Without separating us, he rolled from his knees to sitting and I was in a straddling position over him. His hands met around the back of me, grasping my ass; while his tongue traced one of my nipples. As I felt that glorious pressure build between my legs, I pulled myself into him, wrapping my arms around his neck and held on tight as I exploded and cried out with one of the strongest of my releases yet.

I rested in the same position I climaxed, and with him still inside me and holding me every bit as tight as I held on to him. He nuzzled my neck and lightly kissed my ear as I rested my head against his shoulder. “That was incredible”, he spoke softly against my ear. He then helped me off of him and as he placed himself back inside his pants and zipped up, I cuddled up against him. He wrapped his arm around me and I took his hand and placed it over my abdomen. With joyful and satisfied tears, I whispered, “We have a new beginning.

September 1951

Robert stood at the nursery window in the hospital and gazed over at the crib with his newborn son lying sound asleep. He smiled as he read the name tag aloud – “Robert Maxwell Sterling.” Max slapped him on the back and said, “Damn good thing he’s a boy, now there’s no way that he and his sister can play those twin games with you.” Robert laughed and then looked over at the crib next to his son. “Can you believe it? Vivian and I have one of each!” He exclaimed on the verge of tears. “So did you and Viv finally decide on a name for your baby girl?” Robert pointed to the name tag and asked, “Can’t you read? My baby girl’s name is Gracie Rose Sterling.” Max smiled and said, “She’s as beautiful as her name, my friend. I know that Rose must be after Rosie, but who came up with Gracie?” Still smiling as he gazed at his little girl resting, Robert answered, “Vivian’s mother’s name was Grace.”

October 1951

We had returned home from St. Rose after the baptism of our babies. Later the same evening, Robert had insisted on drawing a bath for me so I could relax, and then he would put the babies down for the night; so I could get my much needed rest. I had finished bathing and crept into our bedroom when hearing Robert talk to Gracie. I stood quietly in the doorway while he rested against the pillows propped along the headboard, and had Gracie in his arms, sleeping on his chest with her face nuzzled close to his neck.

He stroked her back gently and he spoke softly to our daughter. “You know baby girl, daddy loves your brother, RJ every bit as much as I love you, but there’s something about you that has changed my ideas about some things. I look into your beautiful blue eyes, and I realize that the love a father has for his little girl is the most overwhelming kind of love. And I have come to the conclusion that there is no way that I will allow a rough neck like myself in your world.”

Upon hearing these words, I placed my hand over my mouth to suppress my giggle. “No way”, he emphasized. “I’m going to make sure that my baby girl is treated like a princess when it’s time for her to find a man to marry.” He kissed Gracie’s cheek gently, and then added, “I need to show you and RJ both, how a man should treat a woman; that way he will treat a lady with gentleness and respect, and you will know how you should be treated by a man. That’s part of my job as a daddy, and my promise to you is, that I will not fail you.”

After hearing those words, my eyes flooded with overwhelming realization that Robert truly had every intention in leaving the darkness of his past behind him, and together we could find out how wonderful life could really be. Through my tears, I was able to release the ache in my heart from not being able to have that close daddy/daughter relationship with my own father. At that moment I felt nothing but gratitude that God made sure that my baby girl would receive that wonderful daddy that I had missed out on, and that was good enough for me.

"Hi mama", Robert grabbed my attention softly. "Come and sit next to us", he said when nodding to a spot on the bed. I smiled and wiped my tears when sitting next to them. Robert looked into my eyes, and asked, "You heard me talking to Gracie?" I never lost the adoring smile, and quietly answered, "Yes I did."

I gently stroked the thin hair on our baby's head and asked him, "But, why wouldn't you want Gracie to marry someone like you?" He raised an eyebrow and said, "Look at what I've done in my life. I don't want some over-sexed, hot headed lunatic marrying my baby girl." I placed my hand on his leg, and said, "But you've changed a lot, and you love and protect your family. Now, I will admit that you tend to go about things the wrong way, but that's all you knew at the time - and now that you know better; you do better."

He kissed the baby's head and asked, "What are you saying?" I smiled and replied, "Honey, I mean sometimes people deserve a second chance. Look, you told me that you felt you had no choice but to force the issue with my father because you wouldn't take no for answer after I continued to reject your invitations. Again, I will agree it was wrong in how you did it, but that was all you knew." He reached in and captured my lips softly, and told me, "I still won't apologize for doing what I did there, but I do agree that I have learned to allow things to happen naturally, because it was obviously meant to be for us." I nodded in agreement and said, "That's very true, and I learned things along the way too."

***

We finally put the baby in her crib and watched both babies sleep soundly for a few moments before Robert led me out of the room by the hand. "So", Robert said, breaking the silence. "When you said you learned some things, what were you alluding to?" I dropped my heavy robe, revealing my naked body, and asked, "Rub some lotion on me while we talk?" Robert nodded and took the bottle from my vanity. "Sure, Princess." I came to a rest on my belly at the foot of the bed and began explaining as he started rubbing the lotion in my skin.

"I figure God allows things to take place for reasons we may never understand. And I think this was one of those times that he allowed you to force the issue in your way because he had a plan for us. I wasn't open to anything, and I allowed myself to ignore my attraction to you out of fear."

I rolled over and propped myself up with my elbows. "After I had fallen for you, I realized that you did rescue me. I cringe at what my life would have led to had you given up after the last rejection." He applied lotion to my leg and slowly massaged it into my skin, and asked, "You really feel that way?" I shook my head up and down, and answered, "Yes, I do. I'm not saying that it was right that we made love before marriage, but we're flawed; just like anyone else."

Robert gently took my shoulders and laid me back. "Lay back and relax", he told me quietly. I watched as he emptied more lotion into the palm of his hand and applied it to my other leg. "I will admit that I struggled with knowing it was wrong and doing it anyway, but I can't be sorry for it in some ways." I paused when biting down on my bottom lip to stop my tears, without success. "All that we went through brought us here today", I added in a soft tone as my voice broke up.

Robert softly glided his hand up my leg and left it on my abdomen as he came to a rest beside me. "Baby", he said quietly. "I understand – I do", he told me while becoming choked up. "Because of you, I was able to put my demons to rest, and in doing so; I now have the family I have always wanted."

I rose from the bed putting my robe back on; and sat in his lap. "And", I said with a wide smile through the tears, "I have you going to church with us as a family." Amused, he laughed out loud and replied, "Even more miraculous is the fact that my own baptism will be coming up very soon." He shook his head in disbelief and added, "I never saw that one coming." I laughed and tightened my arms around his neck with a hug. "See what happens when God and I team up?" He busted out laughing, and said, "Oh wow, I never had a chance!" I giggled, and then his expression became serious, as he told me, "I wouldn't have had it any other way - because, baby, we are truly living the dream."

www.ingramcontent.com/pod-product-compliance
Lightning Source LLC
Chambersburg PA
CBHW030358310726
48979CB00001B/354
9781987000542